DRONE
WORLD

THE WORLD SERIES

DRONE
WORLD

By

Jim Kochanoff

HOLLISTON, MASSACHUSETTS

DRONE WORLD

Copyright © 2016 by Jim Kochanoff

Cover Art by Chris Gibson.

First printing September 2016
10 9 8 7 6 5 4 3 2 1

ISBN # 1-60975-159-0
ISBN-13 # 978-1-60975-159-3
LCCN # 2016946856

Silver Leaf Books, LLC
P.O. Box 6460
Holliston, MA 01746
+1-888-823-6450

Visit our web site at www.SilverLeafBooks.com

The three essentials to Happiness are:
Something to do
Something to love
Something to hope for
If you're lucky, you'll have all three in your life.

DRONE
WORLD

Prologue

I lived in the safest city in the world... until I tried to leave it.

I could sense the machine on the other side as the ceiling creaked above my head. The metal drone was searching for my body signature. Finding me was its reward. It had been hours since I escaped but it was only moments before it would find me. It's impossible to hide in the city. It's for our own safety, but a warden says the same thing to his prisoners.

A metallic scratch warned me that the drone had turned the corner of the exterior wall. It would look for a point of weakness, find an opening into the building and break through. I moved, realizing that although a sound would alert it to my location, staying still was no longer an option. I scurried around some boxes, heading down to the stairs. I had to cover a lot of distance in a short time. My dad always teased me that I ran around like my life depended on it. For once, he was right.

The stairs squeaked beneath my weight. It wasn't loud, but to a drone it might have sounded like an elephant stomping. The scratching outside stopped. Normally I would have taken that as a good sign, but now I ran. Hard. As I hit the bottom landing, a cutting sound reverberated from the left wall and sparks flashed in the shadows. Sunlight streamed through the crack; I had seen little of it since my base was a windowless room. But I had no time to admire the sun as a red eye gleamed in the hole. In my hesitation, I saw my reflection in its eyes and the drone registered my presence. Once it saw me, then potentially dozens more would be alerted to my presence.

I slid down the stairs like a fire pole. If I tripped now, I was done. If I didn't get away from this drone quickly, I was done as well. *What a lovely set of options.* Boards splintered and cracked from the floor above; the drone had finally entered the building.

Drones come in all shapes and sizes. This one resembled a bumblebee, small, fast, and lethal. Once it sees you, you can't outrun it. It flies through the air at 20 kilometers an hour, and no matter how fast a runner you are, it never slows down. You're only hope is to find obstacles—doors, walls, cars—anything that blocks you from their view. But once it locks onto you, it is only a matter of time before it catches you. The damn things never stop.

I was so exhausted from the day's escape. I would die to rest for just five minutes. The truth was harsher; if I rested for five seconds now, it would be a permanent sleep. A board snapped under my feet, almost wrenching my ankle with my forward momentum. The building was condemned, and with every step I could see why. The structure had four levels, deep in the bowels of the city. The building was made of rusted steel, well past its expiration date.

A red beam flashed from above, its searchlight inspecting the corners of the room. My feet hit the bottom level. I had run out of space, and going back the same way was not an option. I was frustrated. It's funny what emotions take hold when you are about to die. *How has this drone found me? I was so careful to stay hidden! Taking all the precautions, using several disguises, and avoiding the cameras. What did I do wrong?*

Interrupting my thoughts, my foot hit a metal ring. I stooped down, thinking I had found a handle to help my escape. Instead, I triggered a trap as the floor collapsed and I fell into a watery grave.

That was when my world ended.

4 months earlier

1

Sale

I was halfway between the sensation of falling and floating. Warm air blew through my hair. The ground was far below but never seemed to get closer. Every few moments, a gust of wind would blow me higher. I felt like a bird, but I had no wings, no way to propel myself. I was like a feather in the wind floating aimlessly with the currents. I reached up to touch the clouds, and my hand became moist as water droplets appeared on my fingers. I wanted to go higher, to break free of the earth. I just wanted to go anywhere. To see the world. Leave the city.

My eyes opened and my dream was over. I stared up at the ceiling, wondering what I was becoming. I had been dreaming a lot lately, sometimes during school, which always got me in trouble. It's not like I'm depressed; I have friends, my dad and a home. It's not like I lived on the streets. I just always felt like there was more to life outside our city's walls. Our super-safe city, no crime, no trouble, nothing out of the ordinary. Adults told me that we were lucky to live in a place where everyone was so safe. So B-O-R-I-N-G! I pushed up on my arms, turned my head and looked out the window.

A star shone, glowing twice as bright as any other object. Like my dream, I wished I could fly up to it. Grab hold of it and explore its surface. I felt confined in the city and I would do just about anything to get out of there.

It was early; the glow on the horizon meant the sun was about to rise. There was no sense in going back to sleep. My dad would be up soon, and he made enough noise for ten people. I'm sure he didn't mean to, it's just that he had two left feet. And two left hands. But I still loved him.

I slid out of bed, grabbed a towel and headed to the shower. *Maybe if I get an early start to my day, I can walk through the Marks before school.* I undressed, turned on the shower and stepped in. The water was warm as it cascaded down my back. It was one of the few moments of the day when I thought about absolutely nothing. My dad always yelled at me for spending so long in the shower that when I came out I looked like a prune. I squeezed my face together in my hands and looked in the mirror. I looked old and wrinkly.

I pushed open the shower door and grabbed my towel. I wiped my fingers over the steamy mirror. My hair looked dull and lifeless, a wet mop. No matter what I did with it, it just never came out the way I wanted. That applied to just about everything in my life. No matter how hard I tried to study, I was never a top student. Worked my butt off for sports, always second line at best. Tried to be popular, never got into the in-crowd. Maybe that was why I had such a desire to get out of the city, in hopes that I would be special elsewhere.

I threw on a sweatshirt, pulled on my jeans and grabbed my knapsack. I hoped to grab some breakfast and get out of the house before Dad woke up. No such luck.

"You're up early. Big test today?" I turned around and saw Dad reading the paper on his tablet. It was a soft question but I knew he was probing. He couldn't help himself; he was senior counsel, an attorney with the government. Putting away the guilty—like there was anyone innocent in our court system. Everything we discussed was like a cross-examination and lasted at least twenty questions. Sometimes he asked the same question several times but changed the wording slightly, hoping to catch me in a lie. I didn't take it personally—it was what he did for a living. I had to nip this in the bud.

"School project. Hoping to spend some time at the lab before first period," I answered nonchalantly as I downed a glass of orange juice.

"Isn't it easier to do that after school?" he asked and looked away from his tablet while putting down his coffee. Nineteen questions to go.

"Maybe so, but we have softball practice after school. Remember, its Wednesday?" I pulled out yogurt and strawberries from the refrigerator and sat down at the table. Nothing better than to follow up a lie with some truth; keeps the suspicious at bay.

"As long as you're not walking through the Marks on

your way to school." There was his veiled reminder. It didn't matter if he believed my story or not, he intended to make his point.

The Marks was where you could get anything imaginable, sometimes items that were from outside the city. It gave me hope to see items from other places, and I wasn't going to let Dad squash my dream. I turned to face him.

"Yes, Dad. You've told me a thousand times. Doesn't matter that there is almost no crime anymore, don't go to the Marks. Don't go to the Marks." I walked around the kitchen like a Frankenstein monster repeating the warning over and over. I caught a half smile on his face and knew that I had won him over.

"All right. All right. Can't fault a father for wanting to protect his daughter." He shook his coffee cup at me and a drop fell out, almost landing on his tablet. "Just because we can track any criminal doesn't mean crime has disappeared. It means people have gotten better at hiding it. And those people are the ones you meet at the Marks."

"Enough sermons, Dad. I hear what you are saying." *Doesn't mean that I agree.* "I have to go. See you for supper?" I bent down to kiss him on the forehead.

"You bet—crime docket is slow today, just like every day. Are you cooking tonight?" he questioned with a brightness in his eyes. My dad can't boil water without burning it, so I cooked all the meals in the house. Not because I'm a great cook, but my meals won't burn the house down.

"I'll give it a go, maybe a six-course meal?" I teased.

"Make it five. I'm trying to lose some weight." He patted

his stomach.

I laughed and headed out the door. I jumped down the stairs three at a time and felt the sunshine on my face. The morning was quiet but a security drone flew overhead, its red light scanning the ground below. I tried to sidestep it, thinking it was one my Dad had sent after me to spy on me. As soon as I tried to avoid it, it must have picked up my vibrations—since no one else was out walking—and the beam inched towards me.

I stopped, knowing there was no way to outrun it. Better to let it take its reading and then be on my way. I felt the beam cover the back of my head. I closed my eyes, not because it could hurt me, but I preferred that when I opened my eyes again it would be gone. Seconds later, I looked straight ahead and it had already crossed the street, looking for another person's presence to record. I didn't know why they bothered; there were so many security cameras—one on every corner, as the city ads would sing—that they seemed redundant. I headed in the direction of school in case my dad was watching. I didn't look back, not wanting to appear guilty.

Once I was out of sight, I changed direction towards the Marks. I looked up every couple of minutes to make sure no more drones flew overhead. It wasn't like they were tracking me specifically, just thinking of me as a bar code at a grocery store. Recording everything that went through so later they could do a data dump and try to make sense of all the information. I preferred to stay hidden.

The Marks were about a twenty-minute walk to the

north. Not the best side of the city, but with virtually no crime, I never understood my father's concern. Places like the Marks have always existed. A place of barter and exchange. One man's garbage is another woman's treasure. Or something like that. There were rows and rows of stalls, from food to metals to precious stones. The vendors never seemed to stay in the same spot for too long, and the place was a maze of many back alleys and levels. It was always hard to find the ones you wanted, but you got the feeling that the vendors preferred the shuffling around. The most popular ones never stayed hidden for very long.

As I turned the corner, the smell got my attention first. The Marks were in a warehouse district. Hardly anyone lived in the area, otherwise they might be driven insane by the aromas of fresh foods wafting through the air. The Marks had one rule: no credits, only paper money. This was difficult since the rest of the city just scanned the bar code on your wrist and your account was billed. Because some items were a bit on the illegal side—okay, a lot on the illegal side—no one wanted to have their business transactions recorded. Avoiding paying taxes also drove customers here.

The aisles were narrow and many people were bartering with the merchants, creating an obstacle course to duck around. I was not watching where I was going and almost stepped on her.

"Bark!" A metallic, high-pitched whine came from the ground. I stepped back and looked down. "Bark!" the cry came a little louder. I reached down to scoop up the small mechanical dog. Its tail was bent and there were several spots of rust on its hindquarters. Its tongue whipped out as if trying to lick me and it made a contented sound. I patted it on the head, although I doubted it was programmed to enjoy a human's touch.

"Hey that's my dog, put her down!" a boy yelled over the noise of the crowd. I looked up and saw a tall guy about my age with blond hair walking towards me. He walked confidently, like someone who knew the Marks.

"Sorry, she came up to me. She looks like an old model—isn't she illegal?" I asked, handing the little dog over to him. Usually only the police could own and operate drones, although they often looked the other way if the drone wasn't a danger to the public. The mechanical dog scurried along his shoulder and planted her two front legs, looking expectantly at her owner.

"Yah, well, that about describes half of the things you buy here. You know, you shouldn't pick up things that don't belong to you."

"Well, she came up to me. Maybe you should do a better job of taking care of her," I shot back, being a bit rough. But if you walked the Marks, you needed to grow a thick skin. I recovered and tried to be friendly. "She's awfully cute, where did you find her?"

He perked up at my question. "I fixed her up from a scrap heap. Don't know how much life she has in her. There are so few living pets around these days, thought I'd program my own." I looked at him more closely and saw a bunch of wires sticking out of his coat pocket. *Typical techno geek. Probably here looking for some illegal electronics. Everyone's got to have a hobby.*

"Listen, I'm looking for a certain merchant. Seen a guy by the name of Lou? Sells unusual stuff, things from outside in the city."

"Sounds like a lot of the sellers here. Care to be a little more specific?" he asked while holding the wiggling dog.

"He promotes his goods as 'from another planet,' has a bunch of UFOs and spaceships hanging from his roof. Yells from an electronic megaphone." I could tell from his eyes that he knew whom I was describing.

"That wacko—sure, everyone knows Looney Lou. I do my best to avoid him. He's a fraud, and most of his items are fakes. You don't believe that his goods are from another world?" The cynic in me didn't believe but the optimist hoped to see items made outside of the city. That's why I liked Lou's stall—it gave me hope.

"Not really, but it's a lot of fun to go through his stuff. Can you take me to him?" I asked. He reached down and depressed a button on his dog. She immediately perked up and disappeared into the crowd.

"Lola can find anyone. Just follow her nose. I'm Austin." He offered his hand.

"I'm Pene." I shook his hand. His skin was tough and calloused; he must do a lot of work with his hands. "Where do you go to school?" I sidestepped a couple of people yelling at a vendor.

"Armbrae—out on the north end. School's small but they have a great electronics class. Spend some of my time in the lab." He blushed. "I guess that makes me sound like a geek." His dimples made him kind of cute.

"No, it just means you've found something that interests you. A lot of the guys at my school barely show up for class."

"Where do you go?" Austin asked.

"Vestbrooke—I headed out early so I can spend time here before first period." Up ahead I could see Lola barking at someone.

"Your parents must be pretty open-minded to let you walk around the Marks by yourself." I looked away, not wanting to explain my family dynamics. He wouldn't understand. "Hey, Lola found your vendor!" Austin pointed and I was glad for the change of conversation.

As we approached, Lou turned towards us and smiled. He was a heavyset man with black hair and a beard, slightly balding and always with a huge smile. I wasn't sure if it was a smile for enticing customers or if he really liked people. I had a feeling it was a bit of both.

"Pene! My favorite customer!" *The liar—I've seen him say the same thing to other customers.* "I see you brought a friend with you. Please come with me." He grabbed my hand and gestured me into his stall. He pulled us around a stack of boxes to a table with outer-worldly artifacts and metal objects. He motioned to us to sit. "Several new items this week." Lou reached into one of his boxes and pulled out a strange statue made of iron. It was a creature with multiple limbs and eyes. I ran my hand over its hands. "The man I bought it from says it depicts an alien life form he was captured by." Lou leaned into me. "Apparently he barely escaped."

Austin made a motion twirling with his finger at the side of his head. He obviously didn't have any faith in Lou's products.

"No," I answered. "What else do you have?" Lou proceeded unperturbed. He was the ultimate salesman. He reached into a bag and pulled out an electronic box.

"What's that? I asked.

"This fell out of a spaceship. It has advanced technology." He beamed, seemingly believing it wholeheartedly. "If you touch this button," he clicked on a raised red object, "it will open the spaceship." Unfortunately, there was no way to prove Lou's claim. It didn't interest me, so I waved my hand to pass.

The truth was that I wasn't sure what I was looking for. I wasn't trying to find an object from an alien culture, despite what Lou sold. I wanted an object from outside of our city, recognition that there was more than where we lived.

As I scanned Lou's stall, the sun reflected off glass in the corner. I walked over unobserved as Lou went to work trying to sell to Austin. Several colors shimmered on the wall as the glass acted like a prism. I picked the object up. It was about the size of my hand but looked like a section of a much larger object. It was concave, the glass honeycombed, mirroring a dozen of my faces.

"Where did you find this, Lou?" I held it out. He turned, since Austin had proved very unreceptive to his sales pitch.

"A mountain climber from Logan's Peak sold it to me. He found a few of them on a plateau. Most of the other pieces were shattered but this piece had sunk into a depression. Is it something you would like to buy?" he asked expectantly.

When it comes to the Marks, you never want to look too interested. If you do, the buyer knows he's got you hooked.

"I'll think about it. What's in these boxes?" I pointed to the far corner to divert my interest. Lou wasn't fooled.

"If you take it now, I can let you have it for, let's say twenty credits?" Only a fool or a desperate customer takes the first price offered at the Marks. Some vendors are even offended if you take their first offer; it is an art to bargain and try to read the other's person price.

"Twenty credits? That thing's not worth five," Austin interceded on my behalf. He guessed my price exactly.

"What he said." I gestured to Austin but looked at Lou.

"I couldn't part with it for less than fifteen. I paid the climber a fair price, you know." Lou's smile was fake and we both knew it.

"Maybe seven. I don't think I brought anymore," I lied and then turned away. I'm not the best liar and I thought he could read my face. Lou, on the other hand, was so over the top in his response, I felt he deserved some award.

"How can you do this to me, Pene? We have been friends for many years. Do friends steal from each other?" It was a rhetorical question. "Of course not. I'm beginning to think that our relationship has come to an end. Perhaps I should not try to look out for your special interests anymore?" The look he gave me as I turned back was priceless. His performance was almost worth the price.

"Lou—final offer. Ten credits. Take it or I will never darken your door again. And that's a promise!"

"Sold!" he answered enthusiastically and rushed to wrap it up for me. Austin leaned closer.

"If you ask me—" he started.

"But I didn't," I interrupted, knowing that no one shared my interest of items outside of town.

"Hey, no fair, let me finish," he complained.

"So you can tell me how I wasted my money?" I snapped. "Now I have to hide this from father. He thinks that I should be helping improve the city, not trying to leave it." I didn't mean to take out my frustration with my dad on Austin.

"You're misunderstanding," Austin replied, gathering up Lola in his arms. "I was trying to say that you should always go for the things that are important to you. Most girls find the electronics I buy weird." His phone rang and he turned away to talk. *A jealous girlfriend?* I asked Lou to wait a few minutes and intended to apologize to Austin for acting like a drama queen. But as I turned around, he had disappeared into the crowd. Me and my big mouth.

"Hey Lou, hurry up. I have to catch up with my friend." I laid out my money on the table and he handed me my purchase.

"Come next week," he urged as I dashed away. "I have some items coming in from the underground." His voice melted into the noise of the Marks. I saw Austin disappear into the west end of the stalls and I tried to catch up with him. As I dodged a large woman arguing with a vendor, a head-splitting siren began to screech.

A rush of air gushed past me as a drone flew by. It was the shape of a small motorcycle propelled by jet engines. The heat it gave off was immense. Its robotic driver had head and arms, but the rest of its body merged with the machinery. As people scattered, it hovered above a food stall further down, blowing skewers onto the ground. The robotic head swirled left to right, scanning the crowd. Everyone froze, looking like students in a classroom; no one wanted to be picked by the drone. Behind me a stack of crates fell to the ground. I turned and saw a horrified look on Lou's face as he attracted the drone's attention.

"You!" The drone pointed directly at Lou. "You are charged with theft. Step forward to accept your sentence!" Lou backed away, shocked by the command.

"You're mistaken, I'm a simple shop owner. I have stolen from no one," he answered, almost sobbing. The drone hovered closer to Lou while everyone else tried to blend into the surroundings to avoid detection. Lou's eyes scanned the Marks, looking for some point of escape. He seemed to focus on the right side, which went around a nearby warehouse. The drone's eyes followed his glance, almost daring him to run, knowing that escape was nearly impossible. But common sense was not one of Lou's strong points—he decided to run. Being a large man, he wasn't graceful or fast and the drone merely watched his escape. I looked around; all of the vendors and buyers watched like zombies. No one offering to help, all of us assuming that justice was being served. Or none of us wanting to be recorded for questioning the law.

Lou turned a corner and slammed into another drone. This one was humanoid but a good foot taller and probably a hundred pounds heavier. The drone picked him up as if he was as light as a pillow. The motorcycle drone circled above the stalls, making its announcement.

"Your streets are safe again. Continue your business— know that no crime goes undetected. You are watched for the greater good." Everyone watched the drone as it repeated its message several more times, its voice fading as it disappeared further into the Marks. The larger drone carried Lou unceremoniously, like a sack of flour. I watched as they passed me, Lou's big eyes popping out of his head. As his line of vision crossed my position he begged me, "I've never stolen from anyone. This is all wrong! You said your father was a lawyer. Help me!" And just like that, Lou and the drone disappeared into the crowd. The Marks returned to an uneasy rumble of voices as people ventured back to their business.

There's no way I am mentioning any of this to Dad. If he knew I was here, I'd suffer my own punishment. Sorry Lou, you're on your own.

2

Indoctrination

I made it into school a full minute before the doors were sealed and locked. If you were late, there was no sneaking into school. And you were wasting your time trying to get a drone to open the door by telling your sob story for not being on time. When I was in junior high, one of the boys tried to climb in a second-story window. He made it to class but not without a drone replaying the entire 'break-in' to the laughter of the class.

As I walked the halls, the school's television monitors flashed the latest news on their screens. From meetings to dances to homework, we lived in the age of communication. It was pretty hard to claim you weren't informed of upcoming events. The problem was, with so much information, from homework to online quizzes, school's reach never seemed to end. The end of day bell merely transitioned your studies to a new location.

As I entered the room, I met the gaze of Mr. Stewart, my history instructor. He was around my dad's age but seemed to have more seniority than any teacher at the school. His main feature was his piercing gaze. His eyes were a deep ocean blue and you felt as if they were dissecting you as he watched. I immediately saw him watching me as I walked in and quickly found a position in the middle of the class behind a taller student. His gaze immediately shifted to another pupil, like a hawk watching its prey.

"Did you just feel a chill in the air?" I turned as I sat down, smiling at my best friend, Lacey. She was taller than me, with bright red hair. Some of the boys would mumble "Racey" when she got onto a topic that she had a strong opinion about. Down deep, I think she liked her nickname.

"Try getting into the classroom without one of his icy stares," I replied.

"Sometimes I think Mr. Stewart is a drone—at least he has the personality of one," Lacey teased. I fumbled in my backpack, trying to get out my tablet for class. Lacey spotted my purchase from Lou.

"Where did you get that?" she asked. Before I could answer, a look of realization crossed her face. "Oh, wait a minute—were you slumming it in the Marks this morning?"

"Do I have to answer that?" I replied, red-faced.

"Well, you'll need a better lying face than that. If your dad asked the same question, you'd be toast."

"I wish I was as talented as you," I answered as I covered the glass with a towel.

"Why are you so crazy to find something from outside the city? I mean, when you get older, you can always get a job that takes you out of here. That is, if you can survive living with us commoners," she teased. She waved her hand like a queen addressing her subjects. I squirmed in my chair.

"It's not like that," I said defensively. "I just want to see more than this city. See the mountains, the ocean, see the stars away from the city lights. Travel where there isn't a drone five feet behind me."

"Good luck with that. You know they're here for our protection," she mimicked, repeating one of the public service announcements that we heard over and over. The bell sounded, and we knew better than to continue our conversation in Mr. Stewart's class. We had learned not to draw attention to ourselves—call it a mixture of fear and respect. Two video screens dropped down from the ceiling and Mr. Stewart stood up from his desk. He was pencil-thin and his voice was high-pitched.

"Settle down—get your tablets out. I want you to bring up your history assignments." A collective groan went up from the class. No one thought we were going to be graded today. He seemed to sense our unease. "Relax, I'm not marking today but I will be monitoring your progress." He walked around the room, flicking with his fingers as he passed each student. Each assignment moved from the student's tablet into his own. He did a word count in each and then moved on. I dreaded when he passed my desk. He flicked his tablet from mine to his, waited and then did it a second time.

"Haven't started your history project yet, Pene. Your deadline is next week."

Lacey tried to come to my defense. "She's best under

pressure—nothing like getting it done at the last moment."

"But that's not going to work. I explained at the start of the term how important it was, with the length and research required, that you work on it every week. What is your excuse?" His cold eyes burrowed into my skull, making me even more uncomfortable as the rest of the class waited for my answer.

The answer was actually quite simple. School bored me. To tears. I knew it, my dad certainly knew it and probably half the class had already teased me about it. I couldn't help myself, things just didn't seem urgent until the last minute. And trust me, I'm great under pressure. Once I get rolling, I can accomplish a lot in a short amount of time. When others freeze, I can fly. I'm always able to think quickly to get myself out of a jam. This was one of those times.

"I've been waiting to interview my dad. He's cancelled a few times because of work but he's promised me definitely this week," I lied, keeping my face neutral to contain my emotions. Mr. Stewart looked suspicious but then nodded.

"Then get it done, Pene. With your father a lawyer with the ministry, I'll be expecting a first-rate project. I think I'll let you present first in the class." A faint smile crossed his face, like a cat that had just swallowed a bird and was going to enjoy every moment of eating it. I had the exact opposite feeling. Dad rarely talked about work—conflict of interest was his excuse—and it would be like pulling teeth to get any information out of him. I slumped in my chair as Lacey read my body language.

"Come on," she whispered, "appeal to his ego. Tell him

how interested you are in his job. If you look at him with your big brown eyes, he won't refuse."

"Telling him I'll fail the course would be a better approach," I whispered back just as Mr. Stewart turned, silencing any further conversation.

"Open your tablets to page 355, new legislation on security. I want to review the setup of the ministry." Tablets flashed as students scrolled to the correct page.

"Is it true that until the ministry was formed, crime was at the highest level in history?" asked Cory, a scrawny guy who always asked questions that he knew the answer to.

"That's correct. If you turn to page 358, you'll see a photo from a typical street in the city." We scrolled to look at the photo.

"There's no security cameras. People could do anything and not get caught," a girl named Alyvia commented. Mr. Stewart pulled out his digital wand and circled several buildings in the photo to illustrate her comment.

"Before the ministry was created, there were no cameras to protect society. Crimes went undetected, vandalism, theft, even murder went unpunished."

"Is that when drones were introduced?" Cory asked again, and several groans came from the class. We all knew that he already was well aware of the answer. Mr. Stewart sat on the edge of his desk, looking pleased to explain the security of the city. Again.

"Before you were born, we lived in a lawless city. Criminals could commit crimes undetected, and those that were caught took years to punish or never served time for their crime. People felt unsafe as soon as they left their homes. In an effort to provide safety, security cameras were installed on every street corner, in every store. But we soon learned that they were not enough."

"Why? Is that when the drones were built?" asked Lacey, showing an unexpected interest in the topic. I gave her a glare while she made a face back at me.

"Not quite. Because criminals knew where the cameras were, they could evade or wreck them to prevent being caught on recorders. Then the ministry placed secret cameras, putting them in places not obvious to the public. Unfortunately, camera locations were eventually discovered, and as people became aware of them, they were destroyed or avoided."

"When are we going to get to the drones?" a boy asked from the back to the class. Mr. Stewart raised his head slowly and looked at us, like a politician ready to discuss his main message.

"Drones were introduced by the ministry to watch over citizens. While the cameras were tethered to specific locations, drones could come and go at any location. Their benefits were immediate and the crime rate dropped dramatically. When crimes were committed, they were immediately recorded and the criminals jailed immediately."

"Is it true that court cases used to take years to complete?" a girl behind me asked.

"I'm sure Pene's father could answer that." Mr. Stewart looked at me and then continued. "Yes, with the drone footage, justice is swift and final. Appeals are no longer required as the drone footage is irrefutable. We truly live in a golden age!" I thought that Mr. Stewart was going to start singing the national anthem after his impassioned speech. Silence greeted him instead of a rousing cheer. He looked around the room with his icy stare, driving his point home.

"Can anyone sum up in a few words the differences the drones have made in our lives?" Mr. Stewart looked straight at Cory to begin.

"No crime," he stated.

"No victims," a girl yelled from the front. Mr. Stewart scanned the room, looking for more feedback.

"No privacy," I shot out and immediately regretted my outburst. Lacey gave me a look as if to say, *'What is wrong with you?'*

"Would you like to clarify your statement, Miss Anderson?" His eyes looked as if they would bore through the back of my head. *Oh well, I started this, I may as well see it through.* I chose my words carefully.

"The drones record all criminal activity but they also observe everyone's actions, from eating to walking down the street. Sometimes even when they're not there, I feel like something is watching me."

"Like in the washroom," Cory added. Mr. Stewart gave a cold stare that immediately shut him up, and he slunk down in his chair. Mr. Stewart paced around the classroom.

"A little loss of privacy is a small price to pay for safety. Knowing you can walk the streets without fear, that no criminal can go unpunished." Mr. Stewart walked down the aisle of seats while giving his sermon, looking into the eyes of each student. I remembered Lou's eyes as he was accused and wondered if our society was as safe as my teacher described.

"What triggered the drone act of 2025?" Lacey asked. I was more than happy for the change in focus. Fighting Mr. Stewart was a battle I didn't want. He walked back to his desk.

"A group of anarchists took over the generating plant on the west side of the city. Their demands for a ransom were not met. They triggered an explosion that created a monumental earthquake, making buildings collapse and creating a blackout throughout the city for over three weeks. Instead of causing chaos, this incident galvanized the government to form the Ministry. The drone officers were released immediately, patrolling all streets and helping clean the rubble from the earthquake. Their friendly presence inspired thousands." I thought about the police drones that took Lou away; they seemed neither friendly nor inspiring. Cold and heartless were better descriptors.

"Is that why they say there are underground buildings and tunnels under the city?" A girl in the front row asked. Mr. Stewart fixed her with a glance that said 'What a stupid question'.

"Of course not. Almost all of the old buildings were torn down. The few remaining buildings underground were unsafe and remain condemned in the east side of the city. Whenever you go to the town hall by the Justice Building, you can see the monument that commemorates the drones and the years of peace they have created."

A knock on the window diverted my attention. A bee drone was hovering outside, its eyes scanning the class and then stopping when it saw me. At least that's what it looked like; drones aren't made to find people, only to record what they see. I could almost see some type of intelligence in its eyes, as if was tracking me.

"Hope we aren't interrupting your daydreams, Pene?" Mr. Stewart asked while the class laughed at my distraction. I turned to him to respond but realized any excuse was worthless. I did the only thing I could to salvage the moment.

"Sorry, Mr. Stewart." He dismissed me with his right hand and turned to the front of class.

"Can I get everyone to turn to page 385, to the aftermath of the earthquake and the new government?" Fingers tapped on screens as we searched for the content.

I turned my head to the window but the drone had gone. Typical—when you don't want them, you can't get them out of your sight. And when you want them, they're gone.

I wished I could be gone too.

3

Justice

Snow fluttered through the air, swirling in a circle as it slowly sank to the ground. Flakes touched the castle turret, which was whiter from the snow than gray from the rock foundation. A boy with a sled lay frozen to the ground, his sightless eyes looking forward into space beyond his sphere. I shook the snow globe again, marveling at the detail; a silly gift from my mother before her accident.

I sat down in a comfortable armchair by my father's desk, surveying the shelves of books in his office. Why would you read from these bulky things when you had so much information on your tablet? I pulled one from the wall. It was titled, *Frontier Justice*, with a hangman and noose on the cover. A body dangled from the rope while a crowd watched with silent interest.

"See something you like?" I turned and looked into a drone eye. Its flashing red light swallowed me in its viewer. I was too shocked to answer, so my dad spoke, entering from the doorway.

"You remember Lord Morall don't you, honey?" he asked. "Last time you saw him you were probably in grade three."

"Of—of course," I stammered. "It's good to see you again, sir." Lord Morall oversaw all of the lawyers on the government staff, including my dad. Because safety was all-important in the city, he seemed to have more power than the mayor or other city officials. He was tall and thin, almost like a scarecrow, with cropped gray, thinning hair. His eye was one of the early drone transplants; today replacements were barely noticeable. His presence unnerved me, and although his good eye turned to Dad, his drone eye studied me.

"It's wonderful to see children of our lawyers visiting their parents at work. Makes me think we're training the next generation for our legal system." Lord Morall slapped Dad too hard on the shoulder and a pen came tumbling out his hand. As Dad stooped down to pick it up, Lord Morall stared at me with a pleasant smile, but his drone eye seemed to dissect my innermost thoughts. I shuddered uncontrollably.

"So what do I owe the pleasure of your visit, Pene?" My dad half smiled and then reconsidered. "You didn't get into any trouble today?"

"No, Dad," I answered, "I have a school project on the evolution of the legal system and my teacher kind of wanted some information straight from the source." Before he could answer, Lord Morall intervened.

"Well, you've come to the right place, young lady. Since

the great earthquake, the legal system has evolved into a flawless, efficient machine. Do you know that your dad has a 99% prosecution rate?"

"He's mentioned once or a hundred times," I replied, a smile cracking my face. Lord Morall sat down on the couch in the corner, folding his long, thin legs.

"You live in exciting times. Do you realize that we have thousands of cameras strategically placed throughout the city at most major intersections and venues? Coupled with satellite footage, no crime goes undetected. The crime rate is single digits, and justice is swift." Lord Morall looked satisfied with his lesson.

"Imagine before you're born," my dad added. "Trials could take years, and many times criminals went free. I received footage from a crime today. Trial will be tomorrow and the sentencing the day after. Our justice system is fair and swift." A question bubbled up from my thoughts. I hesitated, since it was something I would usually ask Dad when we were alone.

"Do many crimes go undetected? I mean, we can't have cameras everywhere." My question seemed to energize Lord Morall, who jumped up from the couch like a man half his age to respond.

"Excellent question, my dear. I can see you following in your father's footsteps." He beamed. His smile was sharp, though, like a politician's, and I doubted his sincerity. "One of my jobs has been to lobby our government for more drones, more cameras to watch over and protect our society. Their costs are expensive but the benefits of a safe society can't be measured in dollars and cents. The Justice Committee has even explored 'other avenues' of observation." His eyes shone as if we were discussing a favorite hobby.

"Such as...?" I leaned in, hoping for a hint in his cryptic description.

"Pene!" my dad interrupted, embarrassed at my forwardness.

Lord Morall laughed. "Ah, the youth of today, always so inquisitive." He stepped up to leave. "I can't give all our secrets away—we don't want the criminals to learn how to evade them." He leaned forward to tap me on the shoulder. I'm sure he thought it was a fatherly gesture but it just felt creepy to me. I involuntarily shivered. His grin was piecing and his drone eye scanned me once more as he exited.

"Evan, don't forget to review the latest case before you go home." He waved and disappeared into the hall. My dad fixed me with a reproachful stare.

"You know that he is one of the most powerful men in the city," he said as he sat down at his desk. I slumped into the couch across from him.

"I'm sorry. He scares me with his drone eye. It throws me off."

"Well, just remember he protects people like you and me. Just because his eye is a machine, it doesn't make him any less human. Come on, they must teach you something in school about treating people equally?" I made a face at him. He began to sweep his fingers over the computer tablet and then stopped. "How come you came to see me at work? You haven't done that in years. Do you need money?" I could see he was jokingly trying to get under my skin.

"No, Dad. Can't your lovely daughter come see you at work?" I batted my eyelashes to add to the exaggeration. My dad simply stared at me, waiting for me to come clean. "Okay." I slouched further into the couch. "I procrastinated and have a history project due on the evolution of justice. My teacher requested," I lied, "that I interview you to get details on how the justice system has changed over the years. I know how tired you get at home so I thought I'd catch you at work." I raised my eyebrows in the insane hope that I was making my eyes bigger and my face cuter. It had the desired effect.

"When's it due?" he asked.

"Next week, and he wants about 5,000 words." Now it was my father's turn to raise his eyebrows.

"Well, you have some work ahead of you. Pull out your recorder and get your list of questions out. I just need five minutes to scrub through this footage." He pointed at his tablet. "And then we can get started."

Someone knocked on the door.

"Come in," my dad commanded. I felt wary that Lord Morall had returned, as if his drone eye wanted to examine me further. Instead, a younger man came in with a stack of papers.

"Sorry to interrupt," the clerk said to Dad. "I need you to sign off on the footage from the last case."

"Just send it to my tablet, I'll sign," my dad said without looking up. The clerk seemed embarrassed.

"I can't, server problems—can you come down to my

office? It has to be finalized today." My dad leaned back in his chair, resigned. He turned to me as he got up. "Be back in a few minutes, stay out of trouble?" He grinned.

"Yes—Dad." I faked exasperation as the two of them left the office. I pulled out my tablet and looked around the office. Dad was very old school—lots of artifacts from the legal system over the years. Most things were ancient: a set of scales, an old wooden gavel and a bunch of paper books lined the top shelf. I grabbed a book and blew dust off the jacket, and some of it blew back in my face. I coughed and opened the front cover. There was a picture of a person on a wooden stand surrounded by a group of people ready to judge him. Justice seemed strange back them, having your peers try to decide your fate. Today's drones played back your crime and the lawyers gave their foregone conclusion. Neat, clean and final. No appeals required.

I looked over at my dad's desk, and an image caught my eye. I turned to the door and didn't hear any footsteps in the hall. I went over to desk, where Dad's tablet lay. A familiar face stared out at me, frozen in terror. *Lou! Could Dad have been assigned his case?* Dad always made it clear that his work was private, that I was never allowed to see his cases. My fingers tapped the screen, if my dad caught me scrubbing through the footage, I was worse than dead.

Seconds later the familiar images of the Marks scrolled through the tablet. The grungy stalls, customers haggling over prices, the resolution was so vivid, I felt I was there. The camera angle was high and erratic, probably from a flying drone. Below, I could make out Lou's form, stocky and balding. He was walking down an aisle and then turned ninety degrees into a nearby stall. The camera angle changed and was fixed, likely mounted on a wall. Lou sat at a table and pulled out a metal box. The camera cut to a close-up of his hands, taking cash from the box and stuffing his pockets.

I sat back in the chair, saddened by my discovery. I didn't know Lou well but I thought I was a good judge of character. Why would he steal? He knew the penalty if he was caught. He was either desperate or stupid. 'Course, I was one to talk; unless you were a lawyer authorized by the ministry, it was a crime to view criminal footage. And I was probably a minute away from being discovered. Besides, I had discovered what I wanted. Lou was guilty and probably deserved his punishment.

I looked at the tablet and noticed there was extra footage time. Curious, I pushed my luck and tapped the scroll bar. The footage was shot from above and showed the central area of the Marks. My heart leapt into my throat as I could make out my backpack in the corner of the footage as it scrolled the scene. It was quick and you couldn't see my face, but it was me. *Pray Dad doesn't recognize me.* The camera panned and I recognized Lou running through the aisle. I recognized his lumbering pace, and then the drone caught up and lifted him like a feather. Then the camera closed in his mouth as he yelled, "I stole it! I'm guilty!"

I stopped the footage and rewound. *Did I hear that incorrectly? Lou never confessed – he claimed he was innocent!* I played it again, but the audio was the same. *It doesn't make sense, that didn't happen.* I slowed the footage down but the audio matched Lou's mouth movements. If the footage was doctored, they sure did a good job. If I hadn't been there, I would have believed it. *Except it's fake.* And then I thought of something else that seemed wrong. I looked up, knowing I had to look at the footage again, even if Dad walked right in at that moment.

I scrolled the footage again from before, watching Lou walking, turning into a stall, and then stealing from the cash box. Something bugged me. Why did the camera angle change? I looked closely. The arms in the close-up seemed off. Lou's a hairy guy and these arms seemed almost normal. Obviously, I couldn't prove it unless I had Lou's arms to compare with, but to the uninformed you'd never know. Except I knew now—but what could I do with the information? Dad would never believe me; the law was perfect in his eyes. And I would be grounded for life. There was only one thing I could do.

"You ready to go?" my dad said, entering the room. I didn't turn right away, trying to compose my face. "You okay?" he asked while picking up his tablet. I looked up from the couch and smiled.

"Everything's great, Dad. If you have twenty minutes, I have a few questions for you for my assignment."

4

Game

School was a bigger waste than usual. I couldn't focus on any subjects. My mind kept racing to the footage I had seen yesterday. Faked! The crime scene footage wasn't real, and now Lou was going to serve time for something he didn't do. What if other sentences were set the same way? What if other people were being charged for crimes they didn't commit? All of a sudden, our safe society looked like a lie.

"Ouch!" My tablet went flying as I walked straight into Lacey.

"Where's your head today, girlfriend? You look like you're a thousand miles away." Lacey smiled at me as she helped pick up my stuff. As I put the tablet back in my pack, a question crossed my mind.

"What if you could help someone but it'd get you in a lot of trouble?" I asked.

"That's easy—unless she's your best friend, you do nothing. Look after yourself. It's not worth the trouble." We started walking down the hallway towards the main sports field.

"So, except for you, I should keep my mouth shut?"

"Exactly. Why rock the boat? Hey, is this something to do with Mr. Stewart's class?"

"Maybe," I answered coyly, deciding it was better to deflect the conversation. "Where are we heading?" I'd noticed that most students were walking in the same direction.

"You know," Lacey answered as if I was pretending to forget, "it's time for the re-enactment!"

I cringed. Every month, our school faced another school in the aftermath of the great earthquake, simulating the attack by the terrorists that blew up the power plant, sending the city into darkness. Each school fielded a team. One had to be the terrorists and the other was the citizens fighting back. No one enjoyed being the terrorists but everyone had to take their turn. It was a true school activity because unlike most sports, where only a few elite athletes got to play and the majority watched, in the re-enactment we all could be participants. Teams could be as large as an entire school, and spectators were the participants who were knocked out of the game.

"Come on, let's head to the game grid." Lacey grabbed my hand and pulled me through the crowd. We entered into main field, the length of a city block, and a covered huge transparent dome. Bad weather never cancelled one of these games. In the distance I could see hundreds of participants from the opposing school.

"Who are we playing against?"

"Not sure, but I know we're home team."

Home team meant that our school played the role of the city while the visitors played the role of the terrorists. No school liked to play the role of the terrorists and usually that meant not a lot of players would come from the other school. Most times the home team had a two on one advantage. Today didn't look much different. I recognized most of the people from my class. Many were stretching and talking strategy. A few had changed into more comfortable running attire and a few girls were still wearing heels, which would put them at an extreme disadvantage. I looked to my right and saw a familiar face.

"Austin!" I yelled. He turned and looked at me. From the distance I couldn't tell if he was happy to see me again but he walked over.

"How do you know him?" Lacey giggled.

"I met him at the Marks, he helped me find a vendor."

"Well introduce me—he looks like a bargain." As Austin stepped up to us, Lacey intercepted him.

"Hi I'm Lacey, Pene's best friend. Have any buddies that you want to introduce me to?" She winked at Austin, who warily regarded her.

"Nice to meet you. I'm Austin." He turned and looked at me. "Are you two competing? I'd hate to hear any excuses after we beat you," he said confidently. Lacey made a face.

"Why would you want to beat the good people of the city?" she mocked as if repeating one of Mr. Stewart's classes.

Austin rolled his eyes. "Don't tell me you listen to all the propaganda about the terrorists?"

"What do you mean?" I asked, not understanding his comment.

"Please." Austin blew out a burst of air, looking incredulously at me. "Don't believe everything your teachers tell you about the great earthquake." He leaned closer to both of us, and his voice wasn't much louder than a whisper. "I've heard a much different story where the government caused the earthquake and created the terrorists as scapegoats."

"Seriously. You're telling me that the Ministry of Justice made all of this up. Who believes that?" Lacey said, her demeanor changing to disbelief, but she kept her voice down. None of us wanted to be recorded by a drone.

"I do. They used the earthquake to push through the security legislation. Don't you think it's convenient that everything became so safe once the M-O-J took charge?"

"Say something, Pene, he's calling your father a liar." Lacey nudged me while waiting for an answer. I was perplexed. A week ago I would have yelled back at Austin, telling him to keep his lies to himself. Instead, all I could think of was the fake footage of Lou. Maybe what he was claiming wasn't so farfetched.

"Ha. Nothing to say. That's answer enough." Austin dismissed us as he headed back to his school. "See you on the field." He pointed and gave me a mischievous grin that made me want to wipe it off his face.

"Why didn't you say anything, Pene? Don't tell me you like him?" Lacey screwed up her face.

"No!" I answered a little too strongly. "Let's line up, the game is about to start." I ushered her over to a line of classmates putting on their headgear. We stood behind them until an equipment manager handed us our crowns. They fit snugly over the top of our heads, with a mouthpiece trailing down from our left ear. They were lightweight and you barely noticed them once the game began. Over my head on one of the bars was a kill switch. If I was hurt or needed to leave the game at any time, I just had to tap it.

The re-enactment was virtual reality but played very specific parts in our city's history. The crown stimulated electronic images to the brain that superseded the images seen by your eyes. You could be in a classroom but your eyes didn't send images of the room to your brain; the process was reversed. The images fooled the brain into thinking it was someplace else. Computers generated a three-dimensional environment for you to move around in and interact with. It was fully immersive, and you could see yourself and others in the game. The technology evolved from multiplayer shooter games where people played in clunky computer-generated environments. Now the environments were so real, you swore you were there.

Although it was playing back a specific part of history, you could interact with the computer-generated participants or other players. Although you couldn't change history, you could change a specific chain of events. So if a building was destined to explode, you couldn't change the event, but you might be able to rescue different people each time you played. The thing that blew a lot of people's minds—especially adults—was that people you interacted with seemed real. If you touched their arm, you felt the sensation of touching skin. I didn't understand the process, but somehow neurons in your brain were being fired to complete the illusion.

Your environment also felt real to your touch, from the ground under your feet to the solidness of walls. When the wind blew, you could feel it on your face. If you touched a hot oven, you would feel the heat and instinctively pull your hand away. The game designers who created the technology were multimillionaires now. Some people even argued that the generated world was better than our own. It was so easy to lose yourself in the game, your brain was a willing participant in believing whatever the program was telling you to see and feel.

During the game there was no lag time—it felt like real life. Sometimes you looked around, trying to find the edge of the image, some seam in the computer-generated environment. But try as you might, the illusion was perfect. The resolution was the same as life, and you didn't feel like you were viewing the world from a screen. What better way to learn about history than to experience it first-hand? Some adults found the environment too realistic and got motion sick. And you had to be careful not to get hurt.

The re-enactment replayed past events and you had a chance to interact with history. In these events you could potentially influence the outcome, which was why people participated. To win.

The speakers in my earpiece came to life.

"Your attention please. Students, the game is about to begin," the voice commanded. It was Mr. Stewart, charged with observing and starting our match. He never missed a re -enactment or the chance to explain how important the game was. "The time clock will start the moment you are immersed in the game and begin carrying out your tasks in the re-enactment. If you are hit, you will be out of the game and must remove your headgear. You may leave at that time or wait until the conclusion of the game, when the winning school will be decided. An attacker can be subdued with your weapon. Ammunition will be placed around the game stage. If you run out, you must take the weapon from one of your opponents. Fellow teammates cannot give you their weapons. Time limit is sixty minutes. Are there any questions?"

The entire dome was silent. No one asked any questions. We had all played the re-enactment since we were kids. Only an idiot would ask a question now, with the entire student body listening.

"Then let the game begin!" Mr. Stewart tried to be dramatic but several of my classmates rolled their eyes. I winked at Lacey and looked up. The entire top of the dome turned black and the playing field turned into a city block. I looked down at my clothes. I was wearing a standard city uniform, as was the rest of my class. I had some type of rifle with a strap around my shoulder. I was ready for the battle. That was when the ground rumbled and the building in front of me fell and swallowed about a third of my classmates. Instant fatalities.

That was just one of the interesting things about the re-enactment. No two were alike. Although the general story was the same, earthquake, terrorist attack, the city residents rising up, the flow of the story changed. Attacks could occur at various points in the city, forcing teams to converge at different locations. The number of combatants was different every game; sometimes the home team had a big advantage, while other times it was more even. But the most important aspect was what students liked to call the "Random Factor." At any point the computer could add random effects, causing a game to swing into the other team's favor. Obstacles could appear, like a building or an exploding car, your gun could have a malfunction or the ground could fracture so that you would fall to your death.

I looked at my weapon. It shot electronic bolts, like a taser gun. Bullets were strictly taboo in the re-enactment; nobody died a gruesome or bloody death, but once shot, you exited the game.

"I think Cody disappeared in the rubble," Lacey commented casually.

"Good," I answered, "he was always a bad team player." I looked ahead, trying to see the opposing team, but the collapsed building blocked our view. "Which way do you want to go?"

"Most people are going to the right, towards the West Mountains. Shall we follow?"

"Like lemmings over the cliff. I hope this game ends quickly. I want to get home." We followed our group forward, watching tentatively for the visitors.

"You used to enjoy this last semester. Acting out the role of our forefathers. Living the dream, Pene!" We both broke into a mini giggle fit realizing neither one of us had embraced our history lessons. Someone told us to be quiet. Then a student next to me was shot. He vanished, taken from the game. He was likely taking off his headset and being ushered to the stands to watch the rest of the re-enactment. Our group broke off in a run, skirting the building and heading to the center of the town.

As in history, the power plant was the key to saving the city. If our team was able to turn the electricity back on, the city was saved. If the visitors were able to permanently disable the plant, then darkness remained and the city would descend into chaos. Game over.

"Guys, come over here," a tall blond kid whispered and motioned us to the wall. I looked at our group. There were twelve of us, five girls and seven boys. He drew on the ground. "We're here," he marked with a stick, "and we need to get there."

"Who died and made you the leader?" A stocky guy moved to the front of the group.

"Can you guys not do this right now?" Lacey gritted her teeth in exasperation. "You're not impressing us." The stocky guy made a face but motioned to the blond kid to continue.

"If we cross here and here," he traced his stick in a zigzag fashion and drew a central square to symbolize the power plant, "we should be able to enter the power plant from the front in about ten minutes."

"Won't the other team be expecting us here? We'll get caught in the crossfire," the stocky boy asked. He seemed to be expressing his opinion now instead of trying to show up the blond.

"Exactly!" the blond answered. "That's why you should take five of our group and go through the underground mall on the side entrance."

"Underground mall," I said. "What are you talking about?"

"In history class, we covered the blueprints of the old city before the earthquake. There were underground tunnels with stores where people would go to shop, mostly in the winter months." I saw a number of heads nod, which made me think I really needed to start paying better attention in Mr. Stewart's class. "Since the earthquake, the ground is too unstable, but during the game there is a good chance this area is still safe."

"That means there could also a good chance the ceiling will come crashing down on our heads. No thank you," Lacey said as she stood up.

"Oh come on, the worst thing that will happen is we'll be knocked out of the game. Let's go for it," I said, intrigued by the tunnels.

"Fine," Lacey answered with resignation.

"Okay, you five," the blond kid pointed to me and Lacey, the stocky kid and two other guys, "head over to this building and then go underground to the power plant. The rest of us will head to the main entrance. We should be first but if the other team is there, we'll attack and draw their attention." He looked us over, making sure everyone understood.

"Let's go make history!" The stocky boy grabbed his weapon and two other boys charged after him. Lacey and I hastily followed after them as the rest of the team veered right up a side street.

"Are we having fun yet?" Lacey smiled and her weapon almost hit her on the side of the head from the forward motion.

"Can't stop smiling," I answered dryly, trying to keep the three boys in sight. We turned the corner and watched as a door slowly closed on the side of the building. I grabbed it just before it shut.

"You idiots want to slow down! We can barely keep up," I yelled. The footsteps stopped below and one of the boys looked up.

"Come on! It's not our fault you can't keep up." He shifted his gaze at Lacey. She made a face but you could tell she silently agreed. We dropped down three flights of stairs and then entered a hallway. I looked across and saw a long tunnel that must have led several blocks ahead. The tunnel ceiling was painted with murals of clouds and a blue sky. *I guess people who worked down here all day wanted to see the sky.*

We caught up with the guys and walked past a number of locked-up shops along the walls, everything from coffee shops to clothes to electronics. The tunnel reminded me of an upscale Marks. I turned and realized that Lacey wasn't with me.

"Stop staring at those shoes! They're not real!" I yelled back to where Lacey had a red high heel in her hand from a shoe boutique. The boys snickered and Lacey dropped the shoe. She gave me a mischievous look. Sometimes I felt she did things just to get a reaction out of everyone else.

The boys stopped suddenly as I almost bumped into their backs.

"Listen—do you hear that?" one of the boys asked. Our group was quiet, and seconds later our silence was rewarded. Laser fire could be heard from above ground, likely a block away.

"Sounds like those guys are in a fight. Come on, let's restart the power plant," the stocky boy commented.

"Look over there!" one of the boys yelled. The ceiling had cracked earlier from the earthquake and debris was spewing down.

"Tell me we don't have to go that way?" Lacey asked.

"We have to go that way!" the stocky boy responded. "If we don't, we have to go above ground right into the firefight. Hurry!" he commanded. Our group ran full-out past the cave-in. Pebbles tumbled past my head; one knocked my arm. A boulder narrowly missed Lacey's head.

"That would have hurt," she quipped. The dust in the air was thick and all of us were coughing. About a hundred feet ahead we could make out the tunnel that led to the power plant. Lacey tripped over her shoes and almost fell.

"Come on!" I grabbed her hand and dragged her into the tunnel past the ceiling collapse. "Don't be lame by dying now." The five of us stopped, out of breath but safely past the debris.

"We did it!" One of the boys punched the air. We all smiled and then fell back to the ground as a boulder the size of a small car crushed him. His form flashed out as he left the game and went back to the safe zone.

"And then there were four," the stocky boy announced. We looked at each other and regrouped, heading into the bowels of the power plant. We activated a motion detector and two doors slid open. We walked into the cool darkness. Just as the darkness made it too difficult to see a flashlight beam kicked on.

"Each of your weapons has a flashlight mounted above your scope," the stocky boy's voice boomed out the darkness. I reached down and flicked a switch. Another beam powered on after me. In seconds there were four beams dancing on the tunnel wall.

"Wait a second. Do you guys hear something?" Lacey asked from the darkness. We were silent and the world seemed quiet.

"Nothing," the other boy answered. "Do you think the fight's over above ground?"

"If it is, who won?" I asked.

"Doesn't matter. We keep going, we're almost there," the stocky boy answered. "Look ahead!" I gazed forward, my night vision ruined by our flashlights. At first I didn't see anything but darkness, but then I saw a row of red lights flickering along the ceiling, like a runway strip beckoning us to approach. The four of us ran towards the light, realizing our time was running out.

Then the darkness exploded with light. We had been discovered.

Lacey and I ducked behind a stairwell just as a section of

wall collapsed and smashed to the ground about five feet from us. The weapons lit up the darkness like fireworks—reds and blues illuminated the shadows. They would have been pretty to watch if their impact didn't eliminate you from the game. The stocky boy pointed his weapon out around a crate and took multiple shots. It looked spectacular but his aim was poor. He got lucky and missed our attackers but the shot dislodged a huge piece of ceiling. A muffled scream meant that our attacker was crushed.

"Booyah!" the other boy yelled. My flashlight shifted over to him as he was jumping in celebration. "You did it! You took him out, man. You rock!" Then an electrical net came flying through the air and wrapped itself around him. The look on his face went from jubilation to frustration. He vanished as he returned to the game area. The stocky boy fired his gun at the origin of the flash of light. A scream and then silence confirmed that he had found his mark.

"Guess there was more than one," Lacey added while sliding her gun back into position.

"Thanks for the obvious," the stocky boy answered from the darkness. "Head for those doors." He pointed with his light. We crossed the tunnel and doors opened automatically. The room beyond bathed us in a sickly fluorescent glow. The area was the size of a warehouse, with large turbines whirling at the far end. The noise was deafening—an army of tanks could crash through the wall and you won't hear them coming. Our fearless leader pointed to a group of machines that were in darkness about halfway down the corridor. He didn't have to explain. We just needed to reach them, turn on the power, and we would win.

He dashed ahead of us while Lacey and I smiled.

"Looks like we won this one!" she yelled over the roar of the noise. I smiled back at her. The stocky boy stopped in from of the dark turbine. I could see him reaching for a handle that was to be pulled down to activate the machine. He turned his head and gave us a big smile. Then he disappeared in a blaze of light. My eyes watched the shot as it came directly across the room. Lacey and I dived behind another turbine as mini explosions rumbled from the front of the machine. We hunkered down, knowing that time was against us.

There was a gap in between turbines; if we crossed it, we could get to the machine we needed. I took one step towards the gap and floor melted under my feet. The heat made me fall backwards into Lacey. "We can't go forward," I screamed. "I'll be disintegrated the second I step into the opening!" She looked at me and then cocked her head, as if she had an idea.

She smiled and I realized a second too late what she was going to do. She gave me a stupid salute, like it would be the last time I would see her again. Then she stood up and ran out into the center of the huge room and began to fire wildly in all directions. I had no time to be cross, and if I didn't react immediately, her diversion would be a waste. I crossed the gap, expecting to be shot but made it to the other side without incident. Then there was a popping sound and the room became quiet. I tried not to expose my body as I reached for the lever to activate the power. My hand slapped around the console blindly since I couldn't look where I was reaching. Then I felt a finger on my back.

"We got to stop meeting like this," said a familiar voice. I turned and saw Austin, looking very smug that he had caught me. I knew I was done but it didn't mean I had to be a good sport about it.

"You are going to let the terrorists win?" I asked, trying to appeal to his patriotism.

"Don't believe everything history class teaches you. It's not as black and white as it's written." I wondered about that, thinking about my dad's office and the video evidence. Was anything we were told true? "Nothing personal, just playing the game." He motioned.

"Well, get it over with, game's almost over."

"I don't shoot girls," he said.

"Then how?" I started as he tapped the kill switch on my headband and fantasy melted back into reality.

5

Family

Lacey waved as she walked away from me down the street. A drone bee buzzed over her head and she tried to swat it away. Unlike a real bee, the drone was very quiet. She probably didn't intend to hit it but instinctively hated having an insect flying so close to her head.

As I walked up the steps of my house, I realized the re-enactment was just an hour ago. After the game, I had thought about talking to Austin about his comments that history was biased against the terrorists. After thinking over his words, I felt like my world should be upside down; everything I had been taught seemed less real. But it wasn't. Life had never been as black and white as history had explained. I had always felt like there was something missing in the texts, something more out there than was described. A star sparkled near the peak of the West Mountains. How I wished to leave this city and see beyond the stars.

"How did you do at the re-enactment?" my dad asked, interrupting my thoughts as I entered the kitchen.

"Ah, okay, I guess," I answered noncommittally. I really didn't want to discuss the game.

"Okay?" My dad put down his tablet. A video was playing on the screen. "You were one of the top players from the school? You had quite a game. I was very impressed with your play." He tapped the screen. My body sank; he had watched the whole game. My life had no privacy.

"Bit of luck," I said while sitting down at the kitchen table. "Even Lacey nearly made it to the end."

"You should be proud of yourself. You probably added a few more points to your final report card." He was silent for a second but I knew he had another question. Likely one he couldn't get from his tablet. "Who's the boy from the other school?"

"What boy?" I answered and immediately regretted my response. Dad turned his head to the side, and rather than answer, he simply turned his tablet towards me. The video showed Austin talking to me just before the end of the game.

"Some kid from the other school. Why?" I felt my breath shorten.

"He says something to you but the receivers from the game don't pick it up. The two of you seem to know each other." He tapped the tablet screen.

"Never seen him before today," I breathed out. I turned my attention to the pantry as if to make supper. I did not want him to see the lie on my face.

"Good." He seemed satisfied. "I didn't like him. He seemed a little too enthusiastic for the terrorists to win." For some reason his words held less meaning now, and he made me want to know more about my history.

"Dad?" He gave me a look as if he knew what I was going to ask. "How did Mom die?" His face didn't register the question but the weight on his body looked crushing. He turned away from me, as if to collect himself.

"I'll tell you…"

"When you're older," I finished, knowing the drill all too well. "I've listened to that excuse all my life. Guess what, I think I'm old enough now." I looked him in the face and he knew I meant business. I watched him get up and circle the table. He was collecting his thoughts, and I wondered if he would actually follow through with an answer for once. He leaned on the windowsill and looked outside.

"You know, you look exactly like your mother right now. And you act like her too. She always pushed to know the truth."

"So tell me. I think I have a right to know."

"Of course you do. You deserve that and more." He turned from the window and faced me. "Tell me, what's your fondest memory of her?"

"I don't know, Dad. I was two when she died. I barely remember her. When I see her pictures around the house, she seems like a long-lost relative that I vaguely remember."

"Think, Pene. There must be something. She loved you so much. I remember you giggling when she tucked you in at night."

A memory clung to my brain. It was nagging, as if it refused to reveal itself. When I looked at her picture, I felt warm inside but I didn't know why.

"Dad. I. Don't. Know," I spat out, but it was a lie. I remembered a song, something she sang to me, but I couldn't remember the words. For a second he looked relieved, as if he was glad I had no memories of her. It made me want to strangle him. "Tell me how she died right now or I will never talk to you again!" His face pinched and I immediately regretted my hard stance. But I had to do something drastic to make him take me seriously. His mouth moved but no words came out. I knew talking about her caused him a lot of pain. But I had a hole so deep where I should have had a memory of her. How I wanted something to fill it!

"Pene?" Dad motioned to the dining room chair. "Have a seat." I sat down while he fumbled for something in his wallet. I was about to protest that I didn't want him to change the subject by offering me money but he dropped a badge face down on the table. I flipped it over and looked at hologram image of my mother in a lab coat. She wore a faint smile, as if she enjoyed her work. I noticed the badge location stamped in the upper left hand corner.

"Mom worked at the power plant? Was she there when the terrorists attacked?" I blurted out, but Dad's pain gave the obvious answer. He turned to me, his eyes moist.

"Your mom worked as a technician, observing the power levels at the plant. She would help recommend alternative energies to compensate for the peak power level times during the day when the plant was at capacity." I gave him a baffled look, as if I couldn't believe what he was telling me or that he was finally telling me the truth.

"How did Mom die?" I asked.

"You have played the re-enactment enough to know the sequence of events. When the earthquake hit and the plant overloaded, there was a huge explosion. A large part of the plant was destroyed and many lives were lost, but your mother's wasn't one of them."

"How did you know?"

"She called me from the plant. She was tending to several people who were hurt. That's when the plant was overrun and the terrorists made their play to take over the remaining power supply. Your mother was a hostage. Demands were made. The terrorists wanted control of parts of the city in exchange for giving the city back its electrical power."

"And what did the city do?"

"They," he hesitated, "did nothing. The city doesn't negotiate with terrorists. After twenty-four hours of getting nowhere with the city, the terrorists blew up the plant. All the hostages were killed." His voice trailed off. After so many years he had finally told me the truth. And then I realized Dad's motivation at work.

"Were you a lawyer before Mom died?"

"Yes." He nodded. "Fresh out of law school. Articled for a small firm in the west side of the city, did mostly contract law. After your mom's death, the work seemed meaningless. I took a few months off, trying to take care of you, get my life in order. But nothing was ever the same. Your mother never should have died. I quit my firm and went to work with the Ministry of Justice. With the new security protocols with cameras and drones, your mother could still be alive today. To honor her memory, I worked to make sure people like the terrorists were made to pay for their crimes."

His eyes shone with determination. He had dedicated his career to the law. He was still trying to put away the terrorists that had killed my mom. I imagined he saw every case as a chance to redeem himself for not being there for her. He had devoted his life to making the current system work.

"Do you ever think that the law could be wrong? That something could be done to make a suspect look guilty of a crime that they didn't commit?" My dad looked puzzled but took a second to think about my question.

"Pene, I always want to pursue the truth. I know I can come across a bit overzealous because of what happened to your mom, but I only want to bring guilty people to justice. I work very hard to make sure I review all of the footage before making my assessment."

"And if someone was truly innocent."

"Then I would do everything in my power to make sure he was set free in a court of law. But with our technology, that is so rare nowadays. And any irregularities would have to run by Lord Morall to determine if an alternate judgment is correct."

And with those words I knew I couldn't tell him about Lou's video. There was no way Morall would listen about the system being wrong. My instincts screamed that Morall himself was the source of corruption. I loved my father but I wouldn't endanger us.

"Thanks, Dad. You don't know how much I appreciate knowing the truth about Mom."

"I'm sorry I've waited so long to tell you. I guess I have

to realize that you're not a little girl anymore."

"Seriously, Dad. I haven't been a little girl for a while now." I tried not to sound defensive.

"How do you feel?" He looked at me as if trying to gauge my emotions. "Does knowing how your mom died make you feel any better?"

"Dad," I considered the last few day's events, "right now, I'm a bit overwhelmed by the truth."

6

Visit

The hover bus skimmed the street, the air jets pushing it a few feet off the ground, never making contact. I looked out the window past the old warehouses. This part of the city had fewer residents and was the most damaged since the great earthquake. Patches of weeds sprung around building corners, reaching towards the rooftops. Since my talk with Dad, I had sleepwalked through class the next day, my mind numb and overloaded with information. I asked Dad if I could visit Grandma on Saturday, and he was supportive of me getting out of the downtown core.

The bus had screens on the ceiling that shimmered with news, videos and advertisements. One screen showed the ribbon-cutting for a new park downtown. Another showed news of some football players crossing the end zone. Endless talking heads inhabited the other ones. I wished for a remote to shut them all off.

Then I caught the footage of young man who had just returned back from travels abroad. He had been the lucky visa traveler and had spent four months outside of the city. Four months! I wished I could have been him. He was doing an interview with a journalist and several images came up of his travels. I was so jealous, I couldn't watch any longer. I twisted around, looked through the window and focused on the buildings as they passed by. It wasn't far now.

Grandma was my father's mother, my only living grandparent. Her home was old, on the outskirts of the city. Each lot had an acre of land, and with the trees between them you could almost believe that no one lived nearby. It was a one-level home with a sun porch where she spent a good part of her time reading and putting puzzles together. She loved her puzzles, and on any given visit she might have a dozen different ones in various stages of completion around her home. Some lay on tables, on wooden boards and even a few on the floor that made it difficult to walk around. As the hover bus skidded to a stop, I could make out the outline of her home in the distance.

I walked onto the street, the doors closing behind me, and the driverless vehicle circled around the street before heading back into the city. As I walked down a dirt path, I could hear a buzzing sound from a berry bush between two houses. I turned down a short driveway and instead of knocking on the front door continued on to the back of the house. As I swerved around some overgrown branches, my hands groped for the door of the sun porch. When I entered, I saw my grandma sitting on a flowery couch with a cup of tea on a table. She looked like she had just started a new puzzle.

"Pene!" she exclaimed, putting down her teacup, "come give your nana a hug." Her smile was infectious and I gladly squeezed her. Her body felt thin and brittle, and I tried not to break any bones with my hug.

"Nana, have you lost weight?"

"I might have," she said with a mischievous grin. "You never know when you might catch the eye of an eligible bachelor."

"Nana," I chastised, not knowing if she was telling the truth, "You feel too thin. Have you been taking your medication?"

On the coffee table in front of her, my eyes spied motion. A mechanical drone stomped towards her with a pill on his tray. It stopped before her as she plucked the pill from the tray and inserted it into her mouth.

"Pretty hard to miss my schedule with these things marching about." Her fingers flicked the drone, which tipped over with its legs kicking. She seemed not to notice. "Sit down, honey, let me look at you. You look more like your mother every time I see you." Her smile was creased with wrinkles framed by kindly eyes. A bee buzzed overhead and tried to land on her face. I instinctively tried to swat it away.

"Damn drones," I exclaimed angrily, "can't leave us alone for a second!" My grandma's expression turned to bewilderment and then to realization.

"Oh dear, you misunderstand. Not every one of these mechanical wonders is watching you. Some are assigned very specific tasks. Take this little guy." She plucked a flower from a vase and the bee flew around her hand before resting on her finger. Its little legs scurried as it dug into petals, its body shaking in the flower.

"When I was a child, I couldn't do that with a real bee. I'd either be too scared or it would consider me a threat. These new mechanical bees are trained not to hurt, and without their help, half of our crops, from apples to blueberries, would never get pollinated."

"I've never seen real bees. Where did they go?"

"They died," she answered flatly, as if their extinction was quite normal. "No one knows for sure. It happened gradually. May have been pesticides or parasites; scientists never confirmed why. Man interfered with things and Mother Nature said we could no longer have bees. Good thing we showed Mother Nature a thing or two." Nana sipped her tea as the bee flew out the window.

"Nana," I reached and grabbed her hand, "Dad told me about Mom. About how she died." Her face was first blank and then realization set in.

"Well, it's about time. You're not a child anymore." She waggled her finger at me. "Your mother was an amazing woman. Smart as all get-out. I used to tease my son and ask him how he attracted such a brilliant woman. If she hadn't died in the power plant blasts, she would have been one of our leading scientists." She picked up a puzzle piece and put it in place. She was a multi-tasker, always doing more than one thing at a time. I was never offended; I knew she was still listening to me even as she did something else.

"Nana. Why didn't you tell me?" I grabbed a flower piece and fit it into her puzzle. She smiled at my assistance.

"Not my place, dear. Your father changed after your mother's death. He became more withdrawn, more focused on the law. He missed her spontaneity and creativity." She looked closely into my eyes. "It was never my story to tell." She was focused again on the puzzle. This topic had come to a close. I thought about something else.

"Grandma, how come you don't live in the city? If you lived any further outside, you would be beyond the hover buses." She focused on her puzzle, and for a moment I thought she hadn't heard me. Then her hand cupped her ear.

"Dear Pene," she didn't raise her head, "what do you hear?" I was silent and confused.

"But Grandma?"

"What do you hear?" She looked up, expecting an answer. I was quiet and closed my eyes. I could hear a bird chirping in a nearby tree. I could hear the hum of the refrigerator. In the distance I thought I heard a mower cutting grass. But if I listened really carefully, I could hear...

"Nothing," I said. "It's so quiet, you can hear yourself think."

She smiled. "Now you know. When your grandfather was alive, we hated the city. Too much noise, too many cameras, no privacy. We always felt like we were under a microscope. Some specimen meant to be examined. Here we felt less studied, freer."

"Why didn't you two move away? See the world?"

"Justin was always a homebody, never had the itch to see beyond the city. During university, I thought about taking the necessary courses to go overseas but...." She trailed off.

"What stopped you?"

"The red tape. There are so many tests and costs, it became so difficult that it made it not worth it to travel. Then your father was born and my priorities changed." Grandma became quiet and I wondered if she ever regretted her choices. Maybe she would have made a different decision now, looking back.

I poured some tea from her flowery pot. It smelled sweet. I dropped a spoonful of synthetic honey into my glass. The drone bee banged on the window from the outside.

"Grandma—what was it like before the drones? Were they all created after the earthquake?" She looked thoughtful, as if imagining a world completely different to the one we lived in now. She put the puzzle piece into the corner.

"The earthquake certainly expedited the drone machines, but honestly, they have been around for as long as I can remember. We have been poisoning our earth for so long, we had been trying to recreate animals in some form or another. Clones were popular for a while but their ability to follow instruction was unpredictable. Drones were used about ten years before the earthquake, simple ones, like robot rats, to sniff for explosive devices. Drone planes eventually replaced fighter pilots when I was a teenager. It was all about dollars and trying to balance government budgets. Countries were so badly in debt. Drone planes were much cheaper to build and fly than human operators. Pilots fought the changes, but eventually defense budgets were trimmed and drones were the most cost-effective option."

"You mean people used to fly in planes?" I asked.

"They used to drive cars and ships as well. But sweetheart, we make mistakes. Thousands of lives were lost each year, from car crashes to airline disasters. You might not like the drones but a lot of accidents are prevented because of their help."

"But when did they start watching us? I can't walk for two minutes without a drone following me." I stood up and knocked over the cup of tea. It flowed towards the puzzle pieces like a liquid snake across the table. As it reached a corner piece, Grandma placed her napkin down, making a barrier and stopping the flow.

"What's wrong with you, dear? I've not seen you this upset before." I cautiously scanned the window to make sure a drone bee wasn't watching me. I choose my words carefully.

"I think I got frustrated with my class project," I lied. "You know how there are rarely any court trials. The sentence is usually automatic once footage of the crime is played."

"Of course, you should have seen it in my day. Trials could go for years. The guilty would often go free on a technicality. The system is so efficient now, and our city is so much safer."

"Yes, but are innocent people being punished? Are we seeing the truth?" I spoke louder than I wanted. And I realized then that I didn't want to tell Grandma all of the details. It would be too much for her to believe. Or worse, she'd tell Dad.

"Truth?" Grandma seemed bewildered. "Of course it's the truth. Just ask your father. Crimes are caught on camera. The guilty acts are captured, digitally recorded. Now people think twice before committing a crime. What seems to have you so worked up, dear? You can tell me." She looked genuinely concerned and I wanted to tell her about Lou and the doctored footage. But it wasn't fair to involve her. I was already in deep trouble if I told others; I wasn't going to jeopardize her.

"No reason, Grandma, just curious, that's all. I'm trying to finish my project in a very short time. Putting me under a bit of pressure." I tried another approach. "Where do all of these drones come from? No one seems to know where they originate. They just seem to be everywhere." Grandma looked thoughtful for a few seconds but then nodded.

"That's an excellent question, dear, but I don't know. I really don't need to know. I don't need to know where the local police station is to know that they are protecting me."

"But—" I tried to coax out a location.

"If I did, I would go see your father. They record and send all footage to the courts. Your father reports to the High Courts—the judges probably know.

I thought of Lord Morall's red eye and thought no one else would know better than he.

"That's a good idea. Maybe it's silly to want to know where they come from." Grandma looked warily around the room and scanned the windows.

"Now, dear, if you ask me, drones aren't the only way they watch us."

"What do you mean?" I asked.

"Drones, cameras, satellites, who knows what else they track us with. With today's technology, no one can truly hide from the law."

7

Chase

"Lieutenant Vaslor, I'd like you to meet my daughter."
My dad directed my attention to a tall man in a blue uniform. His face was kind and younger than my dad's. He had
a rugged handsomeness, with a strong jaw and deep blue
eyes. The only flaw was a scar on the right corner of his
forehead. If Lacey was here, I'm sure she would have made
some comment about his good looks.

"Hi, I'm Pene. I really appreciate you letting me come
here to see the Justice Building. I have a whole list of questions from school I'm hoping to ask." I smiled up at him. He
motioned for me and dad to follow behind. He had a disciplined walk, and we matched his steps.

"Well Pene, you're getting a rare glimpse today. We
don't normally give tours, but your father is such a stand-up
guy, I was happy to oblige. My only problem is my time is
extremely limited. We'll have to walk and talk." We traveled down a long hallway, passing several people. Some
looked like the lieutenant, officers in uniforms with low

black stripes down their legs. Others wore lab coats, probably technicians or investigators examining crime scenes. Still others looked casual, in t-shirts and jeans. One guy looked like he was reprogramming a tablet. A man and woman in suits walked by, likely lawyers like my dad.

"So how do you know when a crime has been committed?" I asked. A door opened to the right and he directed us to follow. I turned a corner and stopped dead in my tracks, looking up at the biggest room I had ever seen. It was several times bigger than a football field. There were banks and banks of cameras, thousands mounted in the walls, thousands more floating in the air. There were hundreds of stations—men and women sat in front of clumps of cameras, examining hundreds of scenes. We walked over to one particular station, and I could see a camera looking down on the street as dozens of people milled below.

"Welcome to the nerve center," began the lieutenant, "where no crime goes unrecorded." Another camera was at street level, where people walked by without seeming to notice it. A third camera was moving past a window as a family were making their supper.

"How do you find a crime amongst all of these cameras? There's so much noise." I pointed high up the wall. It felt like sensory overload, and I imagined that I would go insane trying to sift through so much information. Vaslor motioned to one of the techs assessing the monitors.

"Simpson, show us how you review your data." A skinny tech guy with long black hair motioned to a computer. He flicked his hand down and moved several computer screens to the right so he could focus on two cameras angles on his center view.

"The cameras and drones record terabytes of video every second." The technician turned to look at me and my father. "There is too much information for us to review it all so the computers run scripts listening to keywords, analyzing facial expressions, looking for weapons and so on. Anything that is remotely considered threatening is tagged by the computer." He scrubbed through the screen and brought up one of two camera screens he had saved.

A group of teenage boys was walking down an alley. It looked like the back of a schoolyard. Three of them stood in front of a camera while the fourth looked like he was spray-painting graffiti on the wall.

"Simpson, can you send in a nearby drone to that location?" Vaslor pointed to the computer.

"Affirmative." He tapped a key and an icon of a drone bird flashed on the screen. It was flying above the school and zeroed in on the location of the boys. Its bird's-eye view crossed a football field and then looked down on the boys in between two school buildings. The fourth boy was tagging the wall with some type of signature. It was hard to make out from the angle but the other three were looking around as if making sure no one could see them. Suddenly one of them looked skyward.

"Drone!" he yelled and pointed. The three boys scattered while the graffiti artist froze in place. The drone came up to his head as he tried to cover his face.

"Come on. Smile for the camera. We can wait all day,"

laughed Vaslor. The boy uncovered his face, as if he could hear. His face was crestfallen when he saw the bird hovering in place, a few feet away. He turned and ran towards his friends.

"Transmit the image and send it to the principal of the school. The kids will be disciplined. This was a pretty small-time crime." Vaslor turned to my dad. "Now, your father handles a lot of the serious cases, usually theft over $10,000, fraud and robberies. Once we give him the footage, he always gets his man."

"Or woman," my dad answered, looking at me. "Crime knows no gender."

"Dad, have you ever tried a murder case?"

"No, dear, above my pay grade. Maybe someday."

"As long as my team provides the proof, your dad can bring any criminal to justice," Vaslor bragged. I looked at the dozens of cameras, eyes on the city. As I watched, I noticed a common theme. I raised my hand like an obedient schoolgirl.

"Lieutenant, when a criminal is captured, is it always the drones that go after him?" Vaslor looked thoughtful and sat down in an adjoining chair.

"Good question—wasn't that long ago that I was in the field." He motioned to me to sit down next to him. "When all of our cameras were stationary, detachments were stationed around the city to respond to crimes as they were recorded. I used to be attached to the western precinct about five years ago. When footage for a crime was relayed to us, we'd play a game of follow the crook. Depending on how quick we got the call after the crime was committed, we had a success rate of about 70%."

"Why not 100%?" I asked. My dad gave me a funny look as if I was commenting on Vaslor's ability.

"A number of reasons, actually. Remember that cameras were not on every corner; there were a lot of dead zones where someone could hide from a security cam. Public areas were always covered, but inside hospitals, offices, washrooms etc., some measure of privacy is expected."

"A criminal could just duck into these areas and you would lose the trail?"

"Sometimes. If we didn't get good video footage, the criminal could travel through one of the dead zone areas and change direction or appearance. By the time we figured it out, they would be gone. Now, with the addition of the drones, it's a lot harder for a criminal to disappear. These machines are faster and never tire. They stick to you."

"Like gum on your shoe," my dad felt the need to add.

"So when did you let the drones start pursuing the criminals as well? Was it too dangerous for you?" I asked.

"What my charming daughter is asking," my dad gave me a look, "is when did it become more efficient to have the drones pursue the criminals?"

Vaslor smiled as if he had answered the question many times before. "There is an element of danger to law enforcement—there is always a risk when we pursue a runner. But what people forget is that there is also a risk to the criminal because since he wants to escape, sometimes he'll do things that won't only endanger us but could also hurt bystanders as well."

"Like a car chase?" I offered.

"Exactly! The collateral damage is not worth the criminals' capture if innocent people are hurt in the chase. But what if you could let the criminal run for as long as he wanted, like a fish on a hook? Watching his every move, every decision. Watch the desperation drain out of his body, turn into fear, exhaustion and then acceptance. Then the drones are just clean up, once criminals see them, they are resigned to their fate. There is no struggle, no innocents are hurt, just acceptance."

I thought about Lou's denial and escape—I saw no acceptance for his supposed crime.

"Makes a lot of sense. Must have changed your role a lot. Instead of being on the ground, you have to watch the chase unfold."

"I prefer the term 'directed'. The drones have to be moved like chess pieces on a board. I take a lot of pride from the fact that my team always get its man and no one gets hurt."

"Better yet, the footage enables me to present to the courts actual evidence of the crime," my dad chimed in, proud of the process.

"Well, just don't forget who does all the heavy lifting." Vaslor nodded. "You must be near to 100% with the evidence my team provides."

"Well, 99% to be exact—even your drones have a glitch now and then," Dad replied.

A glitch. Glad to hear the drones aren't perfect, although falsify-

ing footage is no glitch. Someone here in this warehouse must have doctored Lou's footage. But who and why?

"Lieutenant?" I looked up into his blue eyes. "Where are the drones stored? Are they in an adjoining warehouse?" He looked at my dad with a smug grin.

"That's classified information, young lady. We could get into trouble just discussing where they're housed." Simpson gave him a look as if he was enjoying an inside joke. Vaslor leaned in closer, as if to whisper a response. "The fact is, we don't know where they are stored. That information would reside with the Judges." Even my dad looked surprised.

"Really—how do you manage your assets if you don't know where the drones come from?" Dad asked. Vaslor nodded to Simpson, who typed in several commands. A schematic of the city came up, with thousands of flashing dots representing all types of drones.

"Think of the city as a living, breathing chess board. On every street, a pawn is watching, awaiting instructions. Depending on where the crime takes place, those drones closest to the scene are used first. If there is more than one criminal involved, going in several directions," Simpson waved his hand over several dots, "then more drones are put in play."

"But where do the drones go for repairs? Where are new ones built?" I asked. Before he could answer, a siren blared. I cupped my hands over my ears. The sound died down immediately.

"We have got a runner! Sector five—south end of the city!" Simpson pointed at a screen that was flashing red.

"Enlarge image," Vaslor commanded. The camera screen

grew ten times larger, taking up most of the wall. A man was rushing through a crowd of people. The camera cut several times as it tried to predict his direction. I began to get motion sickness from the jerkiness of the camera jumps.

"Are we allowed to be watching this?" I asked.

"Here." Vaslor handed me an eyewear apparatus with a similar setup as the re-enactment equipment. "Don't interrupt us until the criminal is captured."

"Okay." I slipped it over my head and suddenly my view changed and I was no longer in the Justice Building. I looked down at a sidewalk. Just like the re-enactment simulation, I became immersed into the environment as I became a drone bystander watching the chase enfold. The man ran by, knocking into the person behind me. The runner barely glanced at me but in the second I looked at him, I could see fear etched on his face. A drone dog galloped past me, chasing the man. I pursued.

The drone dog was rapidly gaining ground, but fortunately for the man, the street was full and he dodged around people, creating obstacles that prevented the dog from using its full speed. A bus came to a stop on the street and the runner jumped inside, with the doors closing behind him. The dog leaped at the entrance, trying to get in, but the automated driver seemed more interested in keeping its schedule and pulled out back onto traffic.

"Simpson, call transit authority and have them shut down bus 318," Vaslor's voice crackled over my headpiece. "Radio to other drones in the area to converge. The only drone powerful enough to bring suspect down is a K9. Sentry drones are observing the scene." The disembodied voice sounded strange as the bus rumbled by. The dog circled the bus, leaping occasionally at the windows, alarming the passengers. The runner might have been safe for the moment but I had the feeling that the dog was going to jump into the bus at the next stop. I ran to catch up as the bus came to an abrupt stop. The power had been cut.

The top hatch on the roof popped open and the runner climbed up. The dog jumped at the bus but despite its augmented limbs, it couldn't leap on top of the vehicle. The man pulled himself up and stood on the roof. He looked towards a storefront and jumped onto the overhang. But instead of climbing into an open window, he jumped several buildings towards an apartment building, smashing into a second-floor window. *Why would he pick such an awkward entrance?*

I stopped and looked around. People barely watched the runner go through the glass window. It was as if they felt safer ignoring him. Everyone avoided him so they wouldn't risk guilt by association. It was assumed that anyone chased by a drone had committed the crime. I looked at my reflection in the window of the bus.

My red drone eyes glimmered. My body was small and bug-shaped, some type of flying beetle. I almost wanted to reach out and swat myself. It was like having an out-of-body experience but being repulsed by my appearance. I tilted my head to the right and my antenna flicked towards the bus. I desperately wanted to follow the runner. Suddenly my body floated up, as if my brain was controlling the bug's actions. I flew into the window and turned suddenly around a wall. The motion was a bit jarring and I felt sick.

There was broken glass and what looked like a drop of blood. My hearing felt extra sensitive and I thought I could hear noise on the landing above. I flew down the hall, where apartment numbers adorned the doors. People start coming out, attracted by the commotion, and I narrowly missed flying into a mother's apron. I flew on and came to a fire door, metal and heavy, too much for my form to push open. I looked around for another entry upstairs. My head turned back to the door and a red flash came from my eyes.

The glass melted from the lasers in my eyes and smoke billowed from the dripping beads of glass. I flew through the gap, careful that my wings did not touch the molten glass. I heard running on the stairs and flew up quickly, barely making it upstairs before the fire door closed to the top floor. The pandemonium from downstairs had ceased while the top floor was silent. Its layout was different from below; the whole floor was open concept, with few walls and lots of windows looking down below. A fitness area was to the right, with lockers and a change area. To the left was a hallway that opened into a rec room with television, couches and small kitchen. I navigated around some balloons hanging down from the ceiling from someone's birthday.

A tinny galloping sound echoed from behind and I turned to make out a familiar silhouette. *Where have I seen that before?* As I flew after it, a tiny piece of paper floated to the ground. My eyes instinctively looked at the writing. It was a bunch of nonsense words that didn't make sense. I wasn't sure if this was a password, combination or a serial number. Either way, it meant nothing to me. As I decided to pursue the direction of the galloping, the sound of a chair moving came from behind me. As I turned to look at it, my red eyes looked up into the bottom of a foot as it crushed me into the floor. A flick of static and then my camera went black. I took off my glasses.

"Good job, Pene. You're a natural hunter," remarked Vaslor. "Don't worry about the runner, he's trapped in the building. Other drones are on their way now." He turned to the bank of monitors. Dad tapped me on the shoulder.

"Let's go. Vaslor and his team need to finish their capture." I waved my thanks as Vaslor was yelling additional orders to Simpson. On a screen, the man who was being chased was backing into a corner as several drones inched closer. He would not be getting away.

As we walked out of the Justice Center, the shadow's shape became clear to me. I knew where I had seen it before. *I had to find Austin!*

8

Answers

Saturday morning could not come soon enough. The rest of the week had dragged on and I don't think I listened to more than two sentences in any class. Fortunately, most of my classmates were the same. I knew that I had to get back to the Marks, to try to find Austin again. The tricky thing was having a plausible excuse. I couldn't just tell my dad I was going to the library. Since he was a lawyer, he needed evidence to confirm where I had been. I had gotten into the habit of buying things in case Dad ever wanted to check my debit list to verify my location. This time I made a preemptive strike.

I had Lacey leave a message for me at home about meeting for a project. Dad would be nosy enough to review the message. She didn't say a time or where, so I could always see her later in the day and not be telling a lie. *Well, sort of.* Lacey thought I wanted to see Austin because I liked him. I wanted to see him because of the piece of paper I saw when I was a drone. And the shadow I saw in that building.

I started my walk, wary of flying drones and cameras on buildings. The streets were quiet today, but although I thought I heard a mechanical whirl a few times, I saw no spying drones. I guessed even machines rest on the weekends. After backtracking several times, my winding route eventually got me closer to the Marks. I smelled the aromas first, long before I saw any vendors. The air was thick with drones here—now I knew why there weren't many on my streets enroute. All the action was here. I pulled my hoodie over my hair, letting the fabric cover most of my face.

I walked the Marks for a good hour, examining clothing, electronics and food stalls. Nothing carried the oddities of Lou's stall. Despite his effort to overcharge me, I missed him. Soon the food smells became too much for me, and my stomach groaned in protest. I bought some meat skewers and sat on a rock wall facing the sun. The morning had been a bust so far—I'd thought Austin was a regular here. So far he was no-show, or maybe I was missing him in another part of the Marks. Some grease from the skewer dripped down the stick and onto the ground. A familiar shape came scurrying up beside me and sniffed the grease stain.

"Lola!" The little mechanical dog barked softly and rubbed against my leg. I stroked under her chin and her tail wagged happily.

"Don't feed her any food! Or I'll be cleaning her gears for weeks," a familiar voice yelled from the crowd. Austin's grin emerged as shook his hair out of his face.

"Honestly. As if I would feed her real food."

"You'd be surprised." Austin sat next to me. "Some people forget she's not a real dog. A few old guys still look at her strangely, almost as if she reminds them of an old pet." I motioned my skewer towards him in case he wanted a bite. He shook his head. "What brings you to the Marks today? Looking for more crazy objects?"

I put down my food. "I came looking for you. I need to talk to you about something. Can we go somewhere away from prying eyes?"

Austin jumped back in mock horror. "I don't know what the girls in your school have been telling you, but I'm not that kind of guy," he joked.

I blushed then slugged him on the shoulder. "That's not what I meant! I need your help. Something happened this week. Something I think you're involved with."

"Sounds menacing," Austin mocked, not really taking me seriously. "Let's head over to my office." He motioned to the alley. I rolled my eyes but followed him with Lola tailing behind me. The alleyway was shaded but busy. Several people walked past us, heading to the sellers. I scanned upward but saw no cameras or drones. Austin motioned to the ground. "Talk downward—makes it harder for them to read your lips." We walked slowly. There was lots of ambient noise around us that forced me to speak up.

"You need to be truthful with me. I was with my father and was able to watch them chase after a runner firsthand."

"What do you mean? Were you actually involved in the chase?" he asked. His interest seemed genuine.

"Kind of. You put a headpiece on and assume the role of the pursuing drones. It feels like you are actually there."

"Guess you like catching the guilty. And here I thought you liked your shopkeeper friend." Austin was teasing but I thought I could sense some anger in his voice. I pulled him towards me.

"Listen! This is important. When I inhabited the drone's body, there was someone helping the runner. He specifically entered a building that was out of his way, like it was a meeting place. And when he got inside, a message was left to help him."

"So? What does this have to do with me?" He turned his face away so I couldn't read his expression. I made him look at me.

"I saw Lola there. Or at least I saw her shadow. Unless someone is controlling your dog, you know something about what is going on."

Austin pulled my arm off him. "I heard your father was some big lawyer for Justice. Are you some spy for him?" He walked away.

"No, but you are making me so mad!" I yelled a bit too loudly. A couple walked by us, looking at me and then whispering to each other. "I'm not a spy, but I saw something at his office that I shouldn't have." Austin stopped and turned around.

"That's pretty cryptic. What'd you mean?" I walked closer to him and whispered in his ear.

"My dad has footage of the crime. It didn't match. Someone doctored the footage to incriminate Lou." Austin looked at me as if I had grown a second head. I wasn't sure if he believed me or if he thought I was trying to trap him.

"You are in a lot of trouble if that's true," he whispered back. "I bet you're not supposed to see that footage—that's only reviewed in the courts. And the footage is just a slam dunk to prove someone guilty. Does your dad know?"

I averted my eyes. "Oh my god, no. He'd kill me if I told him I reviewed his crime footage. Besides, he'd never believe me if I said it was doctored. He couldn't understand that the justice system could be corrupted. It would shake his beliefs to the core."

Austin considered my words. "Then I can't help you. You want me to tell you about something that could endanger my life, but you won't take any risks yourself."

"Because I don't understand what is going on! If the drones aren't here to protect us, what are they doing?"

"I wish I could trust you. I really do. When you confront your father, ask him for some answers. Then come see me. If your information is useful, I'll answer your question." Austin slipped behind a group of men, heading back to the Marks. Lola barked at me and then chased after him. I decided not to pursue him. I had nothing more to say.

If I wanted to get answers, I was going to have to confront my father.

9

Confrontation

About five minutes after leaving the Marks, I knew something was wrong. I was always careful to keep my face covered to avoid the drones' facial recognition software. Sunglasses and a cap could do wonders to protect your identity. I had rounded the corner when I saw a typical drone bee buzzing about five feet above me. I ignored it while looking in another direction but kept moving forward. Moments later, as I peered back, the bee was slowly following me. It kept a discreet distance, never getting too close but always within my line of sight. I felt like it was playing a game of cat-and-mouse.

I headed to a busy commercial street, hoping that many people and vehicles might help me lose my pursuer. I went into a grocery store and grabbed a cart. The bee hovered at the big bay window, looking in at me and the other customers. I went down an aisle, trying to get as far away as possible from the drone. I ducked around a corner of boxed goods so that it could not see me from the window. *Think.*

Was all this in my mind? Was I imagining the drone was following me? A stock boy came out of a swinging door from the back of the store. As he went down the aisle, I ran towards the closing door and entered the loading bay. The area was silent; no one was unloading packaged goods. *Maybe this is a good omen?* I rushed past some crates towards a back ramp door. As I exited, I could hear it lock behind me. I stepped into the back employee parking lot. There was no one around.

I walked between two cars when I suddenly had to duck down. Drones may be hard to lose but they were never hard to spot. The sun gleamed on its metal body and its red eyes flickered. From my vantage point, I couldn't tell if it was the same drone from the front, or a second one. They all looked the same to me. I didn't think it had seen me as it continued its slow, relentless pace around the corner of the building. As it flew by my position, I crawled past another vehicle. An older woman walked by with bags of groceries. I moved past her, using her as a screen. As I rounded the corner of the store, I sneaked a look back at the bee to see where it had gone.

Bam! All the air was expelled out my lungs as I slammed into the metal frame of a man-sized drone. It barely moved as it reached down to pick me up.

"You are to come with me," it commanded in its metallic tone.

I stared at it with dread. Visions of Lou's arrest filled my head, and I felt sure I was going to be charged with a false crime. I thought of escape, but where could I go? They would scoop me up as soon as I got home. So I tried to reason with it.

"No! I'm not going anywhere. Have I been charged with something?"

"No, you haven't." I waited for some elaboration of its answer. When none came, I pressed further.

"Then why do I have to come with you? I wish to go home." I started to walk away with purpose, but the drone's hand ensnarled my arm. It had the grip of a steel vise.

"Who wants to see me?"

"I am not programmed with that information. Come with me and your question will be answered." Its logic was impeccable and I resigned myself to my fate. I swung my leg over the back of the drone as I straddled the motorcycle portion of its body. The metal was smooth and cool to my touch. I was buckled in, which was necessary as the drone flew at a great speed through the city streets. I worried if someone I knew might see me, and I would be considered a criminal. I would have lots to explain. As the city passed by in a blur, I saw our destination.

We came to an abrupt stop in front of the Justice Courts. The drone must have called ahead, because the person I'm supposed to see was waiting for me.

"Dad," I yelled and dashed towards him. One look at his face brought me to a stop. To say he was not happy was the monster of all understatements. "Dad, I can explain," I stammered. He grabbed me by the wrist.

"Explain? When Lacey's mom called me for your school fundraising, she mentioned that you had not been to her house today! Why don't you explain how you were tracked leaving the Marks when you promised that you would never go there! Explain to me why anything that comes out of your mouth isn't a lie!" His face was flushed red. I hadn't seen him this mad. And honestly, he was right. I turned away from him. He must have expected me to yell back at him because when I didn't respond, he stood beside me. His face looked sad, like all the anger had drained out of him. "Pene, please talk to me."

"You wouldn't believe me," I whispered, resigned to whatever punishment he planned to dole out.

"That's not good enough, Pene." He motioned to me to sit down on a nearby bench. "After your mom died, I made a promise to protect you. To keep you safe. It's part of the reason I'm a lawyer. I want everyone to be safe. To never have to lose someone they love. Pene, you're all that I have—please tell me what's going on?"

"Dad, what if everything you believed in was a lie? What if we're not really safe, that justice isn't fair?"

"You're not making any sense. Try this from the beginning?"

I took a deep breath. "Dad, I have been to the Marks."

"The drones have established that."

"On other occasions."

"I'm listening."

"I watched a shopkeeper get arrested for stealing."

"I have a court case coming up on Monday for that case."

"I know. I watched your case footage." I looked up in his

face, expecting rage. His eyes flashed with sorrow. My heart nearly broke with his disappointment. Rather than yell at me and stop me from talking, he checked his emotions.

"Continue."

"When you were out of your office, I scrubbed through the footage," I said as Dad's eyes raged.

"I know it was wrong, but hear me out. The footage showed things that never happened. It made the shopkeeper look guilty when he wasn't."

"That's impossible, Pene. The court footage is from the crime scene, the drone recorded it live and then it's stored for the courts. It's played at the justice courts for the trial and then the criminal is sentenced."

"There you go. You and the judge are the only ones who see it. How do you know it's the truth? Why doesn't the accused get to see it?"

Dad considered my question. "There is no need. The footage shows the crime. Suspects have always denied being guilty. You can't argue with concrete evidence."

"Unless it's falsified!" I yelled.

My dad threw his arms up in the air. "Then our entire justice system is a farce. Every case I've done in my life is a lie. Do you realize how crazy you sound?"

"Then maybe it's just some cases. Some hidden agenda."

"And who would be doing this?" Dad gave me a dubious look. Lord Morall's drone eye filled my imagination.

"I have no idea," I lied. I wasn't ready to accuse anyone; better for my dad to come to his own conclusions.

"This is... crazy, Pene." He sat down on the bench. He

was overwhelmed but I hoped there was still a small possibility that he might believe me. I had to widen that gap.

"Dad, I'm not making this up. I was there. The footage was different. You're going to punish an innocent man. He'll lose years of his life."

"That is the law. We haven't had prisons for years. The guilty lose years from their life. The machine is quick and painless. In the old days, criminals became worse by living with their peers in inhumane prisons for years. Attacking each other, planning future crimes. Prisons trained criminals to become better at crime, at huge public cost. Now the punishment is immediate and the cost minimal."

"But he didn't do it!" I turned my back to him, as if I could shame him into seeing it my way. It had the opposite effect.

"That's enough! This isn't a negotiation. You were caught lying to me twice. How do I know this isn't an elaborate excuse to get out of your punishment? How could the drone's footage be altered?"

"I don't know, but until today, I didn't think drones had any other task but to observe and protect. How did you change their programming to have one pick me up?"

"Vaslor owed me favor. He was able to divert a couple of drones to hone in your last whereabouts. Nobody stays hidden for long in our city, Pene."

"Is that supposed to reassure me or scare me, Dad?"

"I did what I had to do to keep you safe."

"And someone else is doing the same thing. His definition of safe, on a much greater scale." My dad looked at me in disbelief. "Promise me you'll review the footage. See if you notice any irregularities. You're sentencing an innocent man!"

"Go home," Dad said and dismissed me. "I'll review the footage, but for now you're grounded. And unless you want to be sentenced as well, don't breathe another word of this. Do I make myself clear?"

"Yes," I lied. I turned my back on him and began the long walk home.

10
Class

The weekend couldn't pass any slower. Dad had avoided me for both days. I didn't know if he was so angry that he couldn't be around me or if he was actually reviewing Lou's footage. I didn't ask. For the first time I looked forward to school on Monday morning. I left the house with a quick goodbye, and he acknowledged my departure with a grunt. As I walked to school, I tried to make sense of the last few days. I wish I could go back to being the ignorant girl who just wanted to travel out of the city. If I got into much more trouble, I would never leave this city. I was oblivious to my surroundings and almost bumped into her.

"I've been trying to get hold of you all weekend," Lacey questioned with concern.

"Been under house arrest," I answered, startled by her sudden appearance. "No outside communication." I rolled my eyes.

She grabbed my wrist. "I'm sorry, my mom blew your cover. Her and her fundraising."

"Not her fault." I shook my head. "I was bound to get caught sooner or later."

"No hard feelings?" Lacey asked.

"None." I squeezed her hand. "But I need to talk you." A crowd of boys passed us. I waited until they were farther ahead.

"Shoot. But honestly, you have been acting so strange lately. More secretive than usual. Is it about that boy from the re-enactment?"

"Austin. Kind of. But it's a lot more than him."

"I knew it!" She squeezed my hand so tight that I had to let go. "You were, like, all focused with him. What have the two of you been doing? Is that why your dad has put you in lockdown mode?"

"No! It's nothing like that. Will you shut up for second?" Lacey pretended to be hurt by my comment but I could tell she was dying for details. The girl loved to gossip. I took a second to decide how much to share.

"I got caught going to the Marks. Dad sent some drones to follow me and bring me home."

"Wow! I didn't know your dad could do that. Do you think he would ever help my mom track me down?"

"Lacey!"

"Seriously, how many times do you have to be told not to go there? What does your dad say every time?" She thought for a second then did a horrible impression of my dad. "*The Marks is no place for young girls.*"

"Yeah, yeah. He freaks out over going to the Marks and then tells everyone how safe our city is."

"Well, he is right. It *is* safe. There's nothing that doesn't get captured on camera. Why does that upset you?"

I gripped her hand again. "What if we aren't safer? Sometimes I feel like an animal on a very long leash."

"Pene! You're so dramatic. Don't say that in Mr. Stewart's class. He'll fail you so fast, it will make your head dizzy. I couldn't imagine having to take his class a second time."

"I don't care about Mr. Stewart," I exclaimed, stopping her. "Don't you want to get out of here when you graduate, to see the world?" Lacey shook her head.

"That's your dream, girlfriend. I want to perform, be on stage at the music hall before the city wide re-enactment. Be loved by thousands." She smirked. "Maybe meet a cute boy. Does Austin have an older brother?"

"Lacey!" I yelled. I loved her dearly but she never took anything I said seriously. I could see the school up on our right as we started walking again. "Come abroad with me after graduation—we'll apply for a visa lottery and travel for a few years. What do you say?"

"Tempting. Would we meet any cute boys?"

"What if I said yes?"

"You'd be lying," she smiled. "You are so focused on everything but boys. We'd go to some exotic city and I would just hold you back. I'm a homebody. The world is a scary place. Everything I need is right here in the city." She started up the school steps. "But don't forget to bring some gifts back from all the places you visit. I'll never turn down jewelry or clothes." I laughed and was about to respond when I felt eyes on the back of my neck. I turned suddenly, expecting a drone to be spying on me. Instead I looked up at Mr. Stewart. He glared down from the classroom window. His eyes blazed. I dreaded another dictation of his view of history.

As the two of us walked down the hallway, Mr. Stewart came out to greet us. Actually, greeting is too generous a description; directing was more appropriate.

"Ladies, the two of you will be my actresses in today's class." We both stopped suddenly. His selection was usually a punishment. This was worse than the group re-enactment. Everyone in the class would watch our mistakes.

A couple of times in the school year, Mr. Stewart 'nominated' several students to act out various stages of our history. It was a test that students rarely passed since he would pick the most obscure moments of history. Most of the time you had to guess what actions your character would make, often with the wrong results. Even worse, our classmates observed your every step. Your failures would be played back continually throughout the school year. I remembered how last year, Colin, a fairly quiet boy, had been picked. He made such horrible choices under pressure that he had been ostracized ever since. There had to be a way to get out of this.

"Oh, sorry, Mr. Stewart. I can't." Lacey was quicker on her feet with an excuse. "I'm not feeling well today, and the video imagery would make me sick. The last thing you want is me yakking in front of the class."

"Truly." Mr. Stewart was unfazed by Lacey's comments.

I imagine he had heard every excuse possible. "Unfortunately, unless you have some doctor's excuse, you will be participating." His eyes danced over to me, waiting to hear my excuse. So I didn't give him one.

"I'd love to. I think this is a chance to show the truth about history."

Mr. Stewart seemed confused about my puzzling response. "I appreciate your enthusiasm, Pene. Historical re-enactments are a visit to our past, an opportunity to learn from our mistakes and build on our successes."

"But history is an interpretation, is it not?"

"Based on facts, history can be verified by multiple sources. What is your question?"

"I don't understand your selections. You pick obscure moments in history to test our ability to remember the past. But how do I know the past is accurate?" Mr. Stewart's eyebrow rose, as if I was challenging the accuracy of his course.

"With your comments, I could fail you from this course and expel you from school. Is this how you want your history remembered?" Mr. Stewart looked down at me with cold, hard eyes. Only this time their menace didn't make me shiver.

"Not at all," I answered coolly. "I was just asking a question. As I said, I'm happy to participate. I suggest we get going—I imagine the class is waiting." Behind the classroom doors I could see a number of silhouettes straining to listen in on our conversation. I walked straight into class, not wanting to continue further. If he wanted to talk down to me, I could have twenty witnesses to the event. I walked over by the wall computer screen as Lacey stood beside me. She gave me one of those "Are you crazy?" looks without saying a word. Mr. Stewart interrupted our silent conversation.

"Let's have your attention." He looked at the class, and all talking died immediately. "We are fortunate today to have two volunteers for our next history re-enactment." There was a small smattering of applause; likely they were happy they weren't picked. "Pene and Lacey will be re-enacting the terrorists' ransom demands."

"Boring," one of my classmates whispered. If Mr. Stewart heard, he chose to ignore the comment.

"Would someone in the class like to elaborate on the authority of the city council?" The class was silent. Somewhere crickets were chirping. "Ms. Bennett?" Mr. Stewart stared at one of the girls in the back. She looked a little terrified, and Lacey and I tried to stifle a smile.

"The—the authority?" she stammered.

"I'm looking for the breakdown of the council. How many members? Voting limits? You do remember your assignment from last month?"

"Yeeessss. Ah—the city is divided into 18 wards with the same number of councilors."

"And?" Mr. Stewart made a motion for her to proceed.

"Ah—they are voted in every five years, with a two-term limit. The mayor is elected at the same time to represent our city and be the liaison with other cities." She stopped, hoping she had answered the question completely.

"And?" Mr. Stewart looked around the room. Cory shot

his hand up. Mr. Stewart nodded at him.

"The Ministry of Justice appoints a member to stand for the council, currently Lord Morall. His position isn't voted on, and he can veto any changes that involve the security of the city."

"Does this position have any term limits?"

"I don't think so. He's been there for as long as I can remember."

"Since the earthquake, to be exact," Mr. Stewart continued. "So that's some background on the city's government. We will move to a specific meeting between the city's representatives and the opposing terrorist group." He turned to look at us. "Ladies, do both of you understand the rules?"

Of course we did; only kids in junior high got the game confused. In the re-enactment, the actors you interacted with were records of history. They might seem real but they wouldn't deviate too far from their script. The simulations could only answer things they were programmed to know. Ask them something they didn't know, you'd get a blank stare and then they'd return to their script. They might look real, but it was only your brain making you think they existed. In an earlier class, one of the boys had tried to get a simulation to give him a kiss and learned the hard way that wasn't part of his programming.

We both looked at each other and then nodded.

"Good," he answered. "You will be entering one of the negotiations."

It was an unusual choice. Most historical enactments were battles—people loved to participate in a fight, win or lose. The ransom demands by the terrorists were well documented but uneventful. The terms were unacceptable to the city, which led to the explosion and earthquake. End of story. One side said no and the other side went berserk. Not a lot of history to re-enact. I felt I got off easy. Although I had a good idea which one of us was going to play the terrorist side.

"Ladies, please put on your headsets," Mr. Stewart said, and we reached over to his desk for the apparatus. The two of us would be at the front of the room while the class watched our movements on the viewer screen. "Try to replicate what happened in history to score points. The rest of the class will mark down any mistakes you make for extra points for themselves."

I looked at the sea of classmates staring and smiling at me, happy that it wasn't them. I put on my headset and the classroom disappeared.

Something was wrong. Instead of assuming a historical role, I saw darkness jolted with moments of static. Then I felt like I was watching a television show.

A car was racing across a desert, teenagers out on a joyride. Only instead of having fun, their faces were etched with fear. A huge shadow was blotting out the sun as two girls and a boy looked up. The view panned up to look back at what was chasing the car. A massive dinosaur with jagged teeth, straight out of Evolution class, was pursuing the car, rapidly gaining with its huge strides. It looked like a Tyrannosaurus rex except the arms were much more developed and it ran on all four limbs. The girl in the passenger seat, who didn't seem much older than me, pulled a weapon out of the glove compartment and aimed at the huge beast. A blue laser erupted from the gun, blasting straight at the dinosaur. I couldn't see the impact, but a huge roar blasted out over my speaker and the dinosaur staggered forward. The teenagers in the car screamed and floored the accelerator. Before I could see if the dinosaur landed on the car, the screen went black. What a weird movie.

Then the images faded and the environment changed. Moments later I felt a hard chair as I was sitting in a boardroom. There were several people on my left and a number of city officials across the table from me. I looked up and saw lights dangling down from the ceiling above the conference room. The city emblem was embossed on several wooden chairs and its logo in the center of the table. There were four officials, two older males, one balding and one overweight. Two females, one thin with spiky white hair, and Lacey. She smiled at me and waved.

On my side were three men, two young and one older who seemed to be in charge. I must have replaced the female on the terrorist side. I felt like someone was behind my chair, but before I could look back, the negotiation began.

"The terms are simple," the older man on my side began. "We want control of the city and its resources. If you do not comply, we will take the city by force."

"That's not really a negotiation, Stephan," the woman with spiky hair answered. "You can't intimidate your way through this time. Frankly, I doubt you will endanger the lives in the city just to prove your point."

"Then you would be wrong, Denise. And your mistake will cost lives."

"No! You will be the one responsible for any loss of life,"

the balding man yelled back. "The only person you care about is yourself."

"Let's discuss this rationally. No one wants to see any loss of life," Lacey added. She was playing the role of a mediator, trying to keep both sides talking. Mr. Stewart would give her points for attempting to use negotiating skills.

"There is little to negotiate," Stephan responded. "The city has proven time after time that you are only interested in making yourselves rich. You could care less what happens to your citizens."

"And you do?" said Denise. "The only thing you care about is proving yourself right and you don't care who you have to hurt."

Their argument was nauseating. Both sides seemed deadlocked in their opinions. History showed that the terrorists were set on ruling the city as a series of little kingdoms or gangs. They felt the new administration would be more responsive to people's needs, citing that the current councilors only looked after themselves and their staff. The city argued the exact opposite; they stated they were elected fairly—although there were accusations of vote fraud—and that the terrorists were bullies looking to run the city their way, with little regard for the residents. Neither side would reach out to the state government to mediate a fair decision. It made me angry that adults could act so childish with so much at stake.

History had always labeled them the "Terrorists" but they didn't refer to themselves as that. They called themselves "The Liberators." Freeing the people from the tyranny of the city was their catchphrase. I guess the victors can write history any way they want. Suddenly the unclear nature of the situation got the better of me. Maybe I could rewrite history.

"We should just walk away," I said, speaking as a part of the Terrorist team. "If we attack, the power plant will explode, causing an earthquake that will kill thousands."

The participants stared at me as if I had spoken a foreign language. I had broken the unspoken rule—never talk about what actually would occur as a result of their actions. I was supposed to play-act history, recreate or say what had already happened in the past. Even though I couldn't hear my classmates, I imagined there was an outburst at my antics. Mr. Stewart was probably seconds away from pulling the plug. Lacey stared at me in disbelief.

"Why do we have to destroy the city to prove we're right?" I stood up to make my point. "Can't we share power? Maybe compromise?"

"What's wrong with you, Lilith? When did you become so soft?" Stephan pointed at me.

"Let her speak," a voice from behind yelled. It was vaguely familiar.

"Actually, it's the first sensible thing someone on your team has said," replied Denise. "So far this negotiation has been an absolute waste of time. I almost think you are staging this conflict, Stephan."

"Unless you've paid her off to make our side weak," he retorted.

"Enough!" I yelled. "I watched both sides enough to know there is never a negotiation." That part was true. I had watched a number of re-enactments between the two sides before the earthquake, and neither side would budge. They were like two children in a schoolyard fighting over a stick. Eventually the stick breaks and someone gets hurt. "You need to listen to each other. Instead of listing your demands, actually listen to the other side. Then actually offer something of value instead of empty promises."

The room was silent, and Lacey smiled back at me. For a split second I felt like I had changed history. I had actually made them listen to reason. Things could have been different if someone like me had been there. Then reality set in.

"Take this heretic away. It figures that someone from the city has tried to pay her off. Your group has so much money after stealing from the city, I can only imagine how much you offered her," jeered Stephan. Rough hands grabbed me from behind.

"Or maybe your side can no longer stomach its sad argument. I'd be surprised if others on your side don't begin feeling the same way." Denise pointed at Stephan.

I sagged as I gave up.

"Wait!" a voice from behind me yelled. "What if she's right? What if our inflexibility causes us to hurt the ones we love?" I turned and looked into the young face of someone I hadn't seen in a lifeline. She looked like me. My mother. The way she was fifteen years ago. But what was she doing on the side of the terrorists when she was a scientist for the city? This didn't made sense.

As I stared in disbelief at my mother's face, my headset was turned off and she disappeared for a second time from my life.

11

Court

Three days had passed since my re-enactment lesson at school. I'd had an unexpected burst of popularity since then; my classmates felt I was cool because I tried to subvert history. I had mixed emotions. I hadn't been trying to be disruptive. I didn't have an agenda to teach the system a lesson. I was just angry and confused. I was tired of reliving a screwed-up history. Considering current events, I wasn't sure if history was even accurate.

Mr. Stewart's reaction was over the top. When we came out of the simulation, his eyes looked like they could have drilled into my brain. If I had ever needed to give him a reason to dislike me, this time was a winner. He was even more rigid and cold with me, if that was even possible. Who knows what he told the principal and other teachers? I didn't dare tell Dad that I thought I was going to fail history.

Lacey thought the popularity was hilarious. She had pestered Mr. Stewart for her to try the simulation again, saying she didn't get enough time. Everyone thought she was planning to be more disruptive as a way to curry more popularity. I hadn't confided in her that I'd seen my mother. She hadn't known my mom, and we had so few pictures of her around my house that Lacey wouldn't have recognized her anyway.

I put the whole episode behind me. School had no interest for me; it was a place to spend my day. Where I was going today made school look like a joke. Dad still wasn't talking to me very much but we had come to an agreement. I would stay away from the Marks, and in return I could skip school this morning and see Lou's trial. He still didn't believe me, but he must have felt I would calm down if I saw justice served. The fact was, seeing the trial would do just the opposite.

I arrived at the Justice Department at 10 a.m., thirty minutes before the trail. Crimes were usually punished within ten days since lengthy trial dates were a thing of the past. Yet it was a trial in name only. There was no jury, no cross-examination, and no testimony. Just video footage and a verdict. Unless the camera was in a bad location, the verdict was always 'guilty.' Unlike the court cases of old, there was no public viewing; it was by invitation only.

The main doors slid open for me and I was immediately greeted by a security guard. He looked young and seemed interested in his job. He looked at my papers, signed by Dad.

"Watching your father in action? It's not that exciting but I'm sure he'll appreciate the audience." I smiled pleasantly but said nothing. He waved me on and I passed through three more security gates before I was ushered into a stairwell. I climbed the stairs and entered a small room. I stepped to the far end and looked down through a glass window. Typically, court cases no longer had the public watching the trial. Because the verdict was basically predetermined and took no time to process, trials were no crowd-pleasers.

My vantage point was about twelve feet above the proceedings. A glass window separated us so you couldn't yell or interrupt. However, speakers were fed into the wall so you could hear everything that was said. A huge monitor on the wall played back the footage captured at the scene of the crime. I was the only one in the room and I sat down on a chair by the window. The judge swiveled in his chair, and I shivered at the sight of Lord Morall. He was barking orders to the two security officers, a man and a woman. They stood at attention. Seconds later, the male officer marched out a door to the right of the room.

Lord Morall was alone in the room and pressed a few buttons on a touch screen on his bench. His red eye sparkled as he scanned some documents. If he had noticed my presence, he made no acknowledgement. He looked introspective, as if his thought process had to be sharp to hand down his sentence. I studied his face. There was no malice but I still sensed a menace about him, amplified by his red eye. My thoughts were interrupted as the door on the right opened. The male security guard entered and Lou walked beside him. He had no cuffs on his hands and his eyes looked blankly ahead. He was either drugged or had given up.

Behind them my dad entered as the prosecution and another man, heavyset, a bit older than Dad, stepped beside him. I assumed it was the lawyer for the defense, although that was in name only. Both my dad and the other lawyer stood in front of Lord Morall as Lou tottered for a moment before sitting down. The male officer left as the female officer walked forward.

"Case 39X-45C, Lou Reigns vs. the Crown. Charge of theft and resisting arrest." She stepped back and I waited for Morall to ask Lou if he plead 'not guilty.' The question was never asked.

"Please roll the footage," Morall commanded and the video screen beside him and the one in my room came to life. The familiar scene cut in with Lou and the theft of the cash. Its fakery appeared even more obvious to me but the others in the courtroom watched with muted interest. Lou tilted his head with puzzled bewilderment, as if this was the first time he had seen the footage. Once it was finished, Morall asked the defense lawyer to approach the bench.

"Any comments on the footage shown?"

"None, Your Honor." I doubted he ever answered differently than that. The whole process was a farce. With that comment, Lou seemed to wake up from his daze.

"But that wasn't me. I didn't take any cash!" he pleaded. Morall seemed nonplussed by the outburst. He didn't even look at Lou.

"Counselor, have you explained to your client the proper protocols for addressing this court?"

"Yes, your Honor."

Morall turned to Lou. "I will make this one exception to explain the court procedures. All questions are to be asked through your counsel. Do you understand?"

"Yes," Lou answered, "but my counsel is not asking any questions. He didn't even show me this footage."

"That is because the footage is evidence and cannot be refuted. Do you have any other questions?"

"Yes," Lou stood up. "I did not steal. This footage is wrong!" Morall looked like he had heard the excuse many times before. His expression remained neutral.

"Besides the footage, the prosecution has many verbal witness confirmations that you tried to escape the drones. Do you disagree?" His eye flashed as if it was trying to trap Lou.

"No. That part of the footage is correct. I did try to escape, I was scared and confused. Accused of a crime I didn't commit."

"Are you trying to say that some footage is correct while part of it is false?" my dad interjected. Morall gave Dad a look. Maybe it wasn't his turn to speak.

"The footage is straight from camera, or drone surveillance. Disputing the truth will only lengthen your sentence." The words came smoothly out of Morall's mouth, as if he had recited them many times before.

"So I'm punished if I try to prove my innocence? I used to think that our city was safe from crime. That I was protected. But it's just the opposite—someone is using the system to make me look guilty!" Lou pounded his handcuffed palms on the table.

"Counselor! If you don't get control of your client, you will find yourself relieved of your duties." The other lawyer sat next to Lou. I couldn't hear what they were saying but it looked like he was trying to console Lou. Whatever fire Lou had a moment ago had burned out. His shoulders were slumped as if he had accepted his fate.

"I suggest we recess, give us a chance to review the claims," my dad said to Lord Morall.

"The last time I looked, you were the prosecution, not the defense!" Lord Morall bellowed, his face becoming as red as his eye. "We have heard these statements of innocence many times before. The claims are baseless. Unless there is more evidence to view, there will be no delays."

"No, your Honor," the defense lawyer replied.

"No, your Honor," answered my dad.

"Mr. Lou Reigns, you will stand before the court." Lou staggered a bit and then stood up, his eyes blazing. Lord Morall looked down at his tablet as if reading a recipe. "The drone footage confirms that you have committed theft. Despite the evidence, you have failed to admit your guilt or provide remorse for your crime. As a result, I am forced to sentence you to the full extent of the law. You will lose ten years of your life in the age accelerator. Your sentence is to be carried out immediately!"

"No!" I shrieked. All heads in the courtroom turned up to me. I slammed the glass window with my fist. Although the sound against the glass was muffled, my anguish was not. The security guards and defense attorney looked at me with bewilderment. Lou gaped at me with surprise and ad-miration. My dad looked at me with concern. Morall looked at me with anger.

"Remove her from the building," he commanded the fe-male security guard. "And she is not to return." He looked straight at my father.

Finally I had a realization. The city wasn't safe. It never had been. Its safety had been compromised. And I had to leave. Now.

12

Conversation

I had criss-crossed the neighborhood streets about a dozen times. Each time I acted relaxed, as if I was on my way to somewhere. Once I figured where the cameras were, I walked so that I avoided their field of vision. The only drone in sight was floating slowly down the opposite side of the street, following a group of kids. One of them tossed a small stone. The drone easily avoided it and flashed red. The kids laughed and played a game of cat and mouse, which the drone seemed eager to join. As they disappeared down the street, I turned quickly into an alleyway and walked towards a flight of stairs.

I climbed up two stories and entered an average apartment building, nothing fancy but clean and well-maintained. I walked down the hallway and stopped in front of a scanner. I waited several seconds so the occupant could view my image and decide to let me in. Seconds later, the door speaker squeaked.

"I'm sorry. Do I know you?" A man's face appeared on

the monitor. He looked so much older than I remembered. Lou had been convicted for ten years for stealing. Instead of living in a prison for that time, prisoners were aged with drugs and machines according to their sentence. It saved a lot of money, and criminals were punished immediately. My dad had told me that the part of their memories relating to the crime were wiped, as well as the part of the brain that initiated the 'criminal activity'. People were never the same after the aging process, and anyone they might blame for their capture was immediately wiped from memory. *All in the name of the safety of society.*

"I'm Pene. I used to buy stuff from you."

"Well, dear, I'm not selling anything right now. It may be a few weeks before I return to the Marks." The monitor went black.

"Wait! I was wondering if you have a few minutes to just talk?" The screen remained black, as if Lou was considering my request. Seconds later, the door swung open.

"You're taking a risk, dear. After all, I just finished my sentence. You really don't want to be seen with a criminal." He walked inside with his back to me.

"I'll take my chances." I followed him. If my dad caught me here, I would be grounded for life. As I stepped into his home, I was reminded of his business. Piled in the living rooms were boxes of items. Metal objects spilled out of crates, obscure books were stacked to the ceiling and wooden artifacts hung on the walls. Lou sat down on his couch. His clothes looked ill-fitting, as if he had lost weight as well as gained years. He looked me over, still with the aura of a salesman.

"So what kind of things did I sell you? Nothing illegal?" His question was genuine; he didn't remember me.

"Never," I answered a bit too strongly. "You always found items for me from outside of the city, from places far away." He studied me as he pulled something from one of the boxes.

"You want to leave the city. I used to want to travel when I was younger. Thinking about life on the road. So many opportunities here, though. The trading kept me close to the Marks. Although look where that got me." He stared into the window at his own reflection. He weighed a wooden object in his hands. "Was I good at finding things for you?"

"The best. Although sometimes I had to work to get a good deal."

"Ha! Sounds like something I would do." He looked straight at me. "Are you looking for something now? Probably can't help you." He pulled another box towards him and started to sort it.

"I'm hoping you can tell me where you got this?" I pulled out the glass piece that I had bargained with on that fateful day. He reached over and took it. He pulled out a magnifying monocle and examined it closer.

"Pretty unique—not manufactured in the city. It would have a serial number and the city insignia. I must have gotten it from an outsider."

"Outsider? Who do you mean?"

"Ah, someone from outside of the city. Probably picked

it up along their travels. But you're wasting your time. I don't remember anything I've bought. I can't even remember what I did to get convicted."

"You were tried for stealing." Silently, I chastised myself for volunteering the information. Lou probably didn't want to be reminded of his crime.

"I know that from the lawyer. They said I stole some money. I just don't remember why…" He scratched his chin as if trying to retrieve a memory that no longer existed.

It pained me. I could reassure that it wasn't him. That he was innocent. Maybe it might make him feel better. But it wouldn't make any difference. I had no proof, and even if I did, I would be endangering him. Better to let him believe the lie and move on with his life.

"You know, my short-term memories are spotty at best but I do remember things better long-term. There were a few guys I used to buy from. I guess you would call them unsavory. But they did bring in some unique items. There was one guy, a mountain climber, a bit of a Wildman, used to come in with the craziest things. Some of it was garbage but some of it was worth buying." He screwed up his eye while looking at a computerized snow globe that fit in the palm of his hand.

"Wildman?"

"Yeah—he must have been coming to me for years because I have no problem remembering him. He's big like me, or at least the way I used to be. I don't think he's shaved in his entire life—long beard, unkempt hair, crazy eyes."

"Now you're just trying to scare me," I laughed. "How

does one have crazy eyes?" I rolled mine.

"Well," he pondered my question and raised his hands, "picture this. Have you looked at someone and they looked right back at you, only they didn't really see you? It's almost like they are thinking of somewhere else and not really seeing you." Lou's comment hit home and I released a deep sign. My dad had accused me of that on more than one occasion. Except he had called it my far-off eyes. I was always somewhere else than right there with him.

"Okay, where does this Wildman live?"

"That I don't remember. And the funny thing is that sometimes I wouldn't see him for months at a time. Or was it years? But he'd always be carrying some strange objects and have a story or two about trekking through the woods outside the city walls. Probably brought some things that weren't entirely legal." He paused for a second as if trying to remember something. Then he shook his head and gave up. "Your best bet is to look for him at the Marks. Not too many guys look like him, always carrying a backpack full of camping gear." He paused and looked at me as if he had a question.

"Listen, Pene. I'm having a tough time adjusting to what's happened to me. I've lost ten years of my life for a crime I can't remember. I have to assume that our justice system is right and I deserve what happened to me. But what I'm having the hardest time with, and it's making me want to hide here in this apartment is…" Tears ran down his face. His grief was immense and I could feel my eyes starting to well up also. He stared at me.

"What do you want to know?"

"Was I bad person?" he asked. I reached over, gave him a big hug and then sat next to him.

"No, Lou. You are many things. Loud, sometimes obnoxious, a bit self-serving, a hard negotiator,.."

"Kid, anytime with a compliment."

"But you are always a man of your word. I always knew I could trust you, and I still do." I smiled and he returned the expression.

"Well, I can't let you leave without me giving you something. Take a look around. See anything you like?" He pointed around the room. I hadn't expected this gesture and decided to take some time to explore his belongings. I looked through a box of sparring weapons, probably from a martial arts studio. Underneath it was a box of army fatigues, hats, shirts, pants and belts. I was never a big fan of camouflage.

"What do you think of this?" I turned and almost hit my head on a big eyeball. It was blinking at me at the end of the spyglass. "Bit of an antique, not as visually accurate as a pair of digital binoculars but still in great shape.

"I love it! I'll take it." I slipped it in my bag, gave him a hug and started to leave.

"Hey, wait a second. I remember *some* of my past. Care to make me an offer?"

I smiled and tried not to bargain him too low a price.

13

Wild

The "Wildman" turned out to be remarkably easy to find. The problem had not been trying to find out where he was, it was trying to find out where he wasn't. Every time someone gave me a Wildman sighting, I always got there after the fact. He was everywhere I wasn't. Finally, at the advice of one of the Marks vendors, I found that the "Wildman" climbed the Eaglewood rock face at the east outskirts of the city. On Saturday morning, I didn't bother inventing a lie with my dad, I left without saying goodbye and jumped onto an air bus.

Eaglewood was an expensive and exclusive part of the city. Mega mansions dotted the landscape, and the homes surrounded a large lake. Many homes had docks, boats, power skis and rafts along its lakefront access. But as my bus passed these homes, it was the scenery behind the mansions that caught my attention. The rock face rose up from behind the homes, a park sanctuary dedicated to hikers and climbers. Trails dotted the park. Hikers were the main users except for rock climbers like the Wildman.

As I got off the bus, I looked up at the rock face. In the distance, a climber in a red jacket was about halfway up. I stepped towards a trail on the left and walked upward to get to the top before the climber reached the summit. The air was cool and the woods were peaceful. I passed an empty squirrel feeder mounted to a fence post. I reached into my pocket and uncrumpled a bagful of peanuts. As I dropped a few onto the platform, I heard a chattering from above. I quickly left to let the animal come down from the trees.

I looked back to see a black squirrel jump down from a branch. How I envied the animal's freedom, its ability to go where it wanted, when it wanted. There were so few living creatures in our woods that I marveled at its movements. It scurried onto the platform, grabbed a peanut and disappeared up another tree. I looked around and noticed a camera on a lamppost. Even out in the woods, the 'safety of the people' was maintained. *Gag!* I couldn't even think about the propaganda with a straight face. As I rounded the turn, I came to the top of the rock face.

The view was magnificent, and looking down I wondered if Dad could ever have afforded homes like these. Even if Mom were still alive, the homes were well above anything we could afford. Yet I wasn't envious. I could see a drone cycle driving down a street as kids pointed at it. The rich were under surveillance for their own protection, just like the rest of us. Their wealth didn't afford them any greater freedom.

"Pretty breathtaking, isn't it?" I looked down and realized the climber had reached the peak. The Wildman was in his mid-twenties, with curly brown hair and a shaggy beard. He looked just like described.

"It is. Do you need a hand?" I offered to help pull him up.

"Right on." He grasped my hand and used his other hand to pull up on his rope. He smiled and sat down on rock, his legs dangling over the edge. He pulled out an energy bar and offered me a bite.

"No, thanks," I said as I sat down beside and a bit behind him. I wasn't brave enough to sit so close to the edge. "Ever wish you could ever afford one of the houses down there?" He was silent for a moment, as if he was considering my question.

"No. Never thought about it B. I want to go places. Living down there isn't one them." Okay, now he'd piqued my interest.

"So where do you want to go?"

"There." He pointed to the north. "And there." He pointed west. "And..." I stopped his hand.

"I get the idea. But why? What do you want to see?" He fished out a pair of binoculars from his pack.

"Look over there." He pointed to the West Mountains. I scanned the peaks of lush woods. Their beauty was immense, the land unspoiled, probably less traveled by cameras and drones. I could see the allure.

"So you like to climb?" I handed the binocs back to him.

"B, I love to climb. I live to climb. I want to climb the highest peaks in the world, Everest, K2, Kanchenjunga. I'm going to see them all."

"What's holding you back? Why are you still climbing here?"

"Usual reasons. Need money, lots of it. Need travel visas. Takes time and more money. Need help. Some of these mountains you can't climb alone. You need a team. But I need time and…"

"Money. Yeah, I got that part." I had to admire him. His goal was simple—like me, he wanted out of this city. "By the way, my name is Pene, not B." I extended my hand. Boys in my class had an annoying habit of shortening each other's name and using the first letter instead of the full name. So childish. Jeffrey was J and Thomas was T. It was obvious that despite his age, he still had the mentality of a teenage boy.

"Stu, although my friends call me Wildman." He shook my hand. His felt gritty from dirt and hard with calluses.

"I know, I've been looking for you." If he seemed surprised by this comment, he didn't show it. He started to put some of his climbing gear into his backpack.

"Well, you found me. How can I help you, B?" I wondered if he realized calling a girl a B was rude. I was starting not to like him.

"A friend of mine told me he bought something from you." I reached into my jacket and pulled out the spherical glass fragment. He smiled and manipulated it in his hands.

"Found that months ago, hiking in the west mountains. Went farther than usual that day, barely got back before curfew."

"Curfew?" I asked, surprised.

"Yeah, it's not widely publicized. The idea is that for our safety, everyone should be within the city limits after dark. No overnight camping."

"How would they know? What would they do?"

"Seriously? How would they know? Look around us. The cameras, the drones. They know our every move before we make it. In fact," he leaned in closer, "I've heard guys talk about how everyone is chipped and they have some mega computer that traces our movements every day. With that history, they can predict where you'll be a week from now."

"You're crazy. Why would anybody want to follow me?" I hated the drones but I was starting to doubt his sanity.

He laughed. "They could care less about you and me. We're just cattle in a pen, B."

"I told you not to call me that, what does that mean?" I interrupted, annoyed. Boys are so stupid sometimes.

"Sorry. You did say that. I get nervous around girls. You're kind of a babe so I call you B for short. My mom always said I was a bit thick." *Wow—great mom.* "Didn't mean to disrespect you. You seem pretty cool. Anyway, they keep an eye on us, especially those people who don't play by the rules."

"Like you?"

"Like us." I think he judged me pretty well.

"For our own safety."

"That's the party line."

"And why do you think everyone is watched so closely?" I asked him. He looked at me as if I was conspiring with the government.

"Wait a second, you show up out of nowhere and start asking questions about the city. How do I know you aren't one of them? Maybe you're trying to trap me?"

"Do you think you're worth it?" I leaned closer. He looked at the expression on my face and we both burst out laughing.

"Okay. Sorry, getting a little paranoid. Seems to me that shopkeeper I sold the glass to got into trouble lately. What was his name?" He tapped his forehead to try to jumpstart his memory.

"Lou. He's the one who told me you sold it to him."

"That's right. But he got caught with his hands in the cookie jar. Think he was charged with stealing?"

"That's what they say," I answered nonchalantly.

"Well, he's blacklisted now. I don't imagine anyone will be selling him anything soon."

I thought about his comments and immediately felt bad for Lou. He hadn't committed the crime but had lost ten years of his life and possibly his business.

"So if you sold this to him, where did you find it again?" He pointed to the highest peak in the west.

"Found it with some other debris on the ground. Most of the stuff was smashed up and in pieces, but this piece was intact. Made me think of a fly's eye." He put it near his face for effect, and it reflected a cool blue.

"Where do you think it came from?" I asked as he handed it back to me.

"I don't know. Bigfoot? Aliens? It could have fallen from

the sky. I don't know and I don't care. But I did get a few credits for it towards my climbing trip." Stu grinned and handed it back to me. He stood up and flung his backpack over his shoulder. "Like to stay, but I got places to go. Did you want to walk down with me?"

"Not now." I looked down the trail. "I need a few minutes to think." He looked at me as if I had a question. Which I did.

"You want to know how to get to the West Mountains?"

"Yes," I answered.

"Unless you go through the city gate, the only other way is to climb there."

"I know."

He smiled, pulled out a piece of paper and wrote on it. He handed it to me. I saw a bunch of numbers. "These are the GPS coordinates. Look it up online and you will see where to go. Don't keep the piece of paper—memorize the numbers," he suggested.

"No problem. Thanks for your help. Will I see you around?"

"You never know. It's a free world." He snickered and scratched his beard. He walked down the trail and disappeared between the trees. I watched the road below and a few minutes later saw him walking away into the distance. I considered my options.

I hated school, my dad would never forgive me and the justice system was flawed, possibly corrupt. I really had only one option. I had to leave this city. And I had to do it undetected.

14

Escape

It was an hour before sunrise. I thought it best to escape
before the city came to life. I avoided the idea of running
away at night. Vaslor had mentioned something about night
vision on the drones, and I didn't want to be observed by
machines I couldn't see. I sneaked by Dad's room, I could
hear his snoring through the door. I put some dirty plates in
the sink to fake that I had eaten breakfast and left. On Fri-
days he went to work later than usual, so there was a good
chance he might buy that I had left for school. Considering
how the two of us rarely talked now, I doubted he would
miss me.

I gently closed the outside door, not wanting to alert him.
If he saw me leaving now, he might suspect I wasn't going
to school, or worse, that I was heading to the Marks. It
would probably be midday before he got a call from the
school asking for my whereabouts. I had planned for that
call as I pocketed Dad's phone. The street was quiet, except
for a couple of cars; no foot traffic yet. A robot drone about

the size of a small man marched down the street. His steps were methodical as if he walked a predetermined route. I walked casually, not wanting to attract any attention.

I felt silly running away from home. I had talked to Lacey yesterday, and although she noticed that I was off, she didn't pry. I didn't dare tell her what I was planning in fear she'd be forced to tell my dad, or worse, would laugh at me. It was like something you watched as a kid where a five-year-old left home, only to be found at his neighbor's house a short time later.

This was different. I intended to follow through. My backpack was heavy with clothes, food and water. I had enough supplies to travel for about eight days. I planned on heading west towards the coast and find work at one of the small harbors. My dad had always talked about his trips with mom to the coast when they were young and ambitious. The smell of the salt air, the coolness of the sea breeze, the rise and fall of the waves. So many vivid memories. I hoped to have similar experiences while finally getting out of this city. There was a small problem, though. Like the Wildman said, you didn't leave the city without a travel visa. And you didn't get one without a lot of money and documentation. Since the earthquake, mostly only scientists and dignitaries got to travel. Fortunately, I had a plan.

Instead of running away from the marching drone, I began to follow it. Slowly, I kept the same distance behind, not wanting to attract its attention. Although the drones were meticulous at surveillance, they weren't sentient beings, meaning they could be followed just as easily as a human.

On closer examination, this drone was very predictable. It always marched on the left side of the street. It looked up at every third house and always stopped when someone walked by. The more I watched it, the more I realized that it wasn't controlled by someone to observe—it was programmed. The drones were tools, no more to be feared than a garbage can. However, the ones controlling them were a different story.

The sun was on the horizon and its pink glow illuminated the sky. There were a few more people out on the street now, mostly adults going to work. It allowed me to blend in more easily, in step behind the drone. We were heading slowly westward, towards the mountains in the direction I wanted to go. Then the drone came to a stop. A literal stop—a bus station for drones and people. I never understood why they traveled with us. Maybe the Justice Department was worried about the wear and tear on their joints, and this was a savings measure. I stood in a crowd; most adults looked intense or stressed. No one seemed interested in why I was there so early for school. Minutes later, the air bus came to our stop.

I went to the back but watched the drone plug into the center of the bus. There were four stations and another drone was already plugged in. The drone watched all of the passengers without missing a beat, as if its programming couldn't be interrupted. A mother walked by carrying a small baby. The drone observed her every step as if they were the most important people in the city.

About twenty-five minutes later we came to the edge of

town. Huge walls gated the city from the forest. No one exited the city except through main entrances. *What could get us from outside the city?* I looked at the top of the wall, sharp and sheer. No one was crawling over that thing, and it went well below the surface as well prevented anyone from tunneling under. The red eye of camera peered down as if watching us.

The air bus stopped and shut off its engine. Everyone disembarked, including the drones. Both of them headed to the depot center, a huge warehouse that shipped supplies to other cities. Food, raw materials, trade supplies that kept commerce flowing. I walked with the crowd, shadowing the drones as they walked into the warehouse. I reached into my backpack and put a cap on to obscure my face. I looked around and picked up an empty box then walked with a casualness to my stride, as if I was part of the crew that carried supplies. I learned my first mistake as soon as I walked in.

"You there. What are doing?" I turned, and a skinny guy with long black hair was looking me over. I thought about telling him that I was new and was moving crates to the back of the warehouse. But one thing I have learned that when making a lie is never to blurt out the first thing that comes into your head. If it's wrong, you're sunk. Always buy yourself time. Instead of talking, I just shrugged. "You can't carry anything in here. Drones do all the work." He pointed to one of the drones that I had followed in.

"Just bringing a present for my dad." And I smiled again as I started to walk away.

"Wait!" I could feel his eyes boring into my back. "Not allowed without a pass. Your dad should have told you.

What's his name?" I froze, knowing that my great escape had come to end almost as soon as it had started. His phone rang.

"J-John," I stammered but he waved me off as he spoke on the phone. I tried not to faint and quickly disappeared from his sight. I ditched my box and scanned the interior of the warehouse. The ceiling was high, well over a hundred feet, and the occasional skylight sprayed morning sun on the crates below. Pallets of boxes were stacked up. I climbed a pile to get a better overall view of the building. The view was impressive. There seemed like enough supplies to feed several cities. I looked down one aisle where drones were pushing a wheeled pallet. It took a turn too quickly and one of the boxes fell off. Its lid snapped off and its contents spilled out. The drone picked up a replica of its head and placed it back on top of the box, its sightless eyes watching me. That's all we needed, more drones.

I spied an area of larger boxes and climbed down from my pile. Those crates would be my goal. I walked slowly down the aisle, avoiding being spied by any human or drone workers. I was surprised by the amount of trade between cities; I had no idea how much came from outside. It made sense; although we had a lot of factories in the northwest side of the city, it was impossible to manufacture everything we needed. I imagined the types of things that must come in from distant lands. The foods, the clothes, the precious gems. Things I had only seen online.

I turned right and walked straight into a drone. I fell flat on my butt as if I had hit a truck. The drone didn't move an inch and looked at me as if a bug had crossed its path.

"Crap!" I yelled involuntarily. I was an idiot. How would I ever be able to escape the city when I couldn't stop screwing up in this warehouse? I was my own worst enemy. Because of my incompetence, I had let this metal shell capture me. I looked up ready to yell more profanity at it when it did a curious thing. It ignored me as if I wasn't important. Unlike the drone on the bus, its eyes didn't glow red. They were an ocean blue. It marched on, carrying its crate as if I wasn't part of its programming. Guess there were spying drones and working drones. Maybe they weren't all evil, after all. I got up and decided to stop daydreaming. I doubted I could make a third mistake.

I needed to get to the end of the warehouse as soon as possible. I had overheard Dad mention that shipments went out of the city first thing in the morning, probably because of the distance they had to travel. Today they were going to carry some extra cargo.

I walked down an aisle, taking better care to listen. The boxes were labeled with letters and numbers burned into the wood. They seemed very cryptic. I stopped and looked at the number: BX-W23. Typical adults making everything more confusing that it needed to be. I shook the box, which clanged like metal. *Hope there's no glass inside.* Then I heard a sound from behind. I quickly ducked behind some boxes as the sound of footsteps got louder.

"I swear, I don't understand why we can't open the crates. It's like they don't trust us." It sounded like the man I had met at the entrance.

"Our job's not to inspect the cargo; that's the drones' job. They approve everything coming in and out. Your job is to make sure the trucks make the deadlines." The other voice sounded older, probably my dad's age. They stopped walking nearby and I hunkered down further.

"If you ask me, some of the tech that was just shipped in, I've never seen anything like it. It makes the drones look like antiques."

"You keep looking at what's in the boxes, you either lose your job or go to jail. Leave it to the drones." I peeked up and the two workers were barely ten feet away from me. The younger guy grabbed the older guy's arm.

"Don't you ever wonder where it's all going? Why some cities are more advanced than we are?"

The older guy shook his head at the suggestion. "All I care about is a pay check. If you want to still be working here when you're my age, you'll do the same." Footsteps confirmed that they continued walking and were gone a minute later. I peeked around to make sure I was alone again. My goal was in sight. I scurried into the truck container, which looked to be full of tenting equipment, poles, ropes and tarps. I looked up high and there were several holes to the outside for ropes to lash containers together. I would have enough air. I lay down in the back under some tarps and waited. About thirty minutes later I heard the door latched and the wheels moved forward. There were a few voices outside initially but then it became quiet. I imagined the drones and machines were doing the heavy lifting.

I stood on a box and looked out the holes as beams of sunlight streaked through. The container was pulled forward and I could hear the straining of a crane as it was loaded for transport. Several other containers were loaded on next to mine and then a huge engine roared to life. I heard a loud horn screech and then the truck moved. I leaned back and imagined where I would be at day's end. I had looked forward to this day for my entire life.

My dad had always told me it was common for teenagers to want to leave home and see the world. That we were acting out, trying to get away from our parents and strike out on our own. It was more than that for me. I didn't hate my home or dislike my school or city. I had friends, interests; I loved going through the Marks. And I knew why I had to leave. I needed to see more. I wanted to explore new cultures. I wanted to have new experiences, to try new technologies. I hated routine. Sometimes I walked to school a different way just to see the street in a new way. I must have tried every soft drink possible, always looking for a unique taste.

I wondered what my dad was doing now. Probably already at work, reviewing another case. Another guilty verdict. Despite my anger with the justice system, I knew my dad meant to do what was right. He had undoubtedly brought many guilty people to justice. I had seen enough history videos to appreciate that our society was much safer now. People lived under much less stress knowing that violence was almost nonexistent.

So why did I feel sick to my stomach? Was Lou's case an aberration? Was someone out to get him? He was just a vendor at the Marks—I couldn't see why discrediting him was important. Unless he was one of many. How many times had my dad sentenced people with false video footage? How would one be able to check? Was Lord Morall unwilling to look at the truth or part of the corruption? It didn't matter; I'd be so far away at the end of the day that I'd never have to deal with any of this again.

The sounds of the city streamed through the holes on the top of the wall. I was surprised that we hadn't left the city yet. I assumed we would have exited at the checkpoint at the depot. Maybe we were taking another route? Then the truck slowed down. It was not the slowing down that you did when you rolled to a stop sign but to a complete stop for a longer period of time. I heard commotion outside and then felt a jolt as my container was raised up and then lowered to the ground. Had I miscalculated? Were these containers delivered to the city instead outside of it? I cursed my luck but then listened as the truck pulled away without dropping any more containers. *What's happening?* My answer came seconds later as the container door opened.

"You were lucky you weren't caught. They scan every crate for life signs before they cross the border. If I hadn't diverted this container, you would be going straight to jail." He shook the hair out of his face.

Where did Austin come from?

"Thanks, I think. Where am I?"

"Someplace safe. I made sure the drones didn't detect you."

"How? Were you following me? How did you know I was in the container?"

"I know a lot." He extended a hand to pull me out of the container. "Because of your attempted escape, now I can tell you what's really going on."

15

Explanation

When I looked up at Austin, I was conflicted.

Don't get me wrong, I was happy to see him. I had figured that he had just saved my life. I was naïve to think I could escape on my own. But I was also devastated. I had let myself believe that I would finally get out of the city. See the world, get away from this place. Now, instead of escaping the city, I was in some weird warehouse with a boy who I seemed to know more than anybody else.

"How did you find me?" I asked. He smiled and beckoned me towards a couple of chairs around a table.

"No need to thank me for saving your life," he laughed.

"Assuming you're telling me the truth."

"I am. They scan every box that crosses the border. A mouse doesn't cross without them knowing about it. Surprised your dad didn't tell you about that."

"He doesn't talk to me much these days. How did you find me?" Austin tapped his computer tablet and a map of the city flashed onto the screen. On it glowed dozens of moving green lights.

"The police know the whereabouts of everyone in the city. Drones record the time and direction of every resident. If they want to scrub through time, they can track your movements to days, weeks or months ago. Their only limitation is storage." His statement seemed farfetched, even for the security conscious justice department.

"And how does a teenage boy come across this information?" I raised my eyebrow as if to question his facts. He shook his head as if to say it was none of my business. I shook a finger back at him. "Come on, if you want me to believe you, you have to give me something."

"Fine." He tossed a picture at me. I looked at an older man, the same age as my dad, in a police uniform. He had Austin's eyes and nose.

"Your dad? Does he know what you're doing?"

"No." Austin averted his eyes downward. "He died three years ago."

"I'm sorry." I already regretted my question. "It's none of my business."

"It's okay, it's just the accident was so… stupid. He was chasing a criminal who resisted arrest. Both he and a drone tried to restrain the criminal but the drone was too intense. It missed the criminal and hit Dad on the side of his head with its metal arm. Dad suffered a concussion. He died in his sleep the next night. There was a big inquiry and they were supposed to change the safety protocols of the drones as a result."

"Did they?"

"I don't think so. Dad was an IT expert and had a lot of police equipment at home for testing. I was so angry that I was going to demolish all of his equipment. Funny thing was that for such a computer whiz, he had very poor password protection. I was able to hack in, and the city, in its typical inefficiency, never cut his access off after his death. I've been able to view a lot of things that no one else outside the justice department would ever see. Believe me now?" He pointed at the table.

I looked at the screen and noticed two green lights in close proximity. I touched the screen and it magnified the area. My name—last name first—appeared above one of the green lights. I double-tapped and a word balloon with my age, height and other stats appeared.

"What? They catalogue how I look? They know my weight!" *Lacey would dispute any number they posted on her.* His access made sense but it made me mad. I felt naked. Not only did the machines know where I was every moment of the day, they kept statistics on me. I felt like an athlete with his own collectible card. Except everyone had one. I noticed a light had faded from view.

"What's happening here?" I pointed. Austin leaned in closer to me.

"Our movements are tracked, but not 100% of the time. For instance, if you walk into a building where there are gaps in positioned cameras, your light becomes transparent."

"So you can become untraceable."

"Not quite. Your location is estimated based on your

speed and footsteps. However, if you walk into a basement or tunnel where you can't be seen, you could stop and the map would think you were here," he pointed to the end of a building "when you actually remained still. And there are other ways to evade the drones."

"How?" I moved closer.

"Become someone else." Okay, now he had my attention.

"You make it sound so easy."

"It actually is." He took a picture of me with his tablet and saved the image for his desktop. I made a face.

"I look horrible. It must be the light in here," I said as Austin smiled back at me.

"The human eye can only detect a fraction of the information that a drone can. The drone even has your specs on file. When it scans you, it identifies several of your features, like the color of your eyes, shape of your nose, fullness of your lips." *Is he coming on to me?* "It also measures your height, notes the color of your clothes…"

"Get to the part where I become someone else." Rather than tell me, he showed me. In my digital image he changed the color of my shirt, made me look heavier and lengthened my nose. "If you are trying to make me look better, this is a major fail," I added.

"Not trying to make you better, just different. See, the drones still have you in their system under specific measurements, if you add some platform shoes, change your clothes, stretched your face with some facial prosthetics—you could walk right by under the right circumstances."

"Which are?"

"You need to be in a busy place. You need distractions, and sometimes you may want to carry multiple disguises."

I sat down in my chair and tried to process the information.

"You're the same age as me, yet you know more about this city than anyone. Does your mother know what you are doing?" He shook his head, and judging from his face, it wasn't a topic he wanted to discuss. He was silent for a while, and just when I was going to have to ask him another question, he answered.

"We don't have time to talk about my life. Just be grateful that I saved yours." I could hear frustration in his voice. His dad's death had obviously hurt him. Thinking about my mom filled me with a similar loss. I decided to take another approach.

"Okay. Thank you. I was stupid. If you hadn't redirected that container—however you did that—I would be in a lot of trouble." I turned my attention back to his tablet. "Who are all the lights on the screen?" I pointed.

"Friends, family, persons of interest." The way he said the last phrase, I knew 'persons of interest' weren't the people he liked.

"Won't you get into trouble if you get caught? Never had a stalker before." I tried to make a joke.

"You've always had a stalker, Pene. You just never knew. We all do. I'm just breaking into a feed that the police already use to follow interesting people. To prevent crime. You can imagine what would happen if the public found out about this." He sounded so serious.

"Half the people wouldn't care and would buy the city's propaganda that it was only being done to keep us safe."

"Exactly. But with this knowledge, we can change things. We can make sure we can watch the watchers. And if we get really lucky, change the way the law controls our lives."

I considered Austin's words carefully. He meant well, and he certainly had more going on in his head than most teenage boys our age. I could see the appeal of what he was pursuing. An overbearing police force that was constantly watching over our shoulder. I had to give him credit for what he had accomplished.

"You're dedicated. You know more about how our city works than most adults. I wish you luck in changing things. But I just want to get out of here, away from my teachers, away from my dad, away from this city. Do you know of a way I can escape?" As I looked at Austin, I could see the disappointment in his eyes.

"Do you understand, Pene? I've just showed you how this city works. How people's every move is controlled and observed. We have a chance to change this. To set people free. And your first thought is to run away?"

"Who is this 'we'? Are there more people out there besides you who know what's going on?"

"Yes and no." He sat down and slumped in his chair. "Yes, there are others. But no, I don't know who they are."

"What?" I threw up my hands. "Do they read your mind?"

"I wish," Austin replied, not realizing I was mocking

him. "We have to communicate old school. No technology. There is no electronic communication that the police can't listen in on. So we have to send messages to each other, often in code and never with our real name. That way if the message is intercepted, it won't lead them back to me."

"Lola!" She appeared next to me just as my brain kicked in. "You were trying to send a message to the runner?"

"Exactly. Her programming does not connect itself to the network, so she can't be controlled." He pulled a piece of paper from under her collar. "Read this." I grabbed the piece of paper."

'evlf tusffu tjy bn'. It didn't make sense. I stared at it, but it was gibberish. I'm terrible with puzzles—whatever the code, my brain couldn't solve it.

"Is it English?" I asked.

"Typical teenager, no patience," he added.

"Last time I looked you were a teenager too."

"Relax." He held up his hands in mock outrage. "Maybe you should just take a step back." He walked backwards as if to illustrate his clue. I could strangle this guy right about now. But before I could put my arms around his throat, it came to me.

Go back one letter. I subtracted one letter from the sentence and came up with 'Duke Street six a.m.' It was so simple.

"Pretty clever. So this is how you communicate?"

"Usually. With codes or symbols, and then we destroy the message. Paper, rocks, chalk, anything that won't stick around. I use Lola since she has no network to be controlled like a drone."

"Or noticed in a crowd," I added. Then I thought about what he was saying. "How many of you are there?"

"Maybe six, definitely no more than ten."

"Are they kids like us?"

"Not sure. We don't celebrate birthdays," he mocked. I made a face at him. "I honestly don't know. We don't communicate very much and never meet. A couple seem like adults by the language they use."

"What do you talk about?"

Austin stood up to stretch and started to pace. "Lots of things. Like—are all other cities under the same security? Ways to avoid drones. Is the justice system corrupt?"

"Any answers?"

"Mostly theories. Someone suggested that the terrorists are still directing the city. Another person said there is a master computer that is controlling all computer systems. One of the guys," Austin leaned closer to me, "thinks that aliens are watching us." I rolled my eyes. Although the more I thought about it, who says anyone's guess is any sillier than the others?

"So what do you and your friends want? Isn't it hopeless? We're outnumbered by thousands to one. The drones never sleep, they come in all sizes and shapes. They can fly, they can run and they can swim. They're faster than us. You're kidding yourself if you think you can defeat them one on one." Desperation crept into my voice and Austin moved next to me.

"That's why we need to know where the drones are stored. They must go somewhere for repairs and modifications. No one has been able to follow them to their base. They just seem to appear, and someone must be building them. If I know where they are stationed, then we can destroy that building or disable the whole group of them. Once that's done, you can escape."

I considered his request.

"Put a tracking bug on one of them—see where it goes," I offered.

"Silly girl. If it was that easy, why would I need your help? The drones get scanned at the end of a twenty-four-hour shift. Any foreign bodies are studied and destroyed. It's impossible to follow or bug them."

"What makes you think I can find their location? I tried following a drone today and that was a disaster."

"Your dad! He's within the Justice Department. He can find out—use one of his police or judge friends to find out."

"My dad and I aren't exactly on speaking terms. He's probably not going to just give me the location."

"You're a smart and motivated girl. I'm sure you'll come up with a plan." He smirked.

He was right. I was motivated. And I realized that I wasn't going to get out of the city on my own or without years of wading through red tape. It was a deal worth taking.

"You got yourself a deal." I shook his hand. He smiled back at me as if I had become part of his team.

And then I knew what I had to do next.

16
Past

Monday morning came, and my encounter with Austin seemed like a dream. Or a nightmare, depending on how I thought about it. You'd think that after my experiences, knowing about a secret group trying to undermine the corruption of the justice system would reassure me.

I actually felt worse.

Instead of doubting myself or thinking I was crazy, I wanted out of the city more than ever. But what Austin was asking of me, I wasn't sure I could pull off. Could I find the drone base when no one else had?

"Are we interrupting your daydreams, Pene?" Mr. Stewart tapped me on the shoulder. I looked up and half of the class was staring at me.

"Sorry, Mr. Stewart," I answered sincerely.

"We'll discuss your conduct later. You have a visitor." He motioned to the classroom door. I turned and saw my dad's concerned face. I got up and walked towards him. Dad was pacing in the hall.

"Dad! Why are you here? Is something wrong?" I asked. He motioned me to sit on a bench next to the wall.

"This couldn't wait. I'm sorry I've been so distant lately. I've been avoiding talking to you. I've just been so angry that you lied to me." I could see the pain in his face. I hugged him.

"Well, I kind of deserved it, Dad. I haven't been very open with you lately. I'm just not happy. I feel like I'm being watched and manipulated every day. Something is wrong with our justice system."

"That's why I'm here now. We found something." He placed his hand on my shoulder. "I followed up with the footage that you said was altered. I must have watched it fifty times so far." *He did listen to me.* I started to get excited.

"What did you see?"

"There are some irregularities. I had one of the technicians I trust roll through the video with me from start to end. We examined lighting, audio, skin texture, anything that varied from each camera angle. What we discovered was that some of the cuts had a different time code. They weren't filmed consecutively. The footage was spliced in, and some of the frames did not involve Lou."

"I told you so." I felt vindicated. "Can you get his decision reversed?"

My dad shook his head. "Even if the decision was overturned, there is no way to turn back the aging process. Lou's sentence remains, even if he was innocent."

"Well, that just sucks. Why was his footage changed? Are there other falsified cases?" My dad put a finger to his lips to warn me to speak quieter. As I looked around the hallway, I noticed cameras were in several places.

"I need to ask questions, but slowly and with those who I trust. I don't know if the footage was altered by a camera technician to a supreme judge." I immediately thought of my prime suspect.

"Lord Morall is involved. He acts like someone who enforces his own type of laws."

"And you don't like his red eye," my dad countered.

"It creeps me out! I swear he's either part drone or he's being controlled by them."

"Who's *them*?" My dad made a face as if he thought I was crazy.

"I don't know." I stood up. "I just don't think some camera technician goes around and changes footage. It takes someone in a higher position to make those decisions. And I doubt they'd do it alone."

"A computer glitch is more likely than a city-wide conspiracy."

"You didn't see Lou's face when he was accused of a crime he didn't commit. The words spoken on the video were not his. That's no glitch. I should know, I was there."

"And that's why I was so angry." Dad's face changed. "I've told you dozens of times that I don't want you at the Marks. It's not safe!"

"Dad, we live in the safest city in the world. I don't understand your protectiveness."

"Why don't you tell her the truth, Evan?" We both turned our heads and looked at Mr. Stewart.

"This doesn't involve you, Ben," my dad countered as he stood up. I gaped—I didn't even know the two of them were acquainted. Mr. Stewart began circling us.

"Why don't you tell her what the Marks were really like before this city became safe? During the early stages of cameras and drones, before a swift and just legal system. Why don't you tell what really happened to her mother?" Before the realization of his comment sank in, my dad had Mr. Stewart pinned against the wall, his elbow against his throat.

"Stay away from my family!" he yelled. Strong hands grabbed him from behind and pulled him off Mr. Stewart. My gym and math teacher had heard the disturbance and had stepped in to break up the fight.

"Get off me! You're lucky I don't press charges," Mr. Stewart spat. "I'm sure the justice system won't look kindly with one of their lawyers endangering the citizens they're sworn to protect!" The other teachers pushed my dad onto the bench, where he looked defeated. I didn't think it was Mr. Stewart that made him feel that way. He looked up.

"Stay out of this, Ben. It has nothing to do with you. I have a good mind to report you to the school board for your interference. Our conversation wasn't school business."

"In case you hadn't noticed, there are no secrets here." Mr. Stewart pointed to a camera at the far end of the hall. He looked at me. "How would you like to know why your dad is so afraid of the Marks?" I was mystified. How did my teacher know anything about my dad? The answer came when he dangled one of the crowns from the re-enactment from his left hand. "History has been recorded. How would you like to know the truth?"

I turned, looked into my dad's eyes and saw the realization. Something was recorded that had made my dad fearful of the Marks, and that was why he had wanted me to keep away. I had to know, even if it drove my dad further away from me.

"I want to know," I said and reached out for the crown.

"Pene, I did it for your own good," my dad started to explain and reached for my arm.

"I think she's old enough to know." Mr. Stewart smiled, and not in a nice way. He must be taking satisfaction that either my dad or I was going to suffer. Didn't matter either way. He walked me over to an empty office and opened the door. We both stepped in, but my dad and the other teachers stayed in the hall.

"I've made some adjustments to play back the recording of the day in the Marks in question," he said.

"What day?"

"The day your dad began to hate the Marks." It was just like in class; every answer he gave made me more confused.

"How do you know my dad?"

"We've known each other most of our lives. We made different choices as adults but we share some important memories." I felt like hitting him because his answers only created more questions. But I decided it was time to learn first-hand. Or second-hand, if you wanted to be technical, since I was observing past events.

"Turn it on."

"You'll have twenty minutes," he said as he placed it on

my head. The interior of the office disappeared.

The sun was bright. I screened my eyes and then looked down at the ground. The area was familiar but things seemed out of place. Vendors yelled at me as I walked by, and I could smell baking bread a few stalls down. Yet the items for sale were old and clunky; one electronic device looked four times its current size. People's clothes were out of fashion as well. I laughed at one woman who strolled by me. I could tell she thought she was wearing the cutting edge in clothes, but to me it looked hideous and horribly outdated. This was the Marks about fifteen years ago.

A guy in his mid-twenties bumped into me and almost knocked me down. "Sorry, kid," he yelled back, and he continued on. His face startled me. He looked younger, had more hair and less worry lines, but his smile was my dad's. I gave chase as he almost disappeared around some food vendors. He always gave me a lecture for hanging out around the Marks, but by the way he moved around he was very familiar with his surroundings.

I ducked under an awning and tried to cut into the next alleyway to catch up with him. As I came out, I looked at the end of the alley but my dad did not appear. I looked the other way but with similar results. I began to panic because I knew how easy it was to lose someone here.

"Looking for something?" a familiar voice asked.

I turned and stared into the face of a young, attractive male vendor. He was athletic, with long jet hair. Lou never looked so good. The years had not been kind to his weight or lack of hair.

"Actually, looking for someone. Did you see a guy come by a few seconds ago about this tall, short, sandy blond hair, wearing a red jacket?" I inquired.

"Hhhmmm. Maybe I did." He playfully scratched his head in mock concentration. "Perhaps if you bought something, it might jog my memory.

Wow! Fifteen years didn't change his salesmanship. Since my dad was nowhere in sight, I decided to play along and hope Lou had actually seen Dad. I checked my pocket—I had some money. Didn't matter the year, credits are good anytime.

"Okay," I responded, "show me what you got?" His smile widened as he ushered me into his shop. It was smaller than his current one but probably just as cluttered. On the bottom shelves were the impulse buys and cheaper items. Candies and foods from outside the city—a chocolate liquor looked especially sweet. On the middle shelves, hand carvings and jewelry were laid out, made by craftspeople. A wooden mask stared out at me. I couldn't tell if it was smiling at me or mocking me. I looked higher still to the more expensive items. Electronics seemed to be the most common items; although they may have been cutting edge then, they were way outdated now. But something caught my eye. "Can I try that?" I pointed to the top.

"Of course." Lou smiled and handed it to me. It was a very old, clumsier version of the history crown I was wearing now. Back in the school office, I was wearing it to be immersed in this environment. You couldn't see it or feel it on my forehead, but it was there. Even though this looked ancient, it felt weird to putting a second one on. It was heavy, and a metal brace dug into the side of my forehead. *The earlier versions had some wearability issue*s. "I think you press this." He tapped the side and nothing happened.

"Actually, you press the button right here." I pointed to the metal bar and then Lou's shop disappeared.

The old ship rocked in rough seas. Storm water was crashing over its decks and I was about to fall down from the motion of the boat. The spray hit me in the face and I tasted salt water. I looked around and the crew looked like something from an old pirate movie. They were sickly, with yellow teeth, eye patches, hooks for arms and swords strapped to their waists. A wave crashed again and a brown chest ripped open, spilling its contents onto the deck. Gold coins spilled out and a number of crew members jumped to grab the contents, stuffing what they could into their pockets. Then, to the far right, something breached the water. It was dark but I could make out a mass of arms—probably belonging to a huge octopus or squid. It fixed me with its dark eyes as if it recognized me. The eyes were sad and I felt there was a story behind its sorrow.

From the top of the vessel a ray of fire erupted from a gun on the mast at the monster. Nothing made any sense—no movie I ever watched had pirates with this type of technology. What screwed-up movie was I watching? The flash of the gun ignited the sky as flames rained down on the vessel. I looked up just a piece of the mast turned into a fireball and began to fall. Death was only seconds away.

I blinked and I was back in Lou's stall. He was talking,

and even though several minutes had passed in the crown, only seconds had passed in Lou's reality. *What was that all about? A false reality with a false reality? A crown simulation within another crown simulation.* Although I'd never ask him, I'm sure Mr. Stewart could explain.

"Do you want to purchase this?" Lou rubbed his hands, greedily hoping I would buy the crown, one of his more expensive items. I shook my head and reached for the cheapest candies on the lower level. I brought out my card and allowed him to withdraw credits. If he seemed disappointed with my cheap choice, he didn't show it. I guess a sale is a sale.

"And do you have an answer for my question?" I asked as I was exiting his stall.

"You mean did I see a tall man with short brown hair and a red jacket?"

"Yes."

"When you asked the question, no." I was disappointed. All of this was a waste of time. "But," he continued, "since then, someone who matches your description walked by and is at the far end of the alley." He pointed. I looked and my heart rose.

"Thank you Lou." I ran off.

"But I never told you my name," he said, confused.

I dashed around several people and then came up short when I saw my dad had stopped and was talking to another man. He was thinner, with a severe face. Mr. Stewart had changed little in fifteen years and his mannerisms were the same. But then he did something that I had never seen him do. He smiled warmly back at my dad. Not that fake smile from class, as if he was silently superior to his students, but one of actual friendship. My mouth must have gaped open because the two of them stared back me.

"What are you looking at? Shouldn't you be in school?" the younger Mr. Stewart yelled over. My dad punched him in the arm.

"Maybe she can't get over how good-looking you are?" my dad teased, and the two of them started walking away.

Damn! How am I going to follow my dad when they've spotted me? Seconds later, I realized that was the least of my problems. From behind I could hear a large rumbling, like a motorcycle backfiring. I was half right. I turned and saw a bulky metal drone, a much earlier version of the one that had escorted me to Dad. Its outer shell was gun barrel gray, with so many scratches that I questioned how well it was steered. Everyone around looked and stared at it. It was different from my time; most of us had gotten so used to drones that they were background noise. This one stood out like a sore thumb. From everyone's faces, I could tell that it was not welcome. I wish I had grown up during those times.

Its head turned slowly from side to side. It had red slits for eyes, but its beam seemed weak as it scanned the crowd.

"Go away, tin head," someone yelled.

"Nothing to watch here," another voice said. The drone continued on, oblivious to its welcome. It veered to the right to avoid some crates by a stall and awkwardly moved. Its back end grazed my dad's leg. He went down hard.

"Stupid tin can," he yelled while grasping his thigh.

"Can't you see where you're going?" He seemed to regret his words almost immediately. He stood up and put weight on his leg.

The drone's head turned to the right and looked directly at my father and Mr. Stewart.

"Article twelve point three of penal code. City citizens must give drones at least five feet of distance to allow passage. The error is yours, citizen." It's cold eyes stared back at my dad.

"Please—it was an accident," Mr. Stewart said, trying to reason with it. The drone lacked expression and didn't seem to register the apology. "I know there is a human controlling you. Don't create an incident."

At first I didn't understand the comment, I was so conditioned by the artificial intelligence that controlled today's drones. They didn't care about you, they were just recording your movements. Drones of this time were like remote-controlled robots. Some police officer like Vaslor was controlling it from another location. Just when I thought I couldn't hate drones any more than I did.

"Don't let me see the two of you around here again," the drone said. I imagined the human sneering in the background but the metallic voice carried no hint of emotion. My dad started to limp away with his arm around Mr. Stewart's shoulder. Then a stone bounced off the drone's back. Everyone stopped. The drone turned its head but there were dozens of people in that direction. I hadn't seen anyone throw a stone, and with everyone motionless, I couldn't see the instigator. The drone watched, waiting for someone to try to walk away, to give away their guilt. No one dared to move. Then the drone acted quickly, grabbing my father's shoulder.

"Then I guess you get nominated to be the scapegoat." My father tried to pull away but the drone's grip was too strong. There was angry murmuring from the crowd but no one was brave enough to take responsibility for their actions. I knew what I had to do.

"I threw the rock. I accept your punishment." They were my words but I never had a chance to speak them. The voice was familiar, and then I saw her. It was my mom. I wanted to yell at her, to hug her. Instead I stood frozen to my spot.

"No," my dad yelled. "She's lying. She wasn't even here a few minutes ago." Then he turned to my mom. "Lily— don't do this!" My mom looked back at him confidently. She looked radiant and so young, and then I noticed something. She was carrying a small baby in her arms. It was me! I stepped backwards. It would be too weird to meet myself, even if this was just a recording of the events that occurred.

"If you receive any charges, you'll never graduate with a law degree. I'll be fine." My mom stepped towards my dad as if to hand off her baby.

"Your admittance of guilt is all I need," the drone stated, releasing my dad but grabbing my mother before she was ready. I fell from her hands and dropped to the ground.

"No!" My dad yelled. Inches before I hit the ground, Mr. Stewart's arms grabbed me and stopped my descent. *Who is this guy? How did he change so much?* The crowd turned ugly in seconds. Either they didn't like my mom's rough handling or the accidental dropping of her baby. They no longer cared if they got in trouble. Whoever was operating the drone was about to realize his mistake because seconds later rocks flew from several directions.

"Watch out!" my dad yelled. "You'll hit my wife!" My mom ducked but the drone's grip was too tight. A large rock hit her right temple and blood gushed immediately from the wound. Instinctively, I ran towards her, even though the true nature of my presence would confuse her.

The air erupted with a loud screech like an air siren. Everyone dropped to their knees, including me. The sound made me feel like my head was going to split open; it hurt more than any headache I had ever had. And then it stopped. And when I looked around, there were more drones, each stationed at different exits. Suddenly the fight was throughout the crowd. The main drone with my mom's limp body addressed the crowd.

"This woman will answer for your crimes." He pointed to all of us in turn. "Disperse now or be rounded up for prison." Before anyone could respond, the drone had latched my mom to its body and accelerated. My dad tried to stop it but he was knocked away like he weighed nothing.

"No," he yelled, "don't take her away. I'm the guilty one!" But the drone was gone.

"We'll find her," Mr. Stewart reassured my dad. "Cooler minds will prevail." And he radiated that familiar frosty look at the departed drone.

Dad's hatred of the Marks was starting to make sense now but created new questions. *What punishment was served to my mom?*

17

Truth

The water flowed down the rim of the concrete groove. Drops of water formed on the edge of the fountain before falling onto the concrete tiles. I sat on the bench as people walked by me, busy with their day's tasks. I felt a drone, watching, observing but never interacting.

I was calm yet empty and I really didn't know what to do. Since my re-enactment of Dad's past, he had grown more willing to talk about anything now, except about Mom. He was working hard to decipher who faked the footage and why. I had broached the topic about the drone storage area but he knew nothing. I excluded my conversation with Austin and being saved from the container. A girl's got to keep some secrets. But when I asked about what happened to mom after that day in the Marks, he refused to answer any questions. A lot of what I knew about my mother had changed.

I looked around at my surroundings from my park bench. The parade square was the centerpiece of the city. City hall towered over the wide-open space. A statue of a former mayor was at the south end, and flowerbeds of red begonias colored the north. I sat in the center, watching a sparrow bathing in the water. Around the fountain, children played as jets of water sprayed out from the ground. Their laughter radiated through the gardens but had no effect on me. I looked at the flowers and saw something flittering around the petals. The butterfly was gold and red and it flew towards the fountain. Its wings glistened in the afternoon sun and it flew from the fountain and landed on the bench. I smiled and looked at its antenna. Red lights flickered as they scanned me. My smile went cold. The drones were becoming more real every day. At what point would they replace human life?

"Room for two?" a female voice said from behind me. I turned and watched Lacey sit beside me. I had been so caught up in my problems lately that I had been ignoring her.

"Trying to solve all of the world's problems?" she teased, seeing how focused I was on the fountain.

"Can't even solve my math homework," I replied, "The world's problems are beyond me."

Lacey pulled out her tablet. "Math questions I can help you with. Especially with your absence in class earlier in the week. Everyone wants to know what's going on with Mr. Stewart and your dad?"

"Everyone?" I stared unblinking into her eyes. She avoided my gaze.

"Okay, mostly me. Just to put the rumors down. Some

people are saying that your dad tried to knock Mr. Stewart out. I was rooting for your dad." Lacey pumped her fist, which made me smile.

"Well, Mr. Stewart kind of egged him on. Guess they used to hang out together." Lacey made a face. "I didn't believe it either, but I saw it first-hand through the history simulation." I was silent, and I could feel Lacey trying to find the right words to say.

"The last few weeks we haven't talked much. I can feel you pulling away from me. Like you need to go see the world and your friend is holding you back."

"It's not like that!" I exclaimed.

"Hold on, let me finish." I wanted to apologize, to explain. I stopped myself and let her speak.

"We've been friends since grade four. Remember how we met?" I rolled my eyes; of course I remembered, but she replayed that event anyway.

"I was six and it was summer break. We were swimming at the Sportsplex pool. You were with your dad and I was with my mom. It was near closing time and there were only about a dozen kids left in the pool."

"Of course, they were all surrounding you, little miss popular," I interjected.

"Keep down, this is my story." Lacey tried to look cross and failed. "Anyway, a few of us had started playing a game of Marco Polo and I had closed my eyes. As I yelled 'Marco', I could hear 'Polo' whispered several times around the pool. Except I could hear one girl's voice above everyone else's and I homed in on that voice, determined to catch her."

"Oh, you tried!"

"And I caught you but you led me on the greatest chase. From one side of the pool to the other, you moved so fast. You'd yell and I'd turn and reach for you, but you were gone like a ghost."

"I felt bad for you at the end. I let you catch me."

"And we've been best friends ever since. But even as kids you were always the one exploring, taking me to places I never knew I wanted to go."

"And you always talked us out of trouble when the time came," I added.

"We're a team, but Pene," and suddenly she got serious, "I always knew that there would be a time that you would move on. I'll be here my whole life but you need to see the world. Go wild while you're young."

I punched her on the arm. "I want more than just traveling," I said. "I don't want to be here anymore. The city's not what it seems." I was ready to share the last few weeks with her, but she wanted nothing to do with it.

"I don't want to know." She waved her arms with dramatic flair and arched her head to the right. A drone bird was parked nearby, intent on our conversation. I took the hint. "But if you ever need anything, you just have to ask." We hugged and for a moment I felt like crying. And then he came.

"Sorry to interrupt," a familiar voice asked. We turned and Austin was looking down at us.

"I didn't know you were meeting your boyfriend here!"

Lacey teased. Someone else was standing next to Austin. "I see you brought a friend."

"This is Alex." He motioned to a boy with short black hair who was a few inches taller than him. Austin's eyes gave me a strange glance, as if there was no warmth.

Alex waved to us. "Nice to meet you," he said and gave us a smile that seemed painted on. "Austin and I are working on a class project together."

"What you working on?" I asked. Alex seemed to be quick with the answer, stepping in front of Austin.

"In social sciences, we have a week to show how traffic routes cross the city. We're supposed to pretend we're engineers, and our job is to document the ten busiest bottlenecks across the city. Once we have identified them, we suggest alternate routes or additional infrastructure that could be built to alleviate traffic." Okay, the project seemed innocent enough. So why couldn't Austin look me in the eyes?

"That's a lot of ground to cover. Sounds like you two will be best buddies for the next week," added Lacey. Austin turned to her and his eyes lit up like she had made an important point.

"I'm sure we'll be inseparable," Austin offered, and as if on cue, the small drone butterfly landed on Alex's shoulder. An idea started to form in my mind but I needed confirmation.

"Hey Austin, you're looking a little pale, you feeling all right?"

"Feeling '*desserts*', Pene, couldn't be better," he answered. I cocked my head at him and his cryptic answer. Before I could delve further, Alex jumped in.

"We have to go to the corner of Duke and Grand to work on our project. You girls want to walk with us?" Austin looked ready to retract Alex's offer but Lacey was too fast.

"Sounds like fun, honey. Walk with me so the two love-birds have some time together." Lacey hooked Alex's arm and they started walking ahead. The butterfly flew off Alex's shoulder and stayed with us.

"You okay?" I asked as we started walking.

"I already told you. Think you got it all backwards." He stressed the word backwards. Maybe he was alluding to the code he had explained to me before.

"How much is the project worth?"

"Hundred percent," he spat out with a smile, but I could tell that he wasn't pleased.

"Can we talk?"

"I thought that's what you were doing?" he answered, but concern crept into his voice. *Okay. What's going on? Think about his choice of words. Feeling desserts. Backwards. All right— what is the word 'desserts' spelled backwards?* I thought for a second. *Stressed. That's what desserts is backwards. Austin is feeling stressed. Why? And why speak in code? Is it Alex or the drones?* I needed to find a place where we could speak openly. I saw something ahead that might give us that opportunity.

"Hey, Lacey," I yelled, "I have to use the washroom." I pointed to a public restroom. She turned with Alex.

"Want us to wait?"

"No, go on ahead. Austin will wait for me and we'll catch up." The two of them continued walking and disappeared into a crowd. I looked at Austin, flashed the number three and then walked into the women's bathroom. I looked under the five stall doors. No one else was there. For once, luck was on my side. I stepped into the third stall and waited. Austin stepped in and closed the door behind him about ten seconds later.

"Good plan. Neither the cameras nor drones can follow us in here. We got about two minutes before the others wonder where we are."

"Never mind. I'll tell them I had stomach problems. What. Is. Going. On?"

Austin took a breath and answered my question. "I think someone may have backtracked to my computer. I'm usually pretty careful but the last time I was watching other people..."

"Were you stalking me?"

"Watching other people," he continued without missing a beat, "when I thought I was being traced. The computer started to act up as if it was corrupted, and I thought someone was trying to log into my system. I shut down immediately, but it could have been too late. Ever since then the drones have been watching me nonstop."

"What about Alex? Is he watching you?"

"I don't know." He looked unsure. "I've never seen him before and all of sudden he's assigned to this project and we have to spend a lot of time together. The whole thing doesn't feel right."

"You think the Justice Department has assigned someone to watch you? Do you know how crazy that sounds?"

Austin looked away. "Totally crazy. I know, but the guy shows way too much interest in me."

"Maybe he has no friends."

"Could be. He's kind of goofy. But the drones have also been on me from sun up to sundown. They don't even try to hide from me. Too much of a coincidence if you ask me."

"So you what do you want me to do?"

"You can't say anything to me, phone me, text me, anything that leaves an electronic message."

"So you want me to avoid you?"

"Yes. Leave me paper messages or scrawl our code in the dirt. I can't be caught. I don't want to endanger my family."

"Might be a bit late for that."

"We don't have time for this. The longer we spend together, the more likely you will also become a target. Get to your friend and make some sort of excuse to leave." He looked towards the bathroom entrance. "We should go." He got up and opened the stall door. Before he left, he turned to me. "As soon as you have any information on where these drones are stored, get hold of me. If we can stop them, I have to know where they're coming from. Leave me a message as soon as you know." He started toward the exit.

"How will I contact you?"

"I don't know." He shrugged. "But you're a smart girl, I'm sure you'll find a way." He disappeared out the exit. I had only a few moments before I would have to join him. I looked at myself in the mirror. I was tired. All I ever wanted to do was grow up and see the world. Now other people were depending on me, and even if I left the physical borders of the city, there were other things to hold me back.

What to do? What if I failed Austin—could he be charged? Aged into an adult that I would no longer recognize. I shivered. Did I care about a boy I had only just met? He had saved me once—there had to be a way I could return the favor.

A shadow moved outside, hovering high above the exit. Waiting. Watching. Maybe Austin was right, maybe the drones were watching him. Trying to find out how much he knew about the police's ability to watch everyone's movements. The red eyes transmitting information back to base—a huge database with the latest location of the city's residents. I bet with history stored, they could probably predict where I would be on any given day. My safety stored for the benefit of all.

Then it came to me. An idea of how to find out where the drones were stored. Where they lived. I walked out of the bathroom and stepped into the sun.

18
Base

"I'll be with you in a moment," Lieutenant Vaslor said as his door closed again. I had been sitting in his office for the last thirty minutes, waiting for him to become available. I was bored looking at my tablet so I got up and walked around the office. It was sterile and clean, with bleached white walls. The furniture was sparse, a few chairs, a shelf, some cabinets and a few pictures on the wall. I looked at an electronic picture of Vaslor with a woman and a girl a few years older than me. She had red hair and a forced smile. *I wondered if she liked the drones watching her—probably thought her dad was watching her on dates.* I looked at the slideshow, always action pictures of him, his wife and daughter. I could imagine the family vacation was full of activities.

I walked over and looked at the contents of his desk. It was covered with electronic gadgets the purpose of which was beyond me. *Probably a bunch of outdated garbage, like Dad has in our basement.* A tablet caught my attention. On it was a group of static lights, much like the display that Austin had showed me. I couldn't make out the map. It could be city block, a building or a park. Yet something about it looked familiar.

"Looking for something?" Vaslor asked from behind. My face was hot, as if I was poking around where I shouldn't be.

"Sorry, I was bored. Just looking around. What's your daughter's name?" I pointed at the wall, moving away from his desk.

"Evelyn. She's a senior in high school, talks about following in the footsteps of her Dad into law enforcement." His body arched as he spoke; I could tell he was proud of her.

"Has she ever come in to see you at work?" I asked. Vaslor motioned for me to sit down as we spoke.

"Several times. Kids are so lucky today. When I was her age we had to deal with everything at school. From bullies to drugs to vandalism; it's tough enough growing up with your own body changing. Try having others working against you."

"You mean students could openly hurt people?" The concept seemed foreign since now the slightest hint of violence brought teachers forewarned by drones.

"When I was a teenager, it was common for the bigger guys to terrorize the smaller kids. Kids are smart. They don't bully others when teachers or other adults are around. They wait for kids to be alone or separated from their friends. You don't know how lucky we are to have them." He pointed to the ceiling and I noticed a small hummingbird hovering in the corner. Its red eyes scanned my face as it beat its wings.

It must have flown in with Vaslor.

"Don't you miss your privacy?" I slouched in my chair, wondering if he would take this as a dig at his profession.

"Privacy?" He started walking around his desk as if he was about to give a speech. "What is privacy to the innocent? I can walk down the street in any neighborhood, at any time, and know that I am safe. Let me show you something." He motioned to me to look at a screen on the wall. He picked up a remote from his desk and motioned at the monitor. "If you were to name this picture, what would you call it?"

An image of a crowd of people near the downtown core. Some of the buildings looked different and some of the clothing adults were wearing looked out of date. I noticed kids playing in the lower left-hand corner. People were stepping onto a bus and seniors were sitting in the park. Seemed like a snapshot of life on any particular day.

"I guess I'd call it 'People in the City.' There's nothing remarkable about it." Vaslor smiled at my comment.

"Are you sure?" I wanted to wipe the smugness off his face. So I looked closer. It was like a parade of bodies, arms and legs going off in many directions. Then I spotted an arm where it shouldn't be.

"That man is reaching into that women's purse at the bus stop," I pointed.

Vaslor nodded. "What else?"

I was growing frustrated—I didn't come here to play a game of 'What's wrong with this picture?' I bit my lip and looked closer. A minute passed and I was just about to give up when I caught the expressions between a mother and child.

"Did she hit him?" I asked incredulously. He nodded.

"It's after the fact. If you look closely, you can see the fear in the child's face from being hit and anger in his mother's face. All in all, there are about six crimes being committed in this image alone."

"What?" I started to scan the picture more closely but Vaslor changed the image, having made his point.

"Before drones and cameras, the guilty took advantage of people at every turn. Imagine, even when looking for it, crimes occur all around us, many undetected. Criminals that were caught hid behind expensive lawyers. Justice may be blind but she was also forgetful, as many criminals dragged proceedings on for so long that they never served jail time."

"But today's trial is a formality. There is no opportunity to prove your innocence."

"That's where you're wrong, Pene." He motioned towards the door and we exited his office. I avoided another officer who was charging down the hallway.

"Criminals have several opportunities to admit their guilt. The camera or drone footage proves without a doubt that they were there and committed the offence." I decided not to pursue this explanation. Vaslor took another direction with the conversation.

"But the greatest power of the drones is not recording but prevention. Just the fact that the drones or cameras are there stops crime. A whole generation of criminals has been eliminated because people are afraid of getting caught." Vaslor directed me towards a large set of doors. I chose my words carefully.

"I understand that life is much safer now. But don't you think we are also worse off? They're everywhere," I motioned to the drone flying with us, "wherever I go, they watch and record. Is my life so interesting that they have to document each second!" I raised my voice unexpectedly and Vaslor gave me a stern look as we went through a set of doors.

"The drones are harmless. They record and delete. Only if crime is committed does the footage get stored. Why would you care if they are following you?" Okay, this guy had obviously not been a teenager for a very long time.

"What if your dad followed you every place you went and watched everything you did. How do you think you'd feel?"

Vaslor stroked his chin as if thinking of any answer. "I'd feel trapped," he answered. Finally, an honest response. "But I'd also feel safe." He punched me on the arm like a classmate who didn't take my question seriously. My next question died in my throat as the interior of the room overwhelmed my senses.

The room was huge, similar to the monitoring room, but instead of people there were rows and rows of drones. Shelves of mechanical heads stared lifelessly out at me. If their eyes had been on, I would have run screaming. I was never more scared in my life.

"Your dad said your class project was about how the drones keep our city safe so I couldn't resist taking you to one of the maintenance sites." Vaslor crossed his hands and smiled with a goofy salesman's look. Well, whatever he was selling, I wasn't buying.

"Are there any humans working at a maintenance site?" As large as the room was, it was eerily quiet.

"No, that's the beauty of it. The drones are fully self-sufficient. No human time has to be wasted in maintaining them. Come look over this screen." We walked over to where a huge monitor took up most of a wall. The screen showed a map of the east side of the city. Vaslor touched the screen and the schematic rotated on its axis. A series of red and green lights filled the screen, some at street level while others floated above.

"The city blocks are west to east, the map is of the eastern quadrant. Green lights are recorded activities of people, from kids to the elderly." *This screen and Austin's readout are very similar.* "The red lights are the drones, patrolling and documenting the city. Do you see all the red lights here?" I squinted and noticed a large congregation of red lights. *Do drones have parties?*

"Yes, what's going on?" I pointed at the screen.

"Computer—summarize report on drone footage for Drummond Street 1500 block," Vaslor said to the monitor.

"Processing," a very female-sounding voice responded. Seconds passed. "Possible assault has occurred—two teenage boys. One is running while the other is pursuing. Eight drones are capturing footage."

"Please show footage from these cameras," Vaslor commanded while tapping several points on the screen. The monitor broke up into several mini camera feeds, four on top, four underneath. Most drones appeared to be following the two boys, while several had flown ahead to watch them coming towards them. They were older than me, maybe nineteen or twenty. The runner was short and stocky. Black hair flowed behind him. Seconds later, the chaser, who was tall and lanky, was gaining on him. The chaser was smiling like he was enjoying himself.

"What caused this?" I asked. Vaslor began to work buttons on the touch screen.

"Not sure—no footage available previous to their chase. But they have to be stopped before they hurt themselves, or worse, someone else." He spoke to the monitor. "Police drone—intercept course, stop subjects in cameras 45C-89 and 67B-48 before 2000 block of Drummond Street." The face of the half-man, half-motorcycle filled the screen.

"Affirmative," it replied. The drones continue to record the footage. The pursuer was getting closer and would likely catch up in a few minutes. They were both moving fast, weaving around people like an obstacle course. The pursuer even mouthed 'sorry' to one of the passersby. The runner looked back, his eyes narrowed but showing no fear. As he turned the corner, the camera showed his legs coming to a complete stop while his upper body continued its forward momentum. He smashed awkwardly into the metal drone and I could hear a sickening cracking sound. The runner clutched his arm and cried in pain.

"You are ordered to stop. You are endangering other people with your erratic behavior." The drone motorcycle had intercepted the runner. The pursuer caught up and yelled at the drone.

"What are you doing? You could have killed him! Why don't you watch where you are going?" he yelled at the drone and leaned down by the injured runner.

"You are under arrest! You were trying to hurt this person," the drone pointed.

"Bullshit! It was a race. He had a thirty-second head start and I was supposed to try to catch him."

"Yeah. You drones are always trying to find a crime. It the school hadn't closed the track because of the upcoming Re-enactment Games, we wouldn't have to be running in the street," the injured boy added, clutching his arm. Vaslor turned off the screen, shaking his head.

"Central—send an ambulance to Drummond Street. Victim is male teenager with likely broken arm. Make sure parents are notified."

"Roger that," a female voice replied over the monitor.

"That went well," I commented sarcastically. Vaslor turned to me.

"Sometimes we make mistakes, Pene. Doesn't mean that we scrap an entire system the moment it doesn't work. The boys presented a problem and it was investigated."

"What if the boy was seriously hurt? A head injury?" Before Vaslor could answer, someone entered behind us.

"For a safe society, that's the price of no crime." Our heads turned as Lord Morall entered through the main door. I wasn't sure of how much of our conversation he had overheard. He walked in, his red eye squarely focused on me.

"Vaslor, I'll take her from here."

"Yes, sir." Vaslor turned to me. "Good luck with your report. Say hi to your dad." He saluted.

"Thanks a lot for your time," I gulped, trying desperately to think of an excuse not to be left alone with Morall. Nothing came, and then Vaslor was gone.

"As I was saying, no system is perfect. I am very sorry that one of our drones injured that boy. Criminal, isn't it," he smirked. "But we can't very well sentence a drone for its mistake."

"But the boys weren't hurting anyone. Why chase them to begin with?"

"Pene." He reached his arm around and started sheep-herding me towards a series of drone legs. "The drones react to threats. Obviously the boys' recklessness could have injured themselves, or worse, an innocent bystander. What if you were a senior knocked to the ground by them and breaking a hip? The justice system isn't perfect. What's the saying," he appeared to be thinking of something, "You can't make an omelet without breaking a few eggs?"

"I think the boy who was running broke more than an egg," I challenged. My comment seemed to have no effect on Morall's thinking. I may as well have been talking to a brick wall.

"I applaud your interest in the justice system, Pene. Most teenagers are so focused on themselves, they rarely watch what's going on around them." He picked up a drone head and held it like Hamlet held a skull in Shakespeare. I tried to shake the image from my mind, or I would have started to laugh. I think he caught a glimmer of my smile. "But you really should look at the big picture. Then maybe you could see the greater good."

"Sir, I think you are misunderstanding me. As a judge, I'm sure you have heard every story imaginable."

"I suppose that's true." His composure softened for a moment.

"Then someone younger than you, without your experience, might have questions on how the justice system works. How can I appreciate it, if I don't fully understand it?"

"I never said questioning was wrong, Pene. However, some of the ideas you have put in your father's head could be interpreted as dangerous. Your father is a great man, a pillar of the justice system. I hate to see a pillar fall." Now I grabbed a drone head and tossed it from my right hand to my left while I absorbed his comment.

"One thing I've learned from my dad is that to pursue truth, you must be willing to ask questions. Tough questions that challenge how we think. If the law is truly transparent, I should be able to ask any question? Don't you think?"

"As long as it doesn't jeopardize the security of others, you're right. What do you want to ask?" I measured him, deciding if he was sincere. I had nothing to lose.

"How did you lose your eye?" His red eye blinked. I think I surprised him because he was expecting a question about the law, and I had asked him something very personal. He was silent, and for a second I thought about telling him not to bother.

"Losing my eye was the most painful moment of my life.

I can still feel the scar tissue as the metal eye pushes against my eye socket." He touched the side of his head as if recalling the memory. "Please have a seat." He motioned towards a work bench, and I sat down next to him.

"When I was your age, the city was much different. There were good parts of town and there were bad sections. Unfortunately, the way home from school took me through a bad part of town. I was never popular at school, and I recognized some older boys stalking me. I did what any kid in the same circumstances would do." Morall looked pained, and for the first time, human. "I ran."

"If this is too difficult to discuss…"

"Don't be silly. Memories can't hurt us." He paused. "Anyway, I may not look like it now, but I was in good shape. Never the fastest or the strongest, but my endurance was one of the best. I used to have to walk through here." He pointed at the map on the wall at several blocks of industrial buildings surrounded by residential homes. "This was an old oil refinery here that I used to walk by. Back then they used to pump oil out of the ground and refine to use it in vehicles and heat our homes." I nodded. I had heard of oil. It seemed so barbaric to destroy our earth over it.

"I had started running as soon as I saw them. They often tried to take my valuables from me. I had lost watches, lunch money and even clothes before. I figured that if I ran hard enough, hopefully an adult would see me and they would stop. But I wasn't thinking when I ran through this area; businesses had closed for the day and no one was around. As I tried to get to the end of the street, one of the boys cut my exit off on his bike. As I turned around, three other boys had me surrounded."

I could feel my hatred for Morall starting to dissipate.

"'What have you got for us today?' said Findlay, the biggest of the group and the one who sat on the bike. I felt someone grab me roughly from behind. Usually I gave in. There were more of them, and as soon as they got what they wanted, they would leave. I was frustrated, tired of being picked on. So I fought back. I kicked forward. Findlay had moved in closer and his head was down. I felt my foot smash into his mouth. Blood sprayed and I was sure I had knocked a tooth out. It was the biggest mistake of my life.

"Findlay screamed with rage. He looked at me and his silence terrified me. I knew that he was going to do more than just hurt me; he was going to disable me permanently. He began pounding me in the stomach and then punching my face. The arms behind me let go as the other boys began to regret pinning me from behind. Their voices rose as they tried to calm Findlay down. It had no effect. Something smashed my ankle and I fell to the ground. Unfortunately, because of the nearby factory, the ground was rough and uneven. Rocks and debris were everywhere. When I fell, I landed on something hard, and it protruded into this eye!" He gestured to his drone eye. "The pain jolted me to my brain. When I looked up, I realized that I was going to die.

"My bloody eye had no effect on Findlay's rage. He raised his foot and I didn't know if he was going to crush my jaw or my head first, but I knew I wasn't going to get up again. And then the voice of my savior spoke.

"'Stop! You are committing a crime!' The boys turned, including Findlay. This was the earliest drone version—a remote-controlled robot. Big and slow on tank treads, rotating arms that were easy to elude and red eyes that stared back at you. 'Step away from the victim, medical assistance has been notified!' the computer voice wailed.

"'Get out of here, tin can! You don't belong here,' Findlay warned as he stepped away from me and moved closer to the drone. My vision was blurry but it appeared Findlay picked something off the ground as he approached it.

"Did the drone hurt him?" I asked.

"Drones were pretty primitive. They were used more to dismantle bombs or enter areas with a gas leak that were unsafe for humans. They didn't have many protection capabilities. And Findlay knew this.

"'This is a human-only area,' Findlay yelled. Despite my pain, his voice was clear and crisp. Time seemed to stand still as the rocks crunched under the drone's treads. And then I heard the sound of metal on metal shaking the ground. Findlay had transferred his anger from me to the drone. And it had saved my life.

"I wasn't sure if seconds had passed or minutes. I could barely raise my head. Something fell next to me. I turned my face and looked into the bashed-in head of the drone. Its face was destroyed except for one red eye. I passed out from the pain.

"When I woke up, I was in a hospital bed. My body ached and it took all my effort to raise my head. Tubes came out of me and I could see blood flowing into my arm. My depth perception was off and I banged my head on the side railing. I felt off, and not just because I had my head beaten in."

I pointed at his drone eye.

"Yes—although not this version. My eye had been crushed and the only thing that still worked on the drone's head was its right eye. My right was gone and it seemed like a good fit from the doctor's perspective. It was the early days of robotics, and the surgery had been performed before, with mixed results. I was lucky; the eye was primitive but it worked. It was appropriate because if the drone hadn't shown up, I would have lost more than an eye."

"So it saved your life in more ways than one," I stated.

"And continues to do to this day. How many other little boys have drones saved?"

Suddenly Morall and his eye seemed less threatening to me.

"With today's medical breakthroughs, you don't need a drone eye anymore; they have made many artificial eyes that would work as well as a real one. Your eye wouldn't have to stand out," I commented.

"Pene—maybe you don't realize what this eye means to me. I want to stand out. This eye is a symbol of the sacrifice the machine has made for man. The sacrifice it made for my life. I *want* people to ask about this eye. I see things differently than others, and this eye symbolizes that the drones are here to help us." His gaze was focused. He clearly believed every word he told me. I understood his position, though it blinded him to the truth.

"I appreciate your time. You've given me a perspective I hadn't thought of." I stood up and held out my hand.

"Perhaps drones aren't as bad as you think?"

"Maybe." I smiled and stepped through the door. I stopped, not wanting to miss taking advantage of the opportunity. "One last question for my project. Where are all the drones stored? Vaslor says this is the maintenance center."

"My dear," Morall gestured around the room, "the drones are at work twenty-four hours a day. They only come here for the occasional repairs, and they never stop. You may have seen them on buses or other public places, charging their batteries. Otherwise they have no other downtime. There is no storage center for the drones."

He pulled out a hand-held receiver and punched in a code. In unison, hundreds of drone heads flashed red on the shelves and rotated to look at me. I had never felt more insignificant than I did at that moment.

"Don't worry, Pene," Morall stated. "The drones are always working for your safety. They never rest."

Austin was not going to like that answer.

19
Nightmares

The thunder crackled in the night. I looked out my window, where the long, jagged edges of lightning streaked from the sky into the mountains. The effect was breathtaking. Every year during the summer solstice, the city's weather machine created a thunderstorm. Apparently it was necessary to prevent storms from building up during the year. By allowing the excess energy to be expelled during the summer, it made for more manageable weather for the rest of the year. By most residents' request, rain happened at night while days were mostly sunny. No one wanted one of their events cancelled due to poor weather. I found that while most people hunkered down during this night, I watched in awe since I had a front seat to nature's majesty.

There was another reason I enjoyed this night every year. The lightning, coupled with rain and wind, made it hazardous for the drones. As I looked outside, there were no flying red eyes anywhere in the sky. The air smelled fresh and clean. Just to prove me wrong, I heard metal clanging on the sideway as an older drone rolled down the sidewalk, oblivious to the rain. Although it was expressionless, its slow movements made it look like a creature that was miserable in its task. As I looked down, it stopped and gazed up at me, its red eye searching the dark. Instead of stepping back out of sight, I stared back. With its ultraviolet scanners, I'm sure it could see me. Seconds later, it must have become disinterested because it was first to look away and continued to trudge down the street.

On this night, it was nearly impossible to sleep. I needed to talk to Austin but realized that with the security he was under—and still probably myself—it was hard to talk freely. My conversation with Lord Morall had changed my outlook towards the drones. I was realizing that drones weren't evil or good; they were simply the tools of whoever was using them. Yet my dream to escape remained unchanged. Since I was unable to go to sleep, I pulled out my tablet and looked at the map of the city.

It was large—many millions of people in a huge sprawl of five thousand square miles. It had beauty and it had squalor, and even at my young age I had seen a lot of it. Yet when I looked at the sky each night, I knew there had to be more. Considering the flaws in our society, I wanted to find out if other cities were as security-conscious as ours. Could I simply just go into the countryside and actually be alone, without something trailing me and recording my movements? I looked up other places across the world, the pyramids in Egypt, the jungle in the Amazon, the museums in Paris. There was so much to see. Surely I could get the necessary visas to travel to these places.

I remembered a story my grandmother had told me about their honeymoon in Niagara Falls. The sound of the water was deafening, she said, drowning out all other noise, as millions of gallons flowed over the falls. Now she would barely leave her own backyard, yet she'd had the opportunity. That's all I wanted. The opportunity to visit these countries on my own. To realize that there was more to life than the corners of this city.

"Pene?" A voice made me drop the tablet, which tumbled to the floor. I whirled around to see Dad's scared face. "It's just me, sweetheart. I know how you don't sleep during these annual thunderstorms. I was checking to see how you were doing." He walked into the room.

"Knock first, Dad. You scared me." I lay on the bed while my eyes were still focused on the sky. One star seemed to glow brighter than the rest.

"Here's your tablet." My dad handed it back to me. "Still can't wait to explore the world? Is life here with me so bad?" His expression was pained, as if my need to travel was a slight against him.

"No, Dad. But I want more. There is more to life than this city." I thought about my childhood. "Do you remember my scrapbooking project when I was eight?" He nodded and sat beside me on the bed.

"Like it was yesterday. I think it was called 'Around the World in Eighty Days.'"

"You're right. Together we had to pick out twenty places around the world that we wanted to visit and why. And you know which place I wanted to visit the most?"

"Any place but here?"

"Dad!"

"Joking. You picked the Grand Canyon because it was one of nature's greatest wonders. And because your mother loved it as a girl."

"Whenever I saw pictures, it reminded me of the moon with its huge caverns and rock cliffs. But I especially wanted to go because Mom loved it."

We were silent but I knew we were thinking of the exact same thing. Of her. "Do you still miss her?" I asked, expecting him to clam up or try to escape out of the bedroom. Thunder rolled, and just when I thought he wasn't going to answer, he spoke.

"Time heals all wounds. Whoever coined that phrase didn't know anything about love. How about time is a wound that festers every day, bleeding but never healing." He turned to look at me. "Every day I see you I think of her, and I think of every memory we didn't get to share together, every memory that you lost out on."

"Am I more like her than you?"

"More than you can know. While I was happy with what we had, where we went, who we saw, she always wanted to do more. She was inquisitive and strong, two traits that you share."

"Why did she die? Was there something you could have done?" His eyes became moist, and I knew that I was pushing him. Yet I wanted to know.

"Your mother was a researcher and a lobbyist. She

wanted more for this city. But those that she aligned with, their methods were questionable."

"But I thought she worked for the city. Weren't the terrorists responsible for the earthquake?"

"Officially, yes, once the power plant overloaded and the city went dark. But some felt the city should have had a disaster recovery plan, that the corruption prevented the city from spending on backup generators. It's pointless to blame now. Despite what the history books said, both sides were responsible for what happened. Your mom was an innocent bystander. Thousands died that day, and hundreds of bodies were never found, including your mom's."

"Did you ever think she was still alive?"

"For days the emergency crews searched the rubble. In some cases, people were trapped and still alive. There were dozens of people saved, and most of us held out hope that our loved ones could be alive. But after a week the miracles stopped and body after body was removed from the debris. No more survivors, no more hope. There was mass burial ceremony near the center of town where all the victims were commemorated." I thought of the statue downtown. "The names of the victims were stenciled in the surrounding wall to always be remembered. Like we ever forget."

"Did they ever find her body?"

"No. Over the years a number of bodies have emerged, as well as some unidentifiable remains, but not your mom. But the earthquake was massive. The ground opened up and swallowed buildings whole. It felt like the ground rose into the air, and for the longest time the sky went completely black with soot. Most of us thought that all of our lives were over."

"Can it ever happen again?" I asked.

"Not if we learn from our mistakes. The schools have multiple re-enactments each year to drive home these lessons. Your school finals will explain more on the horrible aftermath. Your generation can't make the same mistakes."

Lightning flashed and my dad's face lit up. For the first time that I could remember, he looked old. The weight of Mom's death, the stress of work, my demands, they all aged him. It's easy to get caught up in your own life's issues and feel the world weighing down on you. Dad's face was the result of a battle fought over many years. It scared me.

"Dad? What will you do when I graduate and move away? Will you come visit me?" I smiled up at him but he didn't return my warmth.

"Well, you know how much red tape that takes. I'm happy to stay here. When you get through all the regulations to travel, you be sure to bring lots of gifts back for your old dad."

I smiled, wondering what I would bring back for him.

"Why is it so much tougher to travel now than before the earthquake?"

Dad slid off the bed and walked over to the open window. "Many of the terrorists came from outside of the city, Pene. Most city officials thought we should be more careful about who leaves and enters the city limits. With the change in regulations, everything we do now keeps us safe."

"Safe? Try suffocating. I'm afraid something is watching

me when I take a shower."

"You're being silly." Dad frowned. "I know you have concerns about our justice system but there is no doubt we live in a safer place. The drones have saved untold lives."

"But are we living?" I exclaimed, feeling my blood rise. "How do we not know that every moment is being recorded? The satellites above could be tracking our every movement, deciding if we're good or bad."

"The drones and cameras don't work that way. They just patrol public areas. Nothing private like our home." I felt like telling him about Austin's computer hacking, the lights on the screen. I couldn't share that with Dad. Instead I looked outside into the drone less sky.

"Dad, imagine a place where you could walk down a street and you didn't have a flying bird track your every step. A city that didn't have cameras spying on your every move."

"Pene," Dad grabbed my shoulder, "I don't have to imagine. The world used to be like that. People got hurt, criminals got away and no one was there to help. Is the loss of privacy so high a price to pay for your safety?"

I realized this was a debate I would never win. No adult who had already experienced the world would ever deny that the city was a better place now. I couldn't agree. Lou's aged face showed me that we were puppets for others to watch and control. How safe was a place that could determine your guilt when you had never committed a crime?

"Do you think Mom would have survived if she lived today under the safety of the drones?"

Dad frowned at my question.

"Your mom's death was an accident, probably not preventable even with today's safeguards. Now try to go to sleep." He kissed me on the forehead and walked out the door. "Big day tomorrow with the finals." And then he was gone.

I barely knew my mom, but somehow I knew she would want me to pursue my dreams. I had to talk to Austin, tell him about the drones and work out some other way to escape the city. The lightning had stopped and the rain had come crashing down, washing away into the sewer drains flowing under the street. The same old drone trudged by, this time going in the opposite direction. Despite the rain and darkness, I knew it was always watching.

It stopped and turned in my direction. I gave it the finger. Let it analyze that.

20
Finals

I knocked on the door then looked around the porch while I waited. Some flowers and gloves—definitely a female touch. The streets behind me were busy; students and parents were everywhere. The sun was low in the evening sky. The door opened and I prepared myself for his reaction.

"Who are you?" the young girl asked. I could have asked her the exact same thing.

"I'm Pene." I smiled.

The girl looked at me with bemusement. "Is that supposed to mean something to me?" *Okay.*

"Is Austin home?" My smile was starting to fade.

The little girl closed the door and stepped next to me. "Austin is acting really weird right now. I think he's in trouble with Mom. You probably should run off to the re-enactment finals without him." With that she turned around, walked inside and closed the door. I was amazed—this kid looked eight but acted eighteen. I was about to knock on the door again when it opened up.

"I see you met my annoying sister," answered Austin as he was putting his jacket on.

"Charming, must run in the family. Are you ready to go to the stadium?"

"Mom!" Austin yelled back into the hallway. "I'm heading down—you guys should go soon if you want to get a good seat."

"We'll see you there. The two of us will be cheering you on," an adult female voice responded.

"Let's go." Austin shoved his hands in his pockets and we walked into the street. Drones hovered above the parade of people, although none seemed to be interested in us. We walked a block in silence.

"So are you ready for the finals? Does your school have any strategy to come out on top?" I asked playfully.

"As if I would tell you," he played along while looking up. "Your school doesn't stand a chance."

"Where's your buddy Alex?"

"Ah, we finished the project a few days ago. Haven't seen him since then. Where's your friend Lacey?"

"She's meeting me there. She's in it to win it." As we entered a main expressway, crowds started gathering along the edge of the street. It became more difficult to walk as arms and shoulders blocked our way.

"What's going on?" I asked.

"Think my school's band is marching down the street to the stadium." As if on cue, a tuba blared and drums began to beat. Through the crowd I could see a number of musicians with uniforms walking in the middle of the street. The crowd began to chant and yell, warming up for the finals. Austin lowered his lips to my ear.

"Chances are the drones can't pick up on our conversation. It's dangerous for you to be around me. Why are you here?" he whispered.

"I have to talk to you about the drones." I leaned back and smiled. If a camera was recording our actions, it would just look like two teens having a normal conversation.

"What about them? Did you find their base?"

"Yes and no."

"What do you mean?" The exasperation grew in his voice.

"I saw a maintenance center, lots of spare parts to replace in drones. I was told that the drones don't have a central base—they work 24/7. There is no place you can infect, destroy or blow up to keep them contained. They're always working." If a drone were watching me now, it would see the concern in my face.

"Are you sure? Is your source reliable or was your dad trying to throw you off?"

"My dad has nothing to do with it. I had a tour with one of the officers when the Chief Judge came by. I don't think he's lying. He said it so casually, like it was a silly question."

Austin was silent. It was as though his big solution to the problem was all smoke and mirrors. I didn't know if he could accept it, at least not right away. He turned away, ready to join the parade. I pulled him back.

"Tell me what you're thinking? I deserve to know. Don't go silent on me once the parade goes by." He looked at me and his face was conflicted.

"I'm lost, Pene! I don't know what to do. We're like chipped mice in a maze. I wish I didn't believe you. It would make things easier. I thought if I knew where the drones where stationed, we could blow up the facility. Or shut it down. It would be months before they could rebuild. Maybe people would adapt to the change and have drones reduced permanently. You could use the time to escape. This was the best way to get you out of the city."

"Then think of another way!" I demanded as Austin considered my question.

"What else did he show you?"

"The maintenance center was huge, with tons of drone heads. At one point he showed me by view of his remote control how they could manipulate all of the drones at once. Hundreds of eyes stared at me. It kind of freaked me out."

"A controller. Maybe there is some way to hack the signal?"

"Really, is that something you could do?" I started to feel hope.

"Probably not—likely beyond my expertise. Just trying to make you feel better." He smiled weakly.

The crowd was starting to thin out. Soon the crowd roar would be gone and our voices could be overheard.

"So what do you want to do? Throw up our hands and give up?" I mocked and raised my arms. I was being unfair by not giving him any time to process the news. But there was no time for pity—we had to decide what to do next. "Leave with me. There has to be a weak area in the city boundaries, some way we could slip through. I trust you more than anyone." *There, I said it. He must know that I consider him more than a friend.*

Austin looked conflicted. "You make a tempting offer. But I can't leave my family. The journey out of the city is yours. But what if I could set up a diversion?"

"Maybe if something big was going on?" I offered.

"You mean during the finals?" he laughed. "Little late for that."

"It's always too late for me." The parade had passed into the next block, and the crowd had followed. "We have to get going." Austin grabbed my hand.

"I would like to go with you. You're the only person I have told about this. My mom won't listen and my friends don't care. Sometimes I feel like I'm crazy."

"You're not, Austin." I cupped his chin in my hand. Then he kissed me. Quickly. I wasn't sure if he was trying to thank me or if he was saying something more.

I had no time to consider it either way as he dragged me into the crowd. We blended into the throng of people and walked towards the stadium. Looking up, I could see the drones in full force, watching us the way people stare down at an anthill. Growing up, I remembered a boy who used to kick anthills to watch the ants try to repair, or try to burn them with a pair of glasses. I wondered if the drones had a chance, would they take a magnifying glass to us?

We walked for fifteen minutes in silence, although the street noise was loud. Students were excited to compete in the finals; it was the one event each year where all schools went against each other at once, instead of two teams at a time. The premise was simple, like a video game. This re-enactment took place right after the earthquake, when buildings had fallen and dust filled the air. Each school was assigned the task of saving as many citizens as possible, and the school collecting the greatest number of survivors was the winner. The going was treacherous; most students would 'die' and be sent out of the game while trying to rescue people. Strategies were diverse. Some schools maintained that you should send everyone out around the city to maximize the number of people that could be saved. Others clustered in a large group, concentrating on high destruction areas that had a large number of survivors in a small area. Our school had a plan somewhere in between.

We were to be divided into four teams, each taking a direction, north, south, west and east. We had even researched specific building sites where we expected to find a lot of survivors. As soon as we entered the game, we would break off into our teams. 'Divide and Conquer' was our plan name. The strategy actually had a chance of working.

As we approached the stadium I was overwhelmed by its size. Seating over eighty thousand people, it was still not big enough to accommodate all of the spectators. Huge video screens adored the side so onlookers could view events from outside the stadium as well. As we arrived to enter the main entrance to the field, the crowd started to disperse away to other entry points. Two large drones, looking like tall grasshoppers, looked down on the crowd and were allowing students to enter. Both Austin and I flashed our school badges.

The drones' eyes scanned the card, their red eyes moving from left to right. Then they scanned our faces. The gate clicked.

"You two can proceed," the drone on the left commanded. We followed other teenagers down a long tunnel. It was well-lit but barren. It was wall to wall with teenagers. Fortunately the flow of people was moving well; I knew I would be claustrophobic if we stopped here. Austin's eyes met mine.

"Look." He pointed as we stepped out onto the field. The view was breathtaking. The stadium was mostly full, each section representing the parents of a specific school. Their roar was deafening; cheers, jeers and screams for their favorite schools filled the air. It was a must-see event—you'd have to be on your deathbed for a family member to miss this. Above the middle of the field hung the largest video screen in the city, four-sided, and each side would document different events during the re-enactment. The best action would feed to the screens, usually pertaining to the parents of the students sitting in that section of the stadium. I looked down the field and saw my school's banner hanging overhead. I turned to Austin.

"Good luck. What do you think your school will do with the prize money if you win?"

"*If* we win?" he smirked. "*When* we win, we'll probably put it towards more useless gear for the school or some boring field trip. You?"

"Our history teacher wants to build a monument in the school courtyard to commemorate the disaster. Probably get vandalized in its first week."

"Naw, I'm sure they'll plant a drone on it the moment it's built." Austin leaned closer as if to give me a goodbye kiss. He was rudely pulled back by several arms.

"Come on buddy, we have to get ready," another boy said while pulling him away.

"See you in the game." He waved. The crowd swallowed him up and he was gone in seconds.

I walked towards my school group and soon recognized several faces.

"About time you got here," a familiar voice said as someone elbowed me in the back. "You must have taken the long way. Your dad said that you had an errand before the game." Lacey's expression was telling. I wondered if she had seen me walk in with Austin.

"Well, I'm here now." I chose to ignore her comment. "Where's the gear?"

Lacey pulled me over to wheeled racks with electronic crowns dangling down. I could see Mr. Stewart making some last-minute adjustments. It had been even more difficult being in his class since the fight between him and my father. I couldn't understand why he wanted me to know past information about my dad, almost like he was taking perverse pleasure in my family's discomfort. As if I could dislike the man any more, but for the sake of our school finals, I pushed those feelings down and concentrated.

He manipulated several small tools on the crowns, like a surgeon working on a patient. Sometimes I thought he was a better electronics expert than a history teacher. He pulled one down and handed it to me without a word. His silence was fine with me. I turned from him and strapped it to my head. The glass lens came over my left eye and a flashing red light signaled that the game had not started yet. I looked up the stadium seating for my school and imagined that my dad was sitting and cheering for me somewhere up there. The stadium speakers barked: "The survivor re-enactment is ready to begin." A face appeared on all the video screens.

"Welcome to the annual school finals!" Lord Morall crowed, and the crowd roared with enthusiasm. Morall had to be the center of attention, and he clearly lived for these moments when all eyes were on him. "Each year, these finals are a testament to the sheer bravery our citizens exhibited during the great explosion and earthquake that rocked our city. Today's children play the role of saviors, recreating the heroism that was exhibited during that time." Morall smiled and his eye flashed on the video screen. "This is also a time to remember the ones who were lost and to make sure that our society doesn't make the same mistakes.

"There are fifteen schools here today. For the parents who are watching, congratulations on having your children participate in such an important event." The crowd cheered. "To the students on the field, on behalf of the Justice department, we appreciate your commitment. Whether your school finishes first or last, the fact that you participated, trying to save citizens of your past, is worthy of pride. To the city, you are all heroes!"

The students on the field raised their arms and screamed their approval. Whatever problems I had with the system certainly weren't shared by the people in the stadium. A band started marching through the center of the field and spectators cheered their music. Mr. Stewart motioned about ten of us into a circle.

"I've spoken to the other three groups. Follow the directions on your crowns. You need to go eight blocks to the west for the Burbidge Building. It was one of the tallest in our city. Run as fast as you can. You only have ninety minutes to secure survivors. Avoid other teams, check out your surroundings; you only have one life. If you die in the re-enactment, you're done. Any questions?" He looked around. It was so close to game time that all questions should have been asked much earlier. A guy named Stuart had other ideas.

"What if another student tries to save the same survivor? I don't want to get involved in a tug of war."

His choice of words wasn't so great but his question was good. We all leaned in for Mr. Stewart's answer.

"Let me make myself clear. You must save the most survivors. Period. If someone gets in your way, do what's necessary to win. Do you understand?" Most of the boys nodded but I didn't think they understood.

"Are you saying we should hurt someone if they're trying to save the same survivor?" I asked. The re-enactment was about to start and I could tell that I was testing his patience.

"No, Pene. You mistake the goal of the re-enactment. Thousands of people perished in the explosion and earthquake aftermath. Many more were saved. You are playing a game—this isn't about winning at all cost. This is about saving lives. If someone else wants to save the same person," he turned to me, "let them. Now get going." Our group broke but his words stuck with me.

Lacey grabbed my hand. "Are you ready?"

"No. But let's do this anyway." Our group held hands and looked up. A mini helicopter drone flew about ten feet above us. Four mini blades swirled in the air. At its base, a lone red eye watched us—it had been assigned to relay our movements back to the crowd. Looking around, I saw dozens of similar drones hovering above other groups. The crowd became quiet, anticipating the start. Lord Morall barked his commands.

"Let. Us. Begin!"

The stadium vanished. I was suddenly transported to the center of the city. Huge, unfamiliar buildings surrounded us and reached towards the sky. Even though there were hundreds of students around me, it was perfectly quiet, like watching a movie with the sound turned off. Then a huge explosion appeared to our left, and the sound of terror filled my ears. The concussive force rattled the air, and seconds later the earth shook, forcing me down. A huge rock erupted out of the ground to my right and three of my fellow students disappeared.

"Run!" Lacey yelled and pulled me down a city street. Three guys and two other girls followed behind us. The ground shook again and I felt myself lifting up into the air. The sky became black, as if a curtain had been thrown over the sky. Streetlights still illuminated this block; the earthquake hadn't knocked the electricity out yet.

"Look at that!" One of the boys pointed. About two blocks away one of the tallest skyscrapers swayed, slowly at first, like a pendulum. But with each swing the arc grew larger and cracks appeared in the structure. A section of the uppermost floor broke away and fell. The impact was loud, and a car alarm sounded. Then the building crumpled like a house of cards, its base imploding from the weight and the rest tipping forward. None of us yelled; this was the area we were supposed to be at. We knew we had to move it or lose the competition. As we rounded the corner, we all stopped and covered our faces and mouths. Seconds later, a dust cloud rushed by from the impact of the collapsed building. My dust mask didn't stop it all, and I could taste dirt at the back of my mouth. We waited at least a minute before moving on; no one wanted to be blinded by the dust. I wished they'd let us wear virtual goggles.

"Help!" a voice squeaked in the distance. I turned my head. Lacey was trapped under a pile of debris, her hair matted with dirt. I began pulled off the rubble. A hand tugged me from behind.

"We have to get to our assignment. We don't have time. Leave her!" one of the boys in my group commanded. My response was to throw a rock at him that bounced off his shoulder.

"I'm staying. The re-enactment is about saving people, even our own. You can go ahead. We'll catch up." He nodded and the rest of the group followed behind him. In moments, they were lost in the dust.

"You're wasting time, Pene. Nothing's going to happen

to me. I'll see you later at the finale in the stadium," Lacey coaxed.

"No!" I pushed rocks away, and an edge gashed the back of my hand. Blood bubbled to the surface; it might not be real but I definitely felt pain. "We do this together." I searched around, found a metal rebar and propped it under the concrete by Lacey's feet.

"Let me know if this hurts." I pushed. Lacey made a face but didn't yell out. A large clunk of stone fell to her left. She wriggled her legs free. As she got up, she gave me a big hug.

"Come on, we're running out of time," she told me. Lacey limped a bit but seemed otherwise okay. We scrambled over to a pile of rocks and headed over to our checkpoint. As we rounded the corner of a building, I saw our team pulling people out of a pit. As each survivor was pulled out of the hole, a boy on our team would touch them. Each survivor would vanish—adding to our school's score total. As we ran closer, the ground rumbled again and my vision went sideways. Everything went black.

After several seconds of nothingness, I felt like I was floating in the air. Not like floating in water, but zero gravity. My body was weightless. The sky became night and I reached towards the stars, which rushed closer to me. It was the closest I've felt to pure joy in my life. With no worries pressing down on me, I felt like nothing was watching me. I felt freer than I had my entire life. Maybe this was how a baby feels in the womb. Then something tugged at my mind. A nagging doubt. A persistent worry. A constant fear. And then I opened my eyes.

I was back where I started, lying prone. I looked beside me and Lacey was gone. I got up and strode towards the hole in the ground. The rest of my team was gone as well. *Had they been knocked out of the game?* I looked into the hole, expecting to find it empty. I was wrong. A middle-aged man and a small boy lay motionless at the bottom.

"You can come up now. I'm here to save you." No response. They remained still. *Are they dead?* All around me was a deathly quiet; it was the opposite of the rage of the earthquake. Only the dust in the air reminded me of what had happened. I grabbed the rope attached to a rock and climbed into the hole. I lay down next to the boy, whose chest rose as if he was asleep. I reached over to wake him and he disappeared at my touch. *Damn—the game is still on.* I looked closely at the man.

"Hey! Wake up. Can you hear me?" Knowing I couldn't touch him, I waved my arms, vainly hoping the wind would revive him. As I walked around him, my foot accidently clipped his arm. He disappeared—another score for our team. I shook my head at my own clumsiness. I was helping the school but why were people asleep? Everyone was very much awake during the earthquake. I wasn't going to get any answers if I kept touching survivors before I could get them to talk. Resigned, I climbed out of the hole and began to explore the immediate area.

I walked around, carefully avoiding the rubble. On a pile a rocks, a rat scurried through the debris. It squeaked, the only noise in the area. *At least animals weren't asleep.* I continued west along one of the main city streets. The roadway was four lanes, two going in each direction. A car was crushed at the start, a victim of a piece of a nearby building. I tentatively looked inside, fearing the result. *Empty. At least no one was hurt here.*

I headed to the Point Park and was amazed by the sight. There were bodies everywhere. Most looked like they were trying to escape into the park since there were no tall buildings adjacent to it. The ground had heaved in a few places and some shards of rock had jutted out of the sidewalk; otherwise the park looked untouched. Except for the sleeping bodies everywhere. A dog lay next to its owner; I stroked its head and it panted happily. I touched the owner and he disappeared. The dog looked confused and circled the spot where its owner had lain, its leash dragging behind. I walked around the park, listening carefully to people's mouths, hearing the air exhaled from their lungs. Then I would touch them and they would disappear. I might as well get points for the school while I figured what was going on. I looked at the monitor on my crown.

The display seemed wrong. I was ninety-five minutes in. The re-enactment was only ninety minutes long. Was that why none of the students were still left in the game? Was I trapped? I looked closer at the counter. Time was going backwards, counting back to ninety. Would the game end at ninety? I quickened my pace, wanting to see more in case time was running out. A pigeon flew by and made me look up again. The sky was still black from debris. I couldn't see clouds or the sun. It felt like looking at a blank screen.

I heard a voice. Four minutes left until ninety. I ran towards the source, eager to seek answers from someone. A school bus was parked at the edge of the boulevard. Its door was closed. It was an old bus with wheels for propulsion. I pushed on the door and it folded to let me in. As I walked up, I saw the driver slumped over the steering wheel. He snored loudly. I looked down the aisle and saw children resting peacefully in their seats. It was almost cute, if I hadn't thought something sinister was happening. This was no Sleeping Beauty, and I wasn't the prince coming to save them.

"Mommy!' I heard a weak voice from the back of the bus. I heard heavy breathing and a whooshing sound. I tried climbing over a kid who was sleeping in the aisle. I reconsidered and touched him, sending him out of the game and out of my way. I could see movement ahead as a small foot shifted from under the seat. I scrambled ahead and pulled out a small girl who was drooling in her sleep. A boy behind her raised his eyes in alarm as the girl disappeared at my touch.

"Don't touch me!" he wheezed, taking a puff from an inhaler. The kid looked like he could hardly breathe. I held my hands up to show I had no intention of touching him.

"It's okay, I won't hurt you."

"H-how did you do that?" he stammered. "Where did Margie go?"

"Don't worry—she just left the game. None of this is real," I explained. "This a re-enactment of a historical event. I mean, you were actually scared at the time and you're replaying history. You're not actually a kid, you're an adult now." The boy stared and blinked. I might as well tell him that we were surrounded by aliens and that a third eye was growing out of the back of his head. I looked at the time remaining, less than two minutes before the time counted back to ninety. "Listen, none of this matters right now. Why are you awake while all of your classmates are asleep?" He took a moment to answer, and even though he was wasting precious time, I resisted the urge to shake him.

"I don't know," he wailed. "Our class went on a school trip to the park when the ground shook. My teacher took us all back to the bus. Everyone was crying and yelling. I couldn't breathe because of asthma. I overused my puffer." He shook it to illustrate. "I think I passed out and then when I woke up, everyone was asleep and the ground was quiet. Are they all hurt?" His eyes glistened with concern.

"No, honey," I consoled, "they're just sleeping. Once they wake up, everything will be okay." Less than a minute left. "Was anything strange before the earthquake? Did they eat something that made them sleepy?" He looked around and pulled out his kitbag. He reached out with an uneaten sandwich.

"I never got to eat my lunch. Does peanut butter make you sleepy?"

This was getting me nowhere. He didn't know anything. He was a scared kid.

"Finish your sandwich. Everything's going to be okay." I resisted the urge to pat him. He started chewing enthusiastically and then raised his finger as if to make a point.

"You know, my teacher did point at the sky." He looked

up.

"Yes?"

"She said it looked strange, as if…"

And the boy disappeared. And the bus. And the entire destruction of the city. I was back at the stadium and I had about six people staring at me. I lifted off the crown as Lacey punched me in the arm.

"Way to go! You were the last woman standing for all the schools. You touched a lot of last-minute survivors. How did you do it?"

"Did it help us win?" I asked.

"Not quite," Mr. Stewart said, pushing through the teen-agers standing around me. "But your last-minute heroics did put our school in second place. Our best showing in years. Congratulations." His smile was genuine, and even though I wasn't trying to win, I accepted the praise.

"Where did you go?" Lacey asked. "One second you were with me, the next you were gone."

"I don't know what happened," I answered truthfully. I needed to talk to Austin again. Maybe he could explain what happened to me. Before I could begin looking for him, announcements for the top schools were made.

"Congratulations to Vermont High, this year's winner!" Lord Morall's voice boomed over the speakers. The crowd roared its approval and stamped its feet on the concrete bleachers. On the screens they listed the schools in order of first place and lower. Sure enough, my school was in second place. *Dad will be proud.* There was a siren coming from be-hind. I turned and watched two large drones walking towards us. They had a police insignia on the side of their tall metal bodies, and a half-man and half-motorcycle drone wheeled in behind them. Mr. Stewart approached them.

"Is there something I can help with?" The police drone on the right simply pointed behind him towards me and Lacey. I couldn't make out what the other drone said but Mr. Stewart made a face in response. The motorcycle drone wheeled up next to me.

"You will accompany me," its human top half said emotionlessly.

"Why? Was she the top scorer? Are you going to parade her around the stadium?" Lacey asked. Mr. Stewart came forward and pushed some of his students back.

"Pene. Please go with these drones. It's important."

Suddenly I had the feeling that my conversations with Austin might not have been as private as we thought. What if they had found his computer? Or worse, found something to incriminate me.

"No. I haven't done anything. I'm not going anywhere until I talk to my dad."

"That's why they are here, Pene," Mr. Stewart answered. "You dad has been arrested for the crime of falsifying evidence. If he's convicted, he could get a life sentence!"

21
Jail

I held my head down to keep the wind out of my eyes. The drone drove fast through the streets. Most people stared or gave us a wide berth. I felt like a leper, everyone wondering what crime I had committed. Other than that my father had been arrested, I knew less than nothing. I didn't know when he had been arrested, where he was being held or who would represent him. Worse, I knew I was responsible. I had identified the doctored footage, and my dad's investigation had caused someone to get nervous. Nervous enough to pin the blame on him.

The crowds from the stadium had let out and the drone was constantly steering around groups of people. I leaned back, strapped in, not wanting to hold the back of its cold metal body. The other police drones had remained at the stadium. Lacey had asked if she could come with me but the drone had refused. It was better to meet my dad alone. I felt guilty enough. I didn't need an audience.

The drone cycled into the center of the city. The Justice

Building loomed high in the distance. Part of the bylaws stipulated that no building could be higher than twenty stories. Somehow the Justice Building had been excluded from this bylaw as it looked down on the rest of the city. Within minutes the drone pulled up at the main entrance.

Wordlessly, it pointed to the main doors. I got off and sneered at it. If I hurt its feelings, it didn't register. The doors opened up for me and I looked for a human attendant. Instead a tiny drone on wheels rolled towards me. I looked at it, waiting for it to speak. Instead a flashing arrow illuminated on it as it signaled me to follow to the right. The drone quickly squealed around a corner and disappeared. As I reached the end of the hall, Lieutenant Vaslor and another officer stood in front of a door.

"Pene! I came as soon as I heard." He motioned to the other officer. "I'll take her in." The officer opened the door as Vaslor and I stepped in.

"Is he okay?" I asked.

"He's fine." Vaslor held my hand. "He's in a holding area waiting to see you." Ahead of us was a series of cells; most were empty. My legs felt weak and my hands reached out as Vaslor caught me before I could fall.

"Do you think they could find him innocent?" I asked but Vaslor said nothing. His silence spoke volumes.

"Pene?" A voice from behind me spoke. I turned and saw my dad sitting at a table, his hands in his lap. I heard metal scrape behind me as Vaslor put a chair in front of the cell. As I sat down, I heard his footsteps disappear down the hall. The jail was barren—no cameras or drones. I had expected a different setup. I looked up at my dad; his eyes were filled in sorrow.

"Dad, what happened? Why are they accusing you of tampering with the footage? Before they wouldn't even admit it could happen." I reached my hands through the cell to hold his.

"I don't know. I pushed hard and checked with all of the tech staff. No one seems to have been assigned to the court case. I couldn't find out who had access. My inquiries apparently were overheard by the judges, who weren't pleased."

"They weren't pleased because you were pursuing the truth or because you were making the justice system look bad?"

"Neither, sweetheart. They couldn't believe my claims, and eventually an investigator was assigned."

"And?"

"The only person who had individual access was myself. All the techs have it recorded when they access a file. Two work in tandem, so no one is every left alone when scrubbing and editing the footage."

"Then that system is wrong, Dad. Two techs could be working together or instructed to alter footage. You can't charge someone just because they had opportunity. You have to have proof!" It felt funny to be lecturing my dad on the legal system.

"But here I am. Opportunity and motive are the keystones of our system. They have proven opportunity and are working on motive." I let go of his hands and stood up, almost knocking down the chair.

"You have to tell them, Dad! You were checking the footage because of what I saw. I should never have looked at your tablet. I caused all of this!" I yelled and looked for something to throw.

"But you did look, and I looked too. And you were right. Something is wrong. And I'm worried that this case might not be the only one that was altered."

I sat back down. "What are we going to do?"

"You are going to go home. Grandma will come to live with you until I can work this out. I have friends who will help."

"Like Lord Morall?"

"Say what you want about him, he's not the enemy. He called me just before the drones picked me up at home. He prepared me."

"Dad, he could be the one who did this. Or he knows who did. Let me know where the footage is. I'll post it to a few websites. Then the truth won't get buried." Dad was silent, as if considering my request.

"Sweetheart, I don't want you involved in this. You have your whole life ahead of you."

"So do you, Dad!" Then I considered something. "How long will the sentence be if you are found guilty?"

"Pene," he signed.

"How long?" I asked again.

"Twenty-five years." He looked down at his feet. If they pronounced him guilty, my dad would age into a grandfather. Who knew what memories he'd lose? I had to stop this.

216 · JIM KOCHANOFF

If Dad wasn't going to help himself, I would have to do it myself.

"Not going to happen, Dad. I'll get you out of here."

"No, Pene. You will not. Whatever is happening is not fair. If you get involved, then you could be sentenced too. I'm not going to see both of our lives ruined because of this. Being your dad better count for something. Do you understand me?"

I understood that no one else was going to help him beside me. Our 'oh so safe' justice system had already pronounced him guilty. I had to get to Austin. He would know what to do.

"I understand," I lied. "But I just can't stand that you are trapped behind these bars. This is worse than the drones watching us."

Dad stood up and walked to the prison door. It swung open. He walked over and squeezed me. "Don't worry about me. There is a reason there are no drones in here. Where would I go?" He motioned around the room. "The city has eyes everywhere. No matter where I went, they'd find me. There is no escape."

22

Homebody

I stared at myself in the mirror. Several days had passed and nothing new had developed in my dad's case. I knew nothing would happen unless I helped. But I knew they were watching me, so I had to take some precautions.

As I left the bathroom, I could smell bacon sizzling in the kitchen. My mouth instantly began to water. I threw on a hoodie and strode down the stairs.

"Good morning, dear," Grandma said as she cracked an egg into a skillet. She had moved in to look after me after dad was detained. I visited him every day but there had been no progress in proving his innocence. It was frustrating to see him so free in the detention center, as if they were daring him to try to escape.

"Stop looking so pensive, Pene. Have some breakfast." She slid a plate over to me. It had more calories heaped on it than I'd eat in a day. But I knew better than to tell her. She'd just smile and tell me to eat my meal; she was used to cooking for my father instead of a teenage girl. The outside door opened and Lacey walked in.

"Don't they knock in your house, dear?" Grandma asked, but her smile showed that she liked Lacey's company. Before Lacey sat down, a plate of food was pushed before her.

"Is someone else eating with me? There's enough food to feed me for a week on this plate," Lacey said. Grandmas kept smiling but didn't respond. Lacey took a mouthful and then turned to me.

"I had company on my way over here today." She nodded to the door.

"That's nice, dear. Was it a bee or bird?" my grandma asked without taking her eyes off the stove.

"Bird. Probably a pigeon. Looked dirty too." Since dad's detention, the drones had become extremely interested in my whereabouts and that of my friends. Sometimes when I went out I could see half a dozen of them flying around, tracking my progress. I guess 'presumed innocent' had changed to 'presumed guilty'. Or maybe they hoped I would do something to prove my dad's guilt.

"I'm glad you're here. I really need to get out of the house," I said.

"Can I help you with your makeup?" Lacey asked.

"I thought you'd never ask."

Fifteen minutes later, I looked back into the mirror.

"Not a bad job," I said, admiring my work.

"Well, you'll never be as good as the real thing but you'd pass from a distance." I grinned at her comment. Lacey would always be Lacey. I adjusted my wig and pulled the ball cap over my head. Sunglasses, makeup—Lacey tended to be much paler than me—swapped clothes, and I was ready to go for a stroll.

"You're the best, Lacey. You realize that you could get into some real trouble if you're caught pretending to be me. And I'm not talking with your mother," I said.

"I'm a big girl, Pene. What they did to your dad is wrong. If you think you can find a way to help his case, then let your best friend help you. That's what besties do." Her smile warmed me and I hugged her tight.

"I'll be back in three hours. Think you can stay indoors for that long?" I asked.

"I brought some homework." She raised her tablet. I looked at her in confusion. "Oh, I didn't say I'd work on it, just said I brought it." She leaned back in a chair. The blind was half open so you could tell someone was sitting there.

"Be careful out there." Grandma kissed me on the head. "Don't do anything that will get you in trouble." *Too late for that*, I thought. I waved goodbye and headed out the door. The sun was bright in my eyes and the sunglasses served their purpose for two reasons. I made every effort not to look at the drones circling the house. Maybe it was a childish belief but I felt that the more interest I showed them, the more suspicious I appeared. Casual and cool was my motto. As I walked out into the street, I looked at the window reflection of the house across the street. Six drones flew over the roof. One at each corner, one at the front and one high up in the backyard. Two of them started to float towards me. A window opened from my house and Lacey poured water into a pot. Both drones hovered and then turned back to my house, interested in her movements. The window closed back up. A bird drone from the front of my neighbor's house picked up in step behind me about twenty feet off the ground.

Okay, one is better than six.

I started walking towards a nearby commercial street. It was Saturday morning and there would be lots of people shopping in the stores. I stole a look to my right and noticed a camera. I avoided looking in that direction; my disguise wouldn't hold up under close scrutiny. I saw a family walking ahead of me and I quickened my pace, trying to join their group. We stopped at a street corner while waiting for a car to pass. The drone floated high ahead, looking back at me, not even trying to conceal its intent. Further ahead, the walkway turned and there was a concrete overpass that allowed pedestrians to cross over the busy traffic of a four-lane street. This would be a blind spot for the drone, which would meet us on the other side. Three teenagers joined the family and myself as we stepped into the tunnel. It was well-lit and only about hundred feet in length. As we walked through, two teenage girls started walking towards me. I stepped behind the family and pulled out a sweatshirt.

I immediately whipped out my wig, replaced my look with red hair and put on a blue hat. I switched glasses, and as the girls passed me, I switched directions and fell into step behind them. They were talking intently, and if they knew I was following them, they didn't look back. I headed to the same entrance I had entered as the family exited the other end. This was the tricky part. I backtracked to a clothing store I had passed earlier and stepped inside.

From my vantage point, I could see the end of the tunnel with the family I had walked with heading down the street. I looked up and could make out a small bird circling widely around. After a few seconds it immediately headed to the other exit. I positioned my back to the store window and pretended to be looking at jewelry in a display. The mirror looked back outside and I could see the drone at the window looking in. *Act casual—don't run away. Hide in plain sight.* Two seconds passed. Then five; it felt like minutes. The drone was still there, looking in. Did it have some way to analyze my body structure, to see through my disguise?

A group of teenagers, girls and guys, ran by the store laughing, and when I looked in the mirror again, the drone was gone. I needed to get as far as possible from this area. I walked slowly out the store and headed towards my original destination.

Twenty minutes later the bus let me off in front of the school. Most of the sports teams had already headed to the locker room. I kept my Lacey disguise on and headed inside the school. A couple of boys bumped into me as they were charging off the field. Cameras watched from several vantage points but as boys passed between me and the camera, I slipped into their locker room. There was steam coming from the showers. I blushed at the idea of seeing the flash of a guy's butt. Distracted, I ran straight into the chest of a large adult.

"No girls—can't you read?" The man looked down at

me. He must be one of the coaches.

"Need to see my brother," I stammered. "Is Austin here?"

"I thought his sister was younger." The coach thumbed towards the back. "Pretty boy is back drying his hair. Give him your message and get out," he commanded. I slipped past the coach and headed to the sound of blowing air. There were two boys. One gave me an odd look and left. The second boy was Austin but his back was turned away from me and he only had a towel wrapped around his midsection.

"Austin?" I asked. He turned and didn't look pleased to see me.

"Who are you?" he asked, momentarily not recognizing me. I took off the hat and wig. "Pene! What are you doing here?" His shock almost made him drop his towel. He regained his composure and grabbed a t-shirt from a hook on the wall. "Did anyone see you come in here?"

"A few," I answered. "I told the coach I was your sister."

"I'm sure he believed that. Did the drones follow you here?" He pointed outside.

"No, I took precautions. Right now they think I'm studying for a test at home." Austin stepped behind a partition and threw his towel over the corner. I turned my head while he put on his pants. He came around the corner seconds later.

"So why are you here? Not to see me play?" I shrugged. I didn't even know what sport he was in, just that he would be here.

"You know my dad is charged? His trial is in three days."

Austin nodded. "I know. I'm really sorry." He put his hand on my shoulder. "I don't imagine that his sentence will get overturned?"

"It's his word against the other tech users. They can't prove my dad did it but they can supposedly prove that no else but him could have had access." Austin turned but I couldn't read his expression. I could read his body posture, though.

"So why are you coming to me?"

I gulped. What I had to ask of him wasn't easy or fair. "Can you track the whereabouts of anyone in the city?" I answered his question with a question.

"Yes. You already saw that. Who do you want me to track?"

"Not just who, but when. Can you go back to the time that the merchant Lou was charged? If your tracking system showed he was somewhere other than where the footage put him, it might show my dad was right." Austin shifted his weight and bowed his head, looking uncomfortable with the request.

"You're asking me to show that I've hacked into the justice mainframe. Either way they won't believe me or they'll sentence me. It's not fair what you're asking me, Pene. I've saved you from the drones! I showed you a part of my life that no one else knows. If I provide the footage, my family will be punished!" His face was conflicted, like he was fighting an inner battle.

"I know, Austin. You're my last hope. Without your

proof, my dad will lose twenty-five years and possibly his life." I turned away, my eyes starting to well up. I barely knew him but he had the key to my dad's life. I had no choice but to ask him. "Please," I begged.

"No. I don't know your dad. I have everything to lose. You're not being fair!"

"So you aren't going to even try!" I glared. "You're just like everyone else. Selfish and afraid. I can't wait to get away from this city and everyone in it." My words were mean but I didn't care. I just needed someone to lash out at. I moved to leave but Austin stopped me.

"This is much bigger than your dad. If we show others that we live in a big fishbowl where everyone is tracked, it could start riots. People could get hurt or die. Are you ready for the consequences?"

I was silent for a moment, considering his question.

"Austin, the truth hurts but it's still the truth. If lies bring this city down, so be it."

23
Sentence

The week flew by without any new evidence on Dad's defense. I heard nothing from Austin so I wasn't sure if he was going to help. Grandma and I sat down on chairs overlooking the courtroom. The room was full; approximately thirty people watched through the plexiglas window. Considering how most of these cases had few or no observers, this was a big deal. Most I recognized as colleagues of Dad from work, including Vaslor. He saluted me from across the room. Lacey and her mom were attending to show support. They sat behind us, and Lacey's mom patted me on the shoulder for support.

"You'll get through this, dear," she said. "They have to realize that your father has committed no crime." I nodded but felt no agreement. Justice would get whatever it wanted, in spite of the evidence. Another familiar face entered the room as Mr. Stewart crossed to the opposite corner. If he saw me, he showed no recognition. I couldn't tell if he was here to support or ridicule. A door opened below as a judge entered and sat down. I was pleasantly surprised that Lord Morall wasn't presiding. The court must have realized the conflict of interest. The judge was younger than I expected, mid-forties with jet black hair and a square jaw. He looked like a man who administered justice. Then he did something I didn't expect. He addressed the gallery.

"With today's swift and thorough justice system, it is unusual to have an audience to the proceedings. Let me make myself perfectly clear. You are observers, not participants. I will not tolerate interference, catcalls, yelling, clapping, banging on the window or noise of any kind. This is your one and only warning—any interruptions will be met with your automatic expulsion." The door opened behind us and two security guards stationed themselves around the room. Their serious expressions reinforced that we would be removed if we broke the rules. A few people nodded. The judge took our silence as acceptance and motioned towards the door in the courtroom.

It opened and a bailiff escorted in my dad, who walked weakly. The stress of the last few weeks had been unkind to him, and he had lost weight. A couple of people who hadn't seen him in a while gasped. Dad looked up at the window at me and Grandma and I waved. A woman stepped towards Dad while a man stood on the opposite side. As my dad's defense attorney, she spoke first.

"As stated in my client's deposition, crime footage appears to be altered. As a representative of the justice system, it was his duty to bring forward this information to address a miscarriage of justice for the client, Lou Reigns. There has been no evidence brought forward that he, himself, altered the footage for his own means. Although the culprit has yet to be identified, it is not his responsibility to bring forward the guilty party. On behalf of my client, I demand his immediate release." She stepped backwards and stood beside my father.

"Thank you, Ms. Bennett. Mr. Martinez," the judge turned towards the other lawyer, "please make your statement."

"Thank you, Your Honor. I agree with part of the statement made by Ms. Bennett. A grave injustice has been made. An innocent man lost a decade of his life that he will never regain. The legal system process of reviewing footage is impeccable. No one can touch drone file footage without leaving an electronic footprint. Everyone who reviews footage before editing is recorded. No technician works alone; all are paired to download and record footage. Once the footage is released, the only people to review the footage are the defense and prosecution. The footage is only screened in the lawyer's office and returned. In essence, the only other person to view this person's footage was lawyer Evan Anderson. By process of elimination, he is the only one who could have altered the footage."

"Objection, your Honor," Ms. Bennett interjected. "Someone else could have entered the office and replaced or altered the footage. We should be searching for that guilty party, not condemning the person who brought this offense to light."

"Only because he was likely worried the true footage

would blemish his otherwise prefect prosecution record," Mr. Martinez countered. "The tracker counter in the footage showed that it never left his office and was never alone with anyone else."

I gasped because I realized that fact was wrong. I had been left alone with the footage for a few minutes. However, announcing that fact might not help Dad's case. Either I would be declared guilty myself or of working together with my dad to distract the technician. My grandma looked at me and raised her finger to be quiet.

"Unless the security protocols you mention are not as infallible as you say." Ms. Bennett glared at the other lawyer.

"Strike that from the record," the judge commanded to a drone recorder. He looked at Ms. Bennett. "One more comment like that and you will be removed from this courtroom. Our legal system has been flawless for the last twenty years. Do not criticize it to create some type of government-wide conspiracy to prove your client's innocence. Now, do either of you have any more facts to provide to this court?"

"No, your Honor," the lawyers replied in unison.

The judge looked up at the gallery. "If there is no other evidence, I am ready to provide a verdict."

My heart thumped twice as fast as panic seeped into my blood. A barking interrupted at the door. One of the guards moved towards it and pulled the handle. A drone dog came running in, holding a small tablet in its mouth. *Lola*! It stopped in front of the guard, dropped the tablet gently on the floor and looked up, barking incessantly. The guard was wary of Lola but picked up the tablet and looked at the screen. After a few seconds, his face became puzzled and he spoke into his radio. He then turned towards the other guard.

"Follow me and bring the drone dog." The other guard looked down and then shrugged. Lola had disappeared through the closing door, eliminating the link to Austin. The guard with the tablet reappeared downstairs and gave it to the judge. Several people in the gallery began to whisper. The guard in the room shook his head and all became quiet. We watched for several minutes as the judge looked at the screen, his face confused and alarmed. He then connected the tablet and its content showed up on the main screen.

"It is unusual for evidence to be provided in this manner. Bailiff, bring in a technician to verify." The judge pointed to one of the guards, who exited the room. Then the judge waved upward. "Look at the screen before you—each light is a symbol for everyone in this room and those above in the gallery." A schematic appeared of the room's interior.

"Are we being tracked?" a woman in the room commented. She moved around the room, and her glowing orange light moved on the computer screen.

The judge clicked on a folder and a video appeared. The footage was dated the same as the date for Lou's supposed crime. The video played, showing Lou working at his stall—time-coded for 3:38 in the afternoon. His light on the screen was magnified and confirmed his location.

The judge then played the footage showing Lou stealing, same identical time! When the location was enlarged, an unknown person was highlighted. Not Lou! The whole gallery erupted into conversation. The judge motioned us to silence.

"Enough! I am declaring this case in recess until this new evidence can be analyzed. This technology," waving to the screen with our lighted locations, "has much greater ramifications than just this case." People in the gallery started to stand up, anticipating the trial was over. The door slammed open below in the courtroom, signaling that it wasn't over. Lord Morall, the bailiff and a man in a lab coat burst through the door. The technician grabbed the tablet and the screen went blank.

"I apologize to the people of the court. The evidence is false. Someone, likely in league with the suspect, has fabricated the evidence. There is *no* ability to track people, and the footage showing the other criminal, Lou Reigns, in another location at the time of his crime is false!"

"No! You're lying!" I yelled. I couldn't take it anymore. No matter what evidence was brought forward, it was immediately dismissed. Someone had to speak up. "This isn't a trial. No one is presumed innocent. The result is predetermined. You're the liar, and everyone who challenges you and your system is destroyed. I don't know what Lou did to be falsely accused but my dad is innocent. You know that!"

I turned around and looked at the wide eyes of the surrounding people. "Our city is safe if we don't ask too many questions. Cameras watch our every move, and if we fall out of line, we become the guilty. Justice doesn't keep us safe. Justice ended when we became controlled by the drones.

Our freedom is a lie." I turned back from the gallery and looked down at Morall's face.

"You're the cause of this!" I yelled and felt heavy arms grab around my midsection and my mouth. The door to the gallery burst open and a number of guards exploded into the room.

"Empty the gallery!" Lord Morall yelled from below as guards began grabbing people and taking them through the door. "Bring the girl down to the courtroom." The arms around me were solid and unbreakable. My family and friends were pulled away from me like leaves in the wind. Although my mouth was covered, I watched as Grandma was escorted away. She didn't resist but nodded in my direction and mouthed "I love you." I looked behind her and saw Lacey fighting unsuccessfully with another guard as she and her mother were escorted out. Then the room was empty, with the door slamming in the silence.

Rough hands took me downstairs, and doors into the courtroom opened. My dad's eyes met mine and he struggled with his guard, on the verge of losing control. I could tell he was panicking that I would be sentenced with him.

"Bring her over to me," Lord Morall commanded. A chair was placed in front of me. When I didn't sit down, a hand pushed down on my shoulder. Morall dropped the tablet into my lap.

"Is this yours?" I remained silent. "It's a crime to create fake evidence. Since your father has been confined, you are the most logical choice. Admit it and we'll go easy on you." His eye shone straight into mine. I stayed silent. He paced and looked at me. "It is your right to remain silent, however, the officer," pointing to the bailiff, "will have to detain you for thirty days until we determine the truth. Unfortunately, your father won't have that time."

"You're disgusting, Morall! Threatening a young girl. When did our justice system sink so low? You want to hurt me, go ahead, but leave her alone!" my dad yelled while one of the guards grabbed his right wrist and pulled it behind his back.

"I don't know who sent the footage," I lied. "Probably someone in your own office. Since you're so defensive, you must agree." I wasn't sure if my lie fooled him. I couldn't get Austin in trouble for the risk he took. Morall seemed to consider my comments. He motioned and Vaslor walked into the courtroom.

"It doesn't matter, we'll find the guilty party…"

"Try looking in a mirror," I yelled. A hand clamped over my mouth.

"That's enough! We'll deal with you later. In the meantime, I am instructing Judge Gabriel to disregard this evidence and make a ruling." My eyes turned to the judge, who looked uncomfortable. He was silent and appeared to ponder his options.

"A decision!" Lord Morall yelled.

"Uh-huh." He cleared his throat. "Based on the evidence, I can only conclude that former prosecutor, Evan Anderson, is the only one with means to alter the footage. He is guilty of falsifying evidence and for falsely accusing the justice system of corruption. Sentencing will occur next week."

My dad looked fairly stoic but his eyes gave away his heartbreak. I tried to scream but the hand was too tightly clasped over my mouth. I tried to bite but quickly realized that the hand was not human but a drone. My teeth weren't going to puncture metal.

"Thank you, Judge Gabriel. The three of you may leave." Lord Morall motioned to the judge and the two lawyers. They glanced at each other and silently filed out of the room. The door slammed behind them.

"Morall! Leave my daughter out of this. If you need to punish someone, punish me!" my dad yelled as one of the guards restrained him.

Morall smiled. "I'm glad we agree on something, Evan." He turned to the right. "Lieutenant Vaslor, bring Mr. Anderson to the sentencing machine."

"But Judge Gabriel said the sentencing would be next week." Vaslor looked alarmed.

"I supersede the judge's authority," Morall stated, "and I will apply the sentencing now."

"Judge Gabriel decides the term sir," Vaslor stated defiantly.

"Since he's not here," Morall stepped within several inches of Vaslor's face, "I will take over that responsibility. If you are unable to carry out my orders, shall I find someone else?"

Vaslor's face looked conflicted. "That won't be necessary." He motioned to the guards. One opened the door as the other pulled my dad with him.

"Bring her with us. She needs to see this."

Vaslor looked ready to question him but thought better of it.

"No! What are you doing?" My dad struggled. "The public do not watch the sentencing."

Morall looked straight at him. "Today they will." The drone pulled me like I weighed nothing. Trying to move away from it was like swimming in cement. The drone separated its fingers, allowing me to breathe more freely.

"Let me go!" I squeaked as the drone dragged me down the hallway. If anyone heard my cry, they ignored me. Seconds passed but felt like hours as the cold sterile hallway passed. The lights hummed but the only other people we passed were other guards. Most stared forward as if they could block us from their minds. I noticed one guard stealing a glance at me. I pleaded with my eyes for help but he swiftly returned to staring forward. Then two sliding doors opened in front of us.

I had never seen the 'Sentencer' before. I had heard enough of it from Dad and seen its results from Lou. We were in a room within a room. It was a small structure with a single bench inside. The front door was glass, allowing an audience to view the process. My dad had described it as a modern version of the electric chair used by the legal system decades before. There was an engine in the back, almost like a huge fan compressor that would suck the years out of the criminal. It was the most horrible sight I had seen in my entire life.

"Put him in there." Morall motioned to Vaslor. He complied, opened the door and escorted Dad inside. My dad's frame was defeated but his eyes still radiated defiance. He would not beg for his release. Vaslor's hand lingered on Dad's shoulder for a moment and then he closed the small chamber. Two horizontal locks fastened immediately and four vertical locks were pulled into place. The cage was set. Morall stepped up to a control panel to the right of the machine.

"As per procedure, the criminal is granted two minutes for any last words. Do you have anything to say?" My dad stood up and put his hands on the glass door.

"Can I speak to my daughter?" Morall nodded and motioned to the drone holding me. Suddenly I could move again and rushed to my father. I placed my hand on the glass, looking at him on the other side.

"Dad," I cried, "why is this happening? You've done nothing wrong!" Tears welled up in my eyes as rage and sorrow mixed.

"It's done, Pene. Right or wrong, it doesn't matter. But you have to listen to me. I need you to promise something for me."

"Anything," I answered. And I truly meant it.

"Stay. Look after your grandma. Finish school. Go to university downtown. Make this city a better place."

"But Dad—you sound like you won't be here."

"I'm not, Pene. They are going to age me twenty-five years! It's going to be too much. I won't make it. Even if I do, I'll be a vegetable and I won't remember what makes you special. Promise me you'll stay in this city for me. I need to know you'll be safe."

I gulped. This city represented everything I hated, everything I wanted to leave behind. And he wanted me to stay.

He thought he was protecting me. If I tried to escape, then I would end up like him. There was no time to think, to negotiate his request. So I said the only thing I could think of.

"I'll stay." My dad nodded to Morall, who immediately directed the drone to pull me back. "Noooo!" I screamed as the drone's hands immediately covered my mouth again.

Morall turned and his hand swept over a console. He pulled down a lever and the chamber hummed to life. The lights above my head blinked as a huge amount of power was being drawn. I turned to look at my dad.

His hands were flat against the window. He looked at Moral, then Vaslor and then finally at me. He smiled. Then his life drained away. The years began adding to his face. His forehead creased, his hair turned gray. His hands became thin as the veins protruded, and liver spots appeared. His smile disappeared as his body sagged and he dropped to the floor. My throat constricted as I watched the years added to my dad's frame. The glass screen shook and his body shimmered. I shook my head, as if my dad's image was disappearing. As he hit the floor, it became clear again.

A large clump of white hair fell off my dad's head. His body was frail, and he looked so thin that he could be broken in two. He was no longer the energetic lawyer in the pursuit of justice. He was no longer the man who cooked me breakfast, who once tossed me on his knee. His face was alien to me; he was a hundred years old. In that moment, I looked at Morall. His face was serene, as if watching a man's life flow out of him was an everyday occurrence. In that moment, I knew that someday I would kill him.

Then I turned and watched my dad die.

24

Endings

I was numb. My brain had been on automatic for three weeks since Dad's death. Besides eating and sleeping, I remembered little. The Justice Department refused to provide his body for the funeral so his casket was closed for the service. Everyone offered their condolences and some offered anger towards the city. No one would do anything about it.

It mattered little to me. One of the few things that was good in this city was gone. And I was more obligated to stay than ever. Grandma came to live with me but maintained her house as well. We had spent a weekend at her home to get away from the drones. Despite the quiet, I could still feel their presence. Behind the trees, I could hear their hum. In the night, I could see their glow. Waiting for me. Watching to see where I would go.

Grandma felt it was time for me to return to school, and I agreed. For the first two weeks, I had spent my time looking at photos of Dad, remembering how he loved me. My eyes had dried up from crying so much, and now I was taking eye drops to replenish the moisture. By the third week I had no more tears to give. With four walls closing in on me, I knew I had to return.

As I entered the school, most people gave me a wide berth. There were some sympathetic looks but no one wanted to be near someone whose father had been sentenced. I was tainted with the same brush. Someone grabbed me from behind.

"I'm so happy to see you."

"Thanks, Lacey." I gave her a big hug. "I was going crazy being home. Sorry, I wasn't really up to seeing anyone."

"Don't worry about it. Considering what you went through, I don't blame you." She looked down the hall. "Want to come with me to class?"

"No, I have study period. I'm going to head over to the lab."

"See you later in Mr. Stewart's class." She waved and walked into a classroom. I headed into the opposite direction towards the main school lab. A door swung open and a couple of guys passed me. Our computer lab was broken into cubicles, each one with a desk and a crown that was connected to the computer mainframe. The power of the mainframe could only be accessed at school; no student could login to the re-enactment at home. I sat down on a cushy chair and sank deep into its foam. It was designed to be comfortable, to help immerse the user in the environment. Sometimes it was too relaxing, and on previous lab days I had seen a couple of students fast asleep.

I pulled out my tablet and looked over a number of missed assignments. Mostly standard stuff before and after the earthquake, negotiation, rescuing the survivors. All stuff I had reviewed several times before. But as I scrolled through the list, one item caught my eye. Most assignments had a standard call number using a combination of the teacher's name and grade number. This had neither.

Thetruth.ent

I looked around the lab, as if I could spot from their guilty appearance the person who had sent the file. No one returned my gaze. I reached forward and slipped the crown over my head. I connected the tablet to the jack and clicked on the file.

I opened my eyes and stared at my surroundings. A rifle fired over my shoulder. The sound was deafening and my left ear rang. A man in a red coat charged out of the brush, his rifle long with a sharp knife fastened to its end. A horse galloped from my right, and a band of soldiers in blue charged towards the red coat man. He smiled—a strange thing for a man about to die. Suddenly, a huge man with a gun belt over his left arm emerged from the forest, spraying bullets from a machine gun. I shook my head. This moment in history didn't match up.

The blue coat riders went down like dominos, no match for the superior weaponry. Bodies fell to the mud as a riderless horse stampeded away. One blue coat aimed his rifle to take down the one-man army. He fired and the redcoat giant was shot in the chest. He stumbled and fell to the ground but did not completely fall. He stood on one knee and grinned. He spat out blood and aimed his machine gun at the sniper, who promptly fell off his horse.

What kind of place was this? The weaponry didn't match the time period! Who was this giant man? Although I didn't make a sound, he started towards me. I ducked down, trying to hide in the roots of a tree. I covered my ears, trying to block out the sound of gunfire. The giant was aiming his gun around the corner of the tree. I closed my eyes, hoping to make the terror go away. When I looked up, it wasn't the gun he was aiming at me, but his hand.

"You should leave this place." He beckoned. I hesitated and as I reached forward to touch his hand, he disappeared.

The sky changed and became concrete. Instead of tree roots I was standing in murky water. I felt claustrophobic as the forest became stone walls and moisture dripped down from the ceiling. I had never been here before but I had seen enough pictures from engineering class. It seemed if I was in the underground storm pipes for the city. Mercifully, the sewage traveled through different pipes or I would have been overwhelmed by the gases.

My head hurt. The last location made no sense. It came from no history lesson I had ever learned, no movie I had ever watched and no book I had ever read. Was this another glitch in the re-enactment machine? What did it mean? Who were those people?

My thoughts were interrupted as shadows appeared at the far end of the tunnel. They loomed large and the poor lighting made them look monstrous. I moved my position and climbed a ladder that overlooked the tunnel. The pipe was rusted and I patted it softly so that I wouldn't cut myself. I lay on top of it and tried to make myself small. Hopefully no one would look up.

The shadows became smaller and I could make out four people stepping through the pipe. I couldn't make out if they were male or female. They were wearing bulky clothing with packs, and two of the figures seemed to be carrying a crate. Besides the movement of the water as they stepped through it, they were silent. As they walked under me, I held my breath, worried they could hear my breathing. They passed without ever looking up. About a half minute later, the crate was lowered as its sound reverberated throughout the tunnel.

"Let's put the last of the charges here," an older male voice said. The crate opened and three of them went to work. I tried to peer over but a lot of the overhead pipes obscured my view. But I listened and could hear the sounds of drilling, as if a machine was spinning in the wall. Sparks flew and illuminated the driller's face. He looked old and worn, as if the weight of world was on his shoulders. The drill stopped and then another box was opened. I leaned my head down, avoiding detection but trying to get a better vantage point.

"We have one hour before the power plant is attacked. Are you sure about the power of the charges we've placed?" an older woman asked.

"We've gone over this ten times. The explosion locations are placed strategically around the city. The main square is just a diversion. All of the simulations show that the city will come loose," the older man responded.

"Yea, we know how well computer simulations and reality compare," a younger male voice chimed in.

"We're well past the time for debates, aren't we, Leah?" The other woman turned and the sight of her face made me lose my grip.

Leah was my mother.

I clutched at the pipe, pulling a lump of dirt, which fell into the water below. All four turned to look at my hiding place.

"Probably rats. I saw a nest earlier in the tunnel."

"I'll check it out. We're done. Go back to the rendezvous place," Leah commanded. The two men packed up the remaining gear in the crate and carried it off between them. The older woman pressed something in the wall and a light appeared in the same spot. She followed the two men, and within a minute, the three of them had disappeared into the darkness. My body quivered as the last person stood up and stared at me through the darkness. Seconds later, her foot splashed in the water as she stopped just below my location.

"Awfully big for a rat, aren't you?" She knew I was there. I wondered if she knew who I was. I reached for the rungs of the ladder and dropped down. I stood before a computer simulation of my mother from when I would have been a child. I couldn't control myself. I hugged her. Strangely enough, she hugged me back.

"Mom?" I whimpered. It didn't matter if she wasn't real. I knew this was a computer representation of what my mom was like. It might look like her and might have been programmed with her basic background and feelings, but it was an empty shell. But I didn't care. This was as close I would ever get to holding her. My eyes filled with tears as her hand cupped my chin.

"It's okay, Pene. I've always been there for you." My eyes flashed open as I realized what was happening.

"What are you? How do you know my name?" I pushed her off at arm's length.

My mom started to smile. "I'm a computer representation of your mom, replaying history."

"But I was a baby when you died. You shouldn't know who I am."

"True. I have been augmented with more recent memories. It was more likely that you would listen to me in your mom's form."

"Did you send me the assignment?" Before she could answer, the tunnel shook and the lights flickered. It felt as if reality was being challenged. My mom looked alarmed.

"There is no time for questions. Just listen. You need to leave, Pene. You don't belong in this city."

"But Dad said…"

"Your father is wrong. He means well but you're not safe here."

"Says you. You're dead. How do I know you're not someone trying to trap me? As far as I know, Lord Morall is controlling this whole conversation." The tunnel shook and faded from view. In a matter of seconds, reality was going to come crashing through.

"Would he know that I sang to you as a baby? That I held you and sang you to sleep? Do you remember?"

Suddenly that nagging memory of my mother came flowing back. No one would know this, and it was long before drones recorded our every move. How did this computer simulation know about my mother?

"Leave the city now. It's only a matter of time before you learn the truth."

The ground shook. The tunnel vanished. I was back in the lab. My chest felt like someone had sat on it; there was no air. No one around me noticed, everyone focused on themselves. I stood up.

My depression was over. I knew what I needed to do. Promise or no promise, I wouldn't deny my instincts. Something or someone was urging me to leave.

And I was going to find out who.

25

Goodbyes

The worst thing about making a decision is delaying when you are going to follow through. Whatever that entity in the computer was, it had revived my need to leave. The problem was how and when. The when didn't really matter because I didn't know how. I had already failed to escape once and unless I spent a couple of years applying for the travel visa, I wasn't going to get out of the city any time some. I needed a plan, and there was only one person who could give me the answers I wanted. The question was how to get him alone.

Fortunately, due to our high standings at the re-enactment finals, our school had planned a celebration party. And all schools were invited. Now I just had to get Austin to attend.

Our celebration entailed an entertainment social in the re-enactment dome. Instead of just being immersed in a false environment, we would be immersed in sound. Famous musicians from our past would entertain and the dome would be played like a rock festival. The school sponsored it because it was a way to learn about the past. Plus it was yet another activity to watch us. The drones and the chaperones.

As I walked down the hallway, I knew this would be my last time here. I wouldn't miss it. Propaganda had replaced learning so long ago, I didn't know what was real or not. I just knew that I didn't belong. Unlike some people.

"Hey, honey." Lacey gave me a hug.

"You're glowing. Hoping to meet someone tonight?" I teased.

"You never know." She smiled and grabbed my hand. "You seem better."

"Maybe I'm just looking forward to something." Lacey must have thought I meant the party as she quickly steered me in that direction. The doors opened and the noise of other students filled the hallway. People gave me looks. They didn't know if they should ostracize me because of my dad or cheer for me for helping the school do well in the finals. Most went right down the middle and didn't engage me at all.

Suited me fine.

We followed the mass of students. Most I recognized but a few wore jackets from other schools.

"Do you see him yet?" Lacey was poking fun at me. "What's his name again? Autumn? August?"

"Austin," I blurted before I realized she was bating me. She knew why I was here and what I needed to do. She might not agree with my choices but she would always support me.

"Don't worry. I'm sure he'll be here." The main doors opened up and a wall of sound crashed over us. The top of the dome matched the sky. Fireworks burst all around in time to the music. Bright reds and oranges exploded, cascading into waterfalls. The sight was breathtaking but I was looking for something else.

Lacey and I pushed through the crowd of students. Non-alcoholic bars lined the edges of the dome. Robotic bartenders handed out a variety of drinks and foods. I watched as a floating drone patrolled the aisle, its red eye scanning the cups in students' hands.

"Alert!" the drone cried, flashing red. Mr. Stewart emerged from the crowd and immediately seized the drink the drone was flashing at. Mr. Stewart raised the cup to his nose and smelled it.

"Mr. Crowell. I see you have added alcohol to your drink tonight." A guy from my grade with long black, curly hair vehemently shook his head.

"No way. I'm just drinking what the bartender drone gave me. Honest." His face looked anything but honest.

"I'm sure you can plead your case to the principal. Come with me." He grabbed the boy by his hoodie and pushed him forward. The boy's drink fell to the floor, the contents flowing away.

"Pene." Mr. Stewart nodded at me as he went by with the boy.

"What about me?" Lacey waved as he passed. "I swear I'm invisible to him."

I wish I was, I thought.

We walked deeper into the dome. The music increased in volume, making it harder to talk. The middle of the dome was the dance floor. As we pushed through the crowds lining the edge, we could make out the entertainment center. The dance floor had many levels. Stairs and ramps covered the field reaching up four stories. Some kids were dancing while others were completely still, perhaps dancing to a beat in the re-enactment machine. Lacey and I went to a metal coat rack, pulled off two crowns and placed them on our heads. Suddenly our perspective changed.

"Whoa!" A boy on skateboard whizzed by us and then defied gravity as he jumped over a waterfall. Suddenly the empty skeleton of framework in the dome looked overwhelmingly full. Hundreds of kids danced that were stationary in the real world. Kids tended to cluster in groups of girls and boys. About a dozen girls were jumping on a trampoline above a watery pool, to the cheers of another group of boys. One girl did a flip and then blew a kiss to the boys. They raised their glasses and cheered as if they had just won a big game. Then I saw the boy I wanted.

"You left me a message." Austin came up to me.

"I was worried you wouldn't get it." I kissed him on the cheek. Lacey winked at us.

"I see someone, I'll be back later," she lied and melted into the crowd. Austin turned to look at me. "You took a chance giving my sister a message." He waved the piece of paper I had written on earlier.

"I said she would get a reward if she delivered." I smiled

and nervously played with my fingers.

"She was motivated. But she thinks I need to reward her. You cost me to keep her quiet." He grinned.

"I'm sorry," I said but I really wasn't.

"Want to dance?" He grabbed my hand and moved onto the dance floor. It was busy but we had enough room that we didn't bump into anyone else. I leaned closer to him.

"Can they hear us here?" I made a circle with my finger.

"I don't think so," Austin answered. "This is all a projection, not a recorder. Do you see any drones?" I looked around and then shook my head. "They are watching us in the real world, but here we've got nowhere to go. They control everything we see. But they can't record us." I looked around, and he was right. Everything we thought was projected from our minds. It made me think, was there anywhere that we were truly free?

"I'm sorry about your dad. I wish my evidence had helped." Austin looked sad.

"You did more for me than anyone else. And it didn't matter. They were determined to make him guilty from the start. He didn't have a chance."

"Why? Were they trying to make an example of him? Were they scared of what he was going to uncover?"

"Who knows? I want to leave the city. And I don't want to wait the years it takes to get a travel visa."

"You not wanting to wait. No surprise there!" Austin's smile was contagious and made me grin. "And how are you going to do that? Your first attempt was a total disaster."

"I need to find some place to hide. Get off of the drones'

radar."

"Well, you better stop eating."

"What?" I stopped dancing in confusion. Austin took my hand and kept me moving.

"Listen, when I showed you the lights of the people that Justice was tracking, I learned how they keep tabs on everyone."

"How? Do we have something embedded in our skin?" I touched the back of my neck as if expecting to feel a bump. "Or is there something in my clothes?"

"Well, you could go around nude?" I punched his shoulder.

"How?" I drew out the word.

"Food. Thru some informal chats with some of the others I told you about, we have come up with a working theory on what travels in each of us. Everything we eat that is prepared seems to have some type of insoluble tracking agent that travels through our system. It gives off some type of field, amplifying your body's signature so a computer can differentiate you from others."

"What? Then why do drones follow us at all? They could track our whereabouts without a simple camera watching us."

"Yes and no. They need the footage and audio to process the crime. Besides, the tracking agents seem to be fairly unreliable. In close proximity the signals can meld together, making it difficult to track you in a crowd. Also, if you're sick, people tend to... expel most of the tracking agents," Austin added uncomfortably.

"You're telling me to go on a diet?"

"Sort of. You'll need to pack fresh fruit and vegetables. Anything that comes out of the ground. Anything processed in a bag or can is a no-no."

"Okay, so I can pack some fresh food. Doesn't give me a long time to stay hidden."

"Not unless you hide under a garden."

"No, I've got somewhere else planned."

Austin pulled away from me. "Don't tell me where. It's better I don't know."

"It's okay." I pulled him back towards me. "Someone gave me an idea of where to go."

"When are you going?" Austin looked at me with his big eyes.

"Next weekend. It's too hard to go undetected for long during a school day." Austin went silent. "What?"

"I'll miss you."

"You don't really know me." I blushed.

"I know enough."

I stopped dancing. The enormity of my decision was starting to sink in. I could stay in the city, with family, go to school and get to know Austin better. It would be the easiest thing in the world to stay. I had everything to lose.

"Before my dad died, he made me commit to staying in the city. Do you think I should break my promise to him?"

Austin's eyes revealed his answer. "You need to live. To see the world outside this city. Go with your heart, Pene. Don't do what everyone expects you to do." Suddenly the dance floor evaporated. The trampoline, the bikers, all disappeared as the crown's images were replaced by reality. As I looked around, I saw Mr. Stewart approach with a tall metal drone accompanying him. He was looking at us. As he came closer, he pointed at Austin.

"This girl is under surveillance for the crimes committed by her father. By associating with her, you endanger yours and your family's safety. Discussing the details of the case is strictly prohibited. What did the two of you talk about during the simulation? Did she tell you who provided the false tracking information at the trial?"

"Please come with me," the drone commanded and reached towards Austin's shoulder.

"Whatever," Austin replied coolly, shaking it off. "She never mentioned the trial. I felt sorry for her. Her dad just died. Sounds like she was trying to follow his last wishes."

"What do you mean?" Mr. Stewart asked, looking curious, but I couldn't tell if he was buying Austin's response. Inwardly I gulped, afraid that Austin might give me away.

"She talked about going to City College, maybe following in her dad's footsteps with a legal degree." Austin was a pretty good liar.

"And what did you tell her?"

"That her Dad was evil. Pure evil. She needs to forget about him. She didn't want to make the mistakes he made." Austin walked up to the drone. "Come on, let's get out of here." Austin started walking and the drone hurried to keep up. Mr. Stewart watched him go. I was unsure if he believed Austin's performance. He turned to me.

"And what *will* you do, Pene?" I considered Austin's comments. His backwards comment of evil reinforced my decision. Evil backwards was 'live'.

"I think he gave good advice. And it's time I followed it."

26
Disappearance

I wanted to disappear. To vanish. The problem was how to evade the dozens of drones and cameras that watched my every move. The first thing I had to do was increase the odds in my favor.

Grandma and I decided to spend the weekend at her home at the edge of the city. Not only did the air seem cleaner but the sky held fewer drones, although I always recognized a few. My own personal friends. The sun was high and the day was warm, a perfect day for the beach. I packed my bag full of fruit, spare clothes and some toiletries. Just your basic running away from home kit.

"You got enough in there?" my grandma asked. I jumped slightly.

"I think so," I answered nonchalantly. "Never can be too prepared." I flashed her a warm smile. She shuffled towards me.

"You know you can always be honest with me." She rested her hand on my shoulder. *She knows.*

"You're all the family I have," I said and gave her a hug.

"Come with me." She beckoned to the bedroom, and I followed her in. She walked over to a jewelry tree full of earrings and necklaces. She pulled a ring from it and flattened my hand out. She dropped it in.

"What's this?"

"A gift from your father to your mother."

"A wedding ring?"

"No, dear—a celebratory ring. Your mother was always after your dad about her present. She said that men had it easy and women did all the work carrying children for nine months. She said she deserved a reward for taking such good care of you before you were born. I think he thought she was joking at the start, but by the time you were born, he knew he had to get her something."

"You mean the ring was to celebrate me?"

"Yes. I know you never really got to know your mother but she wanted to celebrate everything about you. In your first year she had a party every month with other mothers, and they would do crafts and watch you toddlers laugh and cry. I'm pretty sure she would have wanted you to have this." The ring glistened. It was half silver and half gold, twisting around each other like a helix.

"Dad rarely talked about Mom. I can never tell if he missed her or was angry with her."

"A bit of both, dear. He wished she could have watched you grow up. I'm sure she would have been proud of you." She leaned over and kissed me on the forehead. "Enjoy the beach." She followed me out of the bedroom and waved as I exited the front door. For a moment I doubted my plan and the hurt it would cause her. As I walked to the end of driveway, I contemplated delaying my escape. Then I heard a purring to my left.

A cat lay at the corner of the driveway. It licked its paws and used them to wet its metallic ears. It had every mannerism of an actual cat—which were rare—except it lived in a metal body. I resisted the urge to pat it and turned abruptly to avoid it. Seconds later, I looked back. It tilted its head to the side, as if to get a better look at me. It got up and rushed after me, like it was pursuing a mouse.

My walk to the beach was uneventful. The beach was manmade a number of years ago, I remember the bulldozers pushing the sand into huge piles. Beautiful white sand that got hot under your feet. I reached the boardwalk and the cat started circling one of the pillars. I knew it wouldn't follow me; cats aren't welcome at the beach. Even drone ones. Besides, it would watch and wait for me to return through the only exit. I stepped over the dune and looked around. A crowd had gathered to the far right and I knew I only had about ten minutes before I had to join them.

I searched the beach and found some trees to put my knapsack beside to keep it hidden from other beach users. I slipped out of my clothes—I had my bathing suit on underneath—and placed them into the knapsack. I grabbed my swimming cap and pulled it tight over my hair. I put my goggles on and headed over to the crowd of people.

Each year there was an annual fundraising race from the beach out towards an island at the other end. The total distance was about two kilometers, and you had to circle the island six times before returning back to the beach. I had always been a decent swimmer and I could probably place well if I tried to compete. But I was here for other results. I showed one of the volunteers the wristband I purchased from registration yesterday. She marked a check on her tablet and continued to greet other swimmers. I lined up in a queue with about a hundred swimmers. They were of all ages and both sexes, and I tried to lose myself into the center of the crowd. Circling overhead, I could see several drone birds casually floating.

"Please get ready, the race is about to begin!" a woman's voice boomed over a speaker. Everyone's excitement grew quiet as swimmers rotated their arms, necks, legs or all three in anticipation of starting. I focused forward on the island and reviewed my plan.

"Boom!" A pistol blared and everyone started towards the water. A young boy seemed anxious to get to the front and I let him by to avoid his elbows in the water. As my feet stepped from the sand to the water, I could feel them slipping into the mud. Because of its shallowness, the water was warm. The water was a mass of arms and legs and I set a steady pace in the middle of the pack. The exercise was comforting, right stroke, left stoke, all I had to focus on was the island ahead.

Fifteen minutes later we approached the island. Each loop would take about ten minutes each. As we approached the west side of the island, I saw onlookers waving down from a metal bridge. The island was connected to the mainland, and people had crossed to see us. As we came to the bridge, several swimmers dove underneath to avoid the low overhang. I burst under the water and looked at the rocks below. With my right hand I took off my swimming cap and reversed it, turning it from a red to a blue. I rejoined the swimmers on the surface.

As I looked around me, I assessed the swimming groups. There seemed to be an equal number of swimmers ahead as behind me. I thought about my placing if I was actually trying to win. It didn't matter. As I swam around the island, I watched the shoreline. The bird drones continued to float overhead, but past the volunteers on the edge of the island I noticed a few drone policeman stationed at intervals. I wondered if they always helped at these events.

Ten minutes passed as I stroked through the water until I saw the bridge span approaching again. There were fewer people looking down as I dipped below the water. I dove deep, seeing the same rock as before. Beneath was a mesh bag with a snorkel inside. I reached in and put the curved end into my mouth. I swam away from the racers and swam back towards the bridge. I came up just below the surface, blowing water out of my mouth. I gulped fresh air and swam along the edges of the lake, far away from the racers. As I swam, I skirted legs and watched air mattresses float by. Sound doesn't travel well through water but the roar of the race gradually dimmed as I swam back to the beach.

I floated to the surface as I looked straight into the face of a little boy. He stared at me with puzzled eyes.

"You should see the fish in the lake!" I exclaimed and

handed him the snorkel before he could respond. I covered my face and dashed towards the tree with my backpack. I unzipped the bag and reached inside. I quickly pulled on a different shirt and put on a ball cap and sunglasses. I looked back to the lake. I probably had about ten minutes before the lead swimmers landed and then the drones would be watching each swimmer at the end of the race. I spotted a family walking out from the beach and quickly dashed to catch up with them.

I walked to the left of them. The dad was arguing with his son, who was probably a couple of years younger than me. Ahead I saw the drone cat in a sitting position, watching everyone as they exited. I held my breath and pulled my hat lower. The cat veered his head around the dad, trying to get a better look at me. I heard a scream from behind and looked. Two girls were yelling at a mouse scurrying over the boardwalk. The cat was distracted by their cries and I walked fast past him.

Now it got hard. I had about twenty minutes before the drones clued in that I was gone. They would scour everywhere for me and then start to review footage from the beach earlier to observe when I left. I couldn't go on any public transport, and I had to stay away from downtown. I started walking down the sidewalk pretending to be casual, avoiding cameras when possible but trying not to look like I was avoiding cameras. I began heading westward. I noticed a drone bird flying to my right. I slowed and fell into step behind an older couple. They walked excruciatingly slow and it took all my patience not to run ahead of them. The drone bird continued to follow. I noticed a tunnel under the roadway and sped towards it.

The shadows were dark with the sun directly overhead. I figured I could lose the drone in a store on the other side when I saw something that stopped me in my tracks. On the opposite side a drone officer was walking behind a group of kids. They were laughing and ignoring him. I didn't want to be seen by the drone's cameras. I stepped back into the shadows and walked as close to the wall as possible. The girls giggled and the sound reverberated off the tunnel walls. Neither the girls nor the drone officer seemed to pay me any attention. As they passed, I resisted the urge to look over. I felt something sharp at my temple and for a second my vision went blurry. I touched my head and felt nothing. As I snuck a look behind me, the drone officer and kids had exited the tunnel.

As I exited the other end, I began to quicken my pace. Not enough to garner suspicion, but I needed to cover some distance. Overhead, a flock of bird drones flew straight to the beach. It seemed like reinforcements had been called in quicker than I thought. I needed to make it to my safe zone now. And I needed speed to get there. As I turned a corner, I saw my salvation.

The park came into view, and a running group was stretching at the entrance. I looked at my clothes—my sneakers and shirt would pass as a casual runner's. My backpack was a bit out of place—and heavy—but shouldn't warrant too much attention. I followed behind a group of three woman runners and settled into a place about ten feet behind them. I needed to make some distance fast, and the guise of being a runner would be good cover. The park was fairly safe and people ran here at all times of the day. But cameras were placed high up, looking at people's heads. If I kept my head down it might prevent them from getting any facial recognition.

My father took me to this park as a kid. There was a big water park in the center and I would always challenge him to the biggest slides. He'd pretend he was scared and I would have to show him each slide to let him know they were safe. He'd mock his fear and try to back out of taking the slide, and I'd have to force him down. I loved every minute of it. I felt like the kid who was teaching her dad to be a big boy. In the end it dispelled my fears because I felt I was doing it to teach him.

"Watch out!" a man yelled at me. I'd almost collided with him on the trail while I was daydreaming. I veered away from the female runners towards the west gate. The foot traffic was lighter here and I continued my pace as if I was running home. Within a few blocks I veered into the industrial area. This was an older part of town and many companies had relocated to the new southern business park. Several minutes had passed and I'd seen no drones. I looked up. Cameras were still located at the end of each block but there were fewer. I guess safety was less of a concern where foot traffic was nonexistent. I walked behind the buildings to stay out of view of the street cameras.

Ahead of me, my destination loomed. I remembered Morall's story from his boyhood, when he lost his eye in a rundown part of the city. I had done my research, and not much had changed since his youth. The oil refinery he described didn't have a single window intact. I was glad there was still a roof. I slipped into a back entrance and climbed the stairs. I found a dirty, windowless office and emptied the contents of my backpack. My new home.

I laid out my food—likely good for eight days. All natural—I'd had nothing but for the last week. If police could follow me by trackers in the store-bought food, I had expelled them days ago. I was off the grid. If I was lucky, they would not seriously start searching for me for a couple of days. I planned to be gone by tomorrow.

My route was simple. At the end of each month travelers came back into the city at the main north gates. There was no chance I could get near it with the drones following my every move. Now that they suspected I was missing, they might double security at the gate. My plan was to go the exact opposite way. I would go over the cliff face where I met the 'Wildman'. I had visited him recently at the Marks. He gave me a few tips as well as some climbing rope and carbineers. I pretended that I would be climbing much smaller cliffs, and he was happy to give me some pointers.

The landscape around where he climbed at Eaglewood was fairly impassable but poorly secured. There was no wall that surrounded this part of the city because of its ragged cliffs. It wasn't a great chance at success but it was one I was willing to try. The constant surveillance at all other locations limited my options. If only I had tried to escape at the finals, when all eyes were on the stadium.

I leaned back on a dirty chair and tried to imagine where I'd be in a couple of days. Once past the city, if I stayed close to the road, it should be about five days before I hit the ocean. Once I felt the sea spray, I knew I could find passage to other parts of the country. Anywhere but here. I imagined an ocean voyage to exotic lands. The glorious sunset over a different city. The tastes of new foods. The smell of new flowers and... burning metal? My body went rigid as the ceiling above me went red and started to smolder. I wasn't alone, and maybe I never had been.

This is where my story began, and now it was where it would end. I should have learned that running away from the drones was exercise in futility. They were everywhere. Once they had you in their sights, there was no escape. As the frigid water went straight to my bones, the watery grave enveloped my body. I began to become disoriented. I couldn't tell if I was swimming up or down as everything became dark. In the last seconds, I felt eerily at peace. As if everything I had done had worked towards this moment.

Then this world ended.

27

Reality

When I was ten, our Sunday school project was to draw a picture of what heaven looked like. I remember a lot of kids drew the pearly gates, clouds and bright rays of light. Some painted a field of flowers while others surrounded themselves with family and friends. I drew multiple pictures—all of them were places far away from my home. My drawings included drinking tea with the Queen of England, sitting on top of a pyramid and traveling on a cruise ship across the ocean. One picture I drew was of me in a house with my dad and my mom. I figured, like many of us, that I would see her in heaven. Unfortunately, when I opened my eyes, I realized that was not going to happen.

I was blinded by bright lights. But the bulbs were far from being angelic. The room was sterile, like in a hospital. My arms were strapped and a belt wrapped around my waist but my legs were free. Machines were around me and a drone was standing motionless in the corner, watching my motions and likely reporting that I was awake. Definitely not heaven—maybe closer to hell. And then he leaned in.

"Sorry if you're not comfortable but precautions had to be taken. Can't have you running off again. Although your hiding place was ingenious, though. It was nice to know that you did listen to our conversation," Morall commented.

I tugged at my bonds. "How did you find me?" I demanded. Morall turned his back but I could feel his grin from the back of his head.

"You were never lost, my dear. We knew where you were every second. My team had thought that we could have left you out in the open for days to see if anyone was assisting you. However, by watching you at the oil refinery, I realized you were going at this alone. I figured there were better ways to find any co-conspirators. From there I shut the illusion down."

"Illusion?" I ran my fingers along my temple and felt a small welt. Was any of this real?

"In the tunnel, you would have felt a slight prick when a mini crown was planted on your head. Just like a game of the re-enactment. Everything felt real to you."

"But how would you know what environment to set up? Some of my decisions were on the fly?" I remembered my decisions in the park.

Morall's head came closer. "That's the beauty of the simulation. You drive the data creation by the decisions you make. Your brain tells the machine what it expects to see. It recreates it to the final detail. Unlike the historical re-enactments, which have programmed events, you drive the results simply by thinking of where you want to go." I didn't like where this was going.

"How?"

"You walked by a drone in a tunnel. He implanted it on your head as you walked by. The effects should have been instantaneous. One moment you were in the tunnel, the next moment you were walking to this facility. Unbeknownst to you, of course."

The run in the park. Sitting in the abandoned oil refinery. All lies, when I was actually walking into a trap.

"But how? The swim meet. I had it all planned. You should have been following the race. How did you find me at the tunnel?" I raised my head towards him.

"We did lose you. You are a very clever girl, Pene. Your dad would be very proud of your ingenuity. For about twenty minutes we had no eyes on you. Our security leader was a bit nervous. Then, once you left the beach, we matched your movements by your location."

"How? I purged myself for days. You couldn't track me by the food I ate. I checked my clothes—there wasn't anything to follow me with." I gritted my teeth, frustrated at how easily Morall had made my capture.

"Pene." He leaned back into my view. If he were another foot closer, I'd have bitten his cheek. He must have seen me flash my teeth because he leaned back. "We anticipated that you might become a flight risk after your dad's... sentencing." He seemed regretful about Dad's death, as if he had made a mistake. He took a moment to collect himself. "A number of items at your family's homes were covered with tracking beacons. They're so small, you can put them on

266 • JIM KOCHANOFF

anything." He was playing with something in his fingers. He held it still. *Mom's ring!*

"Did my grandmother know?" I asked.

Morall smiled. "I'm the one asking the questions here. Where did you think you were going? The city is secure. You were only delaying the inevitable."

"I wanted to be away from the drones! I'm tired of being studied by them every day. You can't go five feet without one watching me. When I look out my window at night, there is always one staring back at me." I paused, gathering my breath.

"I wanted to be alone. For one day, I wanted to be out of sight of your security. To actually feel at peace. A day to myself. Then I would have returned home," I lied. I breathed heavily, trying to communicate my anguish to see if he would believe that I wasn't trying to leave the city. I tried to sell my response, hoping he wouldn't think I had any help. He tilted his head as if considering my answer.

"Maybe you're right. But you seem to know a lot about how our surveillance works. Perhaps you have some friends helping you?"

"I did this on my own. Even my grandmother didn't know. I don't expect you to understand. You created this nightmare and call it home. You killed my dad to hide your petty secret! I know you are going to kill me!" I leaned my head down. It was hurting to strain upward to talk to Morall. He cradled my hair.

"Pene, you are very convincing. I want to believe you, I really do. But like all of us, I report to superiors and they need proof." Behind him I heard a spinning sound. A metal sphere hung in the air. A slot opened on its side and robotic arm spun out. In its hand was a syringe. A green fluid bubbled in its center. It spun around beside me. Lord Morall leaned in and the drone moved closer to the back of my neck.

"I'm sorry. I know you can't understand this but in order for our city to be safe, certain sacrifices have to be made. Your dad was one of those sacrifices." I spat at him but he stepped back and with my head strapped to the table, it went vertical and landed back on my chin. Morall must have felt pity for me and wiped my face with a tissue.

"Why do you get to decide who lives and who dies," I croaked. He leaned back as if considering my question.

"I do because it is my responsibility to keep this city safe, to provide security. You're young. You don't know what the world was like without the drones. Thousands of people died needlessly. The court systems were mocked for their inefficiencies and for letting the guilty go free. We live in exciting times, Pene. You have so much more now than when I was a child."

"So you keep saying. Too bad I won't get to enjoy this safe world you created," I said sarcastically.

"Come on, Pene. Take some responsibility. You brought this on yourself."

"Yes, I remember strapping myself to the table," I laughed. He touched my forehead. I assumed it was supposed to be a fatherly gesture, but it drove me insane with anger.

"A world without drones would be anarchy. Thousands of people are saved each day because of the system in place." His drone eye shimmered. His words sounded so sincere, I had no doubt he believed everything he said.

"Why can't I leave? Why don't I get a choice of where I want to live?"

Morall stared straight into my eyes. "Is life so bad here? You can walk on any street in the middle of the night in the poorest part of town without fear. You're safe with people who love you."

"There is no safety here. Those who are safe are ignorant of what you do. And anyone who learns about your corruption is dead." I felt the needle pressing on the skin of my neck. "You're too much of a coward to do it yourself. You get your slaves to kill me." He motioned to the drone to stop for a moment.

"It's not going to kill you. I get no pleasure in forcing you to tell me if there are others helping you. You're a teenager—you wouldn't understand. You're fighting with gasoline, eventually you'll make a mistake and burn this city to the ground. I keep us safe." He motioned to the drone to proceed. I heard a rumbling boom in the background. *Or was it thunder?*

Morall looked behind at the drone in the corner and nodded for it to investigate. Unless a rainstorm had descended since I was captured, that was no thunder. It was an explosion. The next rumble was closer, and dust began to fall from the ceiling. Despite the encouraging signs, I knew it would hasten Morall's actions.

Let the torture begin. The drone sank lower and I could see the sickly green fluid ready to be pumped into my veins. I strained hopelessly against my bonds, my mind refusing to give up. As the needle dipped lower to inject me, I accepted my fate. Then the ceiling caved in.

A large chunk of plaster fell down onto the drone, smashing it to the floor. I could see its gears writhing under the plaster, the metal bent.

"Call security!" Morall yelled into his tablet and began pressing buttons. About a minute later two security officers charged through the door. Morall pointed to me and the two of them roughly unstrapped me from the table. I tried to get some circulation by rubbing my wrist but they didn't give me any time to recover. The larger one grabbed me by the arm, pulling me off the ground. The second guard opened the door to direct me into the hallway.

"Make sure you wait for reinforcements—take her to the lower levels," Morall commanded. As we stepped into the hall, there was a flurry of activity. People in lab coats, security and other staff ran by in different directions. In the distance an explosion sounded even closer. We stayed stationary, as if we were watching a movie. Then the reinforcements arrived.

Five drones. Four were aerial—mechanical hawks, their heads swiveling 360 degrees as if assessing their environment. The fifth was man-sized. It looked identical to the one that had arrested Lou. The top part was humanoid, the bottom half resembled an air bike. The two security officers walked ahead, the hawks flew above me in a diamond formation and the man-drone gave me a nudge to move forward. As we stepped down the hall, all others gave us a wide berth. I felt like a prisoner being marched to her last meal. Whatever was going on outside might have saved me from the drone needle, but where would it take me now?

The elevator door opened silently and my captors and I went in. I looked at the larger officer.

"Where are we going?" I pleaded. "What's going on outside?" His expression was neutral, and if he planned to answer my question, he gave no indication. The elevator dropped as we sank below the ground. Moments later, the doors opened and everyone moved out. I could feel the breeze from the hawk drones.

I felt like I had stepped into the apocalypse. Wires were hanging from the ceiling, with sparks floating down. The end of the hall was blackened and a fire raged from a hallway twenty feet away. The two guards looked at each other; obviously this was unexpected. The smaller officer reached for radio.

"Central—level five has been compromised. Requesting alternate directions." I looked up at the officer. He didn't look like an evil person like Morall. He looked ... ordinary and a little conflicted. Like he was trying to keep his job. Not like he wanted to hurt me. The radio remained silent. The other officer chimed in.

"Let's go back upstairs. This floor is a battleground. We'll never make it to the cells in this condition." He went back and pressed the elevator button. A blue flame went into his fingers. The concussive force sent his body flying back into the wall. He slumped, unconscious.

"What the hell!" The other guard panicked and began yelling into the radio for help. As before, there was no reply. One of the hawk drones circled the elevator and tried to perch on the metal rim.

Big mistake. Its circuits fired and it spiraled limply to the ground. Its legs kicked a few times and then its eye went dark. Two enemies down in as many seconds. There was hope for me yet. I looked over at the limp form of the officer.

"Why doesn't your drone," I pointed to the half man half machine floating silently, "pick up your partner? He could be dead if he doesn't get any medical attention," I said. The smaller officer glared at me but it took his attention away from the useless radio.

"Drones have to be given direction. They can't think on their own," he answered defensively.

"Well, your hawk just thought on its own." I indicated the smoking circuits on the ground. One of its feet stirred slightly.

"They have some artificial intelligence, with an innate response to investigate questionable activities."

"Curiosity got it killed," I replied sarcastically.

"Looks like that is going around," he answered. His intent was not lost on me. His radio sparked to life.

"All units to main level. Multiple explosions throughout city. All drones to staging area for assignment. Situation critical." The remaining hawk drones flew out down the hall, having received their assignment. They went into a vent and must have flown up to the surface. The man-sized drone began to move off when the officer placed his hand on its shoulder.

"Stay with us," he commanded. The drone remained in place. I wondered how it decided what commands to listen to and what commands to ignore. We turned to the left, away from the elevator and towards a set of stairs. The officer tried to pull open the door and immediately pulled back.

"It's hot," he said to no one in particular and motioned to the drone to go first. The machine reached with its metal hand and pulled the door handle forward. A great rush of heat burst towards us as the fresh air fed the flame. The drone expelled a white foam at the fire, extinguishing it in seconds. Blue smoke replaced the fire and my throat tightened. The officer opened up the side of the drone and pulled out two oxygen masks.

"Take it." He motioned to me. I coughed and slipped it over my mouth. We climbed the stairs, where the sickly smoke made visibility difficult. There were several minutes of climbing before we reached the ground level, one floor higher than where I was held captive. We opened the door to a courtyard and I surveyed the city. I felt sick. There were fires, a huge crater in a street and people were streaming into the park. *What happened while I was captured? How could the safest city in the world turn to this?* It seemed so unbelievable.

"Stay here." The officer motioned to me and my drone keeper. I was so focused on the city that I barely felt the drone redirect me further out into the courtyard. The officer pulled out his radio and began to speak. I don't think he got two words out before the door from the stairs exploded and flew into his back. He went flying and crumpled onto the lawn. I rushed over to him and turned him over to see his face. His eyes were closed, face cut but breathing.

"Drone! Get over here! The officer is hurt." I heard no movement behind me and turned around. The drone looked at me, tilting its head at an angle. "Come. Now." The drone slid over and stopped beside us. "Do something!" I yelled at it.

"Not programmed to help. Only to pursue." I stared blankly at the drone. I had hated them for so long, and now I could only pity this hunk of metal. I knew nothing about first aid. I couldn't tell if the officer was dying or unconscious. And frankly, it wasn't my concern. A short time ago these people had tried to torture me and then lock me away. I owed this guy nothing. I needed to get as far away from this place as possible. I stood up, and as I stepped away, an arm with a vise-like grip stopped me in my tracks.

"Wait here. You can't leave." I couldn't move, the drone's grip was strong. I tried to reason with it. "Are you programmed to hurt me?"

"No. Only to escort and restrain." Its answers were methodical. I almost felt it would obey me under the right circumstances.

"You're hurting me. Let me go." The drone's grip loosened but it did not let go. "You need to get help. This man will die if you do not leave."

"You will escape if I go." I had to admit, it was perceptive. I just needed to use the right words.

"If you let go of me, I will try to help him until you bring a doctor. Every second you delay, you risk killing him. Do you want him to die?"

"No," was its metallic reply, but it did not let go of me.

"Look at the courtyard, I am completely surrounded. Do you think I can escape?" It scanned the entire area, moving its head from left to right.

"Affirmative," it answered. *Shoot.* My efforts to persuade him by logic were failing. I tried another approach.

"Who do you report to?"

"My tech command."

"What is he telling you to do?"

"I am unable to talk with him. Communications are down." *Good, now to lead him to his next decision.*

"Without his direction, what are you supposed to do?"

"Follow my last order."

"Which was?"

"To escort you to the prisoner cell." *A-ha.*

"Mission complete. You escorted me to that floor. You need to move on to your next order." It was silent. I could sense it processors whirling.

"Communications are down. I have no orders." *Here is my opportunity.*

"Yes, you do. I order you get help. Or this man will die."

"You are a prisoner. You cannot give me orders."

"You won't take my orders. You have completed your last command. You have no communications to new commands. What do you do?" I could swear that for a second the drone made me a facial expression.

"Use logic to decide next move,"

"And what are you next moves?"

"To guard the prisoner or to procure help for injured."
Perfect.

"What do you think you should do?"

"Analyzing." Its eyes scanned the soldier as if trying to determine the severity of his injuries. "Soldier could die if he doesn't receive immediate medical attention. You will likely escape if left unattended."

"What is the worst outcome?" Its brain must have been working overtime. If smoke came out of its ears, it would not have surprised me. It came to the only decision it could make, although it took it long enough.

"I must get help but you must be secured." He grabbed me by the wrist and pushed me closer to the outside wall. The drone took a pair of handcuffs from the officer's belt and placed one on my right hand. It grabbed my other hand, snaked it around a pipe on the wall and clicked the other cuff. I was trapped against the wall. The drone bent down, looking for something from the officer. It turned its head to me.

"I cannot find the keys. I will scan you to match sure you are not hiding them on your person." A bluish ray emitted from its right hand as it scanned me from head to toe.

"Find anything?" I asked.

"Nothing."

"It must have fallen off him in the explosion." The drone nodded as if it agreed.

"You will remain here until my return. I will achieve

both objectives." If the drone could smile, I'm sure it would have done so. It turned around and headed back down the flight of stairs. I counted to a hundred—there was no noise from the stairwell. Unless it was waiting for me, it had gone down below. I shifted my hand and began unscrewing the pipe. I had purposely stood there to allow myself to be strapped to it. In two minutes, the rusty pipe unscrewed and dropped to the ground. My handcuffed hands came out of the bar and I stepped over to the officer. I rolled his body to the left and pulled the key from his boot—an earlier move when I was checking the officer's vitals. It was tricky when my hands were so close together but after a minute I was able turn the key to remove the handcuffs.

If I learned one thing, it was that the drones could be forced to make a decision. I got lucky this time. I looked down at the officer. *Sorry, help is on the way.* I walked into the courtyard. I climbed the wall and looked back to the open door. No drones or security exited.

I leap off of the wall and disappeared into the city.

28

Resistance

Something was wrong.

As I ran through the city, people were screaming. Whatever had caused the explosions had sent them into a panic. People were not used to chaos—they were used to order. The lack of it terrified them.

Drones were everywhere but they seemed uninterested in me. There was something much larger at play. As I turned a street corner, I came upon a large crater in the middle of the street. I stepped over a small pile of debris that had been created by the rupture of the street. There were no bodies or anyone injured near the area. If someone had blown up the street, they had either deliberately avoided hurting people or gotten extremely lucky.

I leaned over the hole and peered into the darkness. I was surprised by the depth beneath the street. The tunnel reminded me of my dream—the passages underground with charges set before the earthquake. I felt a buzzing behind me. I turned and faced a dozen bee drones forming a semi-circle. I had become complacent and they had found me. I was pathetic. I thought I was so smart in outwitting the drone, I was not paying attention to my surroundings. I closed my eyes and waited.

Seconds passed and nothing happened. I looked around and the drones had passed me and were lighting the darkness of the hole. As they zoomed into it, their red eyes illuminated the rock walls. Soon they disappeared and their red glow faded into the darkness. I had gotten lucky. Again. The drones were looking for a much bigger prize than me.

I looked around, trying to decide where to go. I could go back to Grandma's; she'd be concerned but as soon as things settled down, they'd find me there. I could go to the oil refinery—for real this time—to avoid the cameras, but I had given that secret place away. I was alone. I had escaped my prison only to be trapped in another much larger one. I could make a break for the mountain now. They hadn't time to discover that part of my plan. As I made a decision, a hand on my shoulder took it all away from me.

"Pene! Come with me." I looked into Austin's eyes and knew I was going to be all right. Some actions just felt right.

"How did you find me?"

"The drones weren't the only ones looking for you." He grabbed my hand and we started running out of the downtown core. "I went to see your grandmother when I heard you disappeared. She was worried and asked me to find you. We knew that if you didn't escape the city, you had to be downtown in the Justice Building." I stopped moving.

"You never thought I could make it. Did you?" I commented, resisting his pull but preventing my hurt pride from getting in the way.

"We know you can make it. Just not alone."

"Who's we?"

"That's where I'm taking you. We're not alone. There are others like us who know how the city really works. I've finally made contact with them!"

What? I try to escape the city and in the span of a day, a whole resistance springs up?

"You're not making sense. Who is helping us?" I turned and realized this wasn't the time for answers. A motorcycle drone stood at the end of the street, and its red eye was directly focused on me. It revved its engine over the ground once, then twice, like a bull ready to charge.

"This way!" Austin screamed, pulling me into a mall. We ran into the main courtyard. Despite the crisis in the street, there were many frantic-looking people, as if they were rushing to buy emergency supplies. About half dozen alert mall cops were near the entrance, ready to act if looting began. We charged up an escalator, bumping into annoyed shoppers.

"Sorry," Austin said to several people as we reached the top. I turned and watched the drone drive in the main door and scan the crowd. It took seconds for it to notice us on the next floor. It pointed its wrist at the escalator and the upward motion stopped. People yelled at the drone but got off the escalator. The drone pointed its wrist again and the escalator steps flatted so that the stairs became a ramp. The drone gunned it up and was on the second floor in moments.

"Hope you got a trick up your sleeve," I yelled to Austin. "That thing is going to be on us in seconds."

"Fortunately, they gave me this." He pulled us into a small alcove between stores and tossed what looked like a small spherical grenade. Instead of an explosion, a video screen flashed in front of us.

"What is it?" I asked. Austin put his finger to his mouth.

"Quiet. The image won't mask audio. Stand still," he commanded. We were in an extremely tight corner. I don't know who started it, but all of a sudden I was holding him and he had his arms around my back. His eyes stared back at me and for a moment he was the only thing that existed.

Then the whirling engine of the drone came from around the corner. We stood like statues against the wall, looking straight out onto the pedway. The drone flew by us, proceeding to the next store.

"That was close," I whispered. The drone engine slowed and came to a stop. Austin gave me a look as if he was going to kill me if the drone didn't. I watched as the drone came back to our position and stared at us. I don't know what the image was, but the drone was scanning it. It tilted its head in a human manner, as if the visuals were false. I held my breath and closed my eyes. Austin gripped my hand.

I imagined being at home, having breakfast with my dad. Talking about his day. Him asking about mine. Cooking for him. All gone. That life had disappeared. My memories of him were all that were left. A sob escaped and a tear ran down my face. I opened my eyes, expecting that I had given away our position, but the drone was gone. We were no longer hugging each other but he held my hands.

"Are you okay?" he asked.

"No, but it can't be helped. Is the drone gone?"

"Yes." He pointed. "It's heading down towards the other end. We should go." We stepped out of the alcove and looked back. The image was perfect—two still mannequins in a store window. It looked real, even to me, and I knew the difference. Austin bent down and grasped the grenade, turning it off. The image disappeared as he pocketed the device.

"Where to?"

"We need to get below ground. Follow me." We headed towards the stairs and went down to the basement. I scanned our surroundings and noticed a camera at the bottom of the stairs. I put my arm in front of Austin's chest to make him stop, and pointed. He pulled a small tube from his pocket and climbed on the rail, out of sight of the lens. He sprayed black paint over the camera.

"They can't alert a drone to us right away." He grabbed my wrist and we opened the door to a parking garage. There was no one else around. Austin went straight to a heating duct.

"It's going to get warm for a moment," as he pulled the grate open. We pulled ourselves through and closed the grate behind us. The air came from a heat duct. The heat made me feel like I had stepped onto a beach. Austin passed me a small tube. I touched a depression on its surface. The light illuminated the gloomy surroundings.

We moved forward in the cramped area and the sounds

of the garage faded away. Suddenly we crossed over a lip and dropped about six feet until our feet touched water. Inwardly, I grimaced. Austin must have felt my body tense.

"Don't worry, it's not sewage, just water."

"Where are we?" I asked. Inwardly, though, I knew the answer.

He put his light under his chin, trying to create a frightening face.

"Don't you remember the re-enactment games? Before the earthquake there were a series of tunnels under the city. Although most were demolished when the city was rebuilt, some stayed intact. You just need to know which ones are still active." As if on cue, a large piece of cement hung down, partially blocking our route. Austin skittered around its edge and pulled me behind him.

"I get taken away for a day and now you're an expert on escaping the city? What else did I miss?" I was getting frustrated. It seemed like on both my escape attempts I had failed miserably, while Austin seemed to come about information freely.

"It's better that I show you. Follow me, it shouldn't take us too long to get there now." I followed his beam of light as it traversed the concrete tunnel. Twice we had to scramble around debris and once the ceiling had collapsed, but eventually the tunnel opened up and a glow appeared in the distance.

"Where are we?" I asked. Before Austin could answer, the tunnel opened up into a huge natural cavern. The area was the size of a large warehouse, with jury-rigged lighting above us. Computer workstations littered the top portion as well as a number of workbenches with bucket loads of electronics strewn across them. About a dozen people were working diligently on focused tasks. Only a few looked up as we entered, and most quickly returned to their work.

"Remember your success at the school games?" Austin grinned. And he pointed above ground. Suddenly I knew where we were.

"You mean all of this is below the stadium?"

"Hidden in plain sight. Apparently the sound of the crowd is overwhelming down here during the competition."

I pulled Austin closer to me. "Spill. How did you find all of this?"

"It kind of found me. Especially after he saw me with you at the dance. He followed me and figured out I was someone he could trust with the Resistance."

"Resistance? Who is leading it?" A hand touched my shoulder.

"Hi, Pene." Cold eyes bore into me.

The leader of the resistance was Mr. Stewart!

29
Truth

For a moment I stopped breathing and stared ahead. I was in shock and my body was threatening to shut down. I gasped as I forced myself to take some air.

"Are you okay?" Austin reached for my shoulders. I leaned against him.

"I'll be all right. I just need a minute." My brain was reeling. *Is this a trap? How can Mr. Stewart be here to help?*

"I'm sure this is a big shock for her. I'm not who she thought I was," Mr. Stewart commented. He was handling an electronic device.

"What does that mean?" Austin was confused. "I thought he was your teacher?"

"Teacher from hell!" My shock had dissipated and my anger spilled out. "He worked against me all during high school. Always putting me down or embarrassing me. Whatever he's telling you is a lie. How did you find him?"

"I found him," Mr. Stewart answered calmly. "When I saw the two of you together at the dance, I figured he was someone you trusted. Once he opened up to me, I realized he was too valuable not to involve in our group."

"What group?" I yelled. "For years you've rammed down my throat how the city operated. Told us to obey, how safe our city had become. Were you lying to us then? Or are you lying to us now?" I got very close to him, closer than I had ever dared. Rather than flinch, he met my gaze.

"I told you what you needed to know to survive. You may not realize this but I've been trying to tell you the truth."

"How? By embarrassing me in front of the class? Yelling at my father? Pick one."

"Sit down," he commanded and gently pushed me down into a chair. I accepted while Austin joined us. Lola whimpered nearby and I was glad to see the mechanical dog. I gave her head a rub. She seemed to perk up at my touch.

"Didn't you ever question why some of the simulations didn't follow the history you were taught? I spent hours restructuring the visuals to give a small glimpse of how the past actually took place. You saw things and met people that no one else ever did." My thoughts went to the simulation of my mother.

"That was you! Why the elaborate setup? Why not just tell me?"

"You know why." He motioned around us. "Our society watches and records every second of our lives. How long would I survive as a history teacher if I was caught subverting my students?" His cold eyes blazed with fury.

"You're not making any sense. Why tell me about the

city's actual history? I mean nothing to you. You and my dad were no longer friends. Why risk teaching me the truth?" Mr. Stewart looked conflicted. He stood up and started to pace, as if working up the courage to answer my question.

"In one of the simulations, I showed you my friendship with your father and your mother."

I nodded. "It's funny, he never mentioned you before."

"Probably because I was friends with your mother first. I cared very deeply for her. But she cared more for your dad." He straightened up, as if embarrassed by his admission. "Still, I wished nothing but happiness for her and your father. It hurt me just as much when she disappeared."

"Disappeared? You mean died?"

He turned to look at me. "Her body was never recovered. I deal in facts, Pene. Most people's remains have been found since that day of tragedy, but never your mother's. Trust me, I've checked many times."

His concern for Mom was touching but creepy. I began to realize why Dad hadn't talked about him and why he was fixated on me.

"So what? There was tons of rubble. Many of the terrorists' bodies were never found either," Austin interjected.

"What if there were no bodies to find?" Mr. Stewart said as he stared intensely at both of us. One of the technicians behind us had been following the conversation and nodded in approval.

I stood up. "What do you mean? History has always showed the terrorists' demands, the attack and explosions.

Are you telling me that they never existed?"

"No. But I've always felt it was an elaborate ruse. As a historian, I have researched the terrorists' identities extensively. None of them seemed to have any history about twelve months before the earthquake. If they were such passionate people about their cause, they should have shown up in other causes before the attack. But there is nothing, no history; they're like ghosts. They had no families that would carry the shame of their attacks."

"That's not in any history lesson I've ever had," Austin added.

"Why would it? It would dispute everything you knew," Mr. Stewart commented. "The ascension of drone technology came after the attack. What if it was all staged to create our 'safe' society?"

My mind danced. I was overloaded. I had been thinking that the court system might have a few corrupt officials, and now that seemed minor in the overall scheme of things.

"What made you suspect?" I asked. Mr. Stewart seemed excited by the question.

"History is rarely neat. If you get in an argument with someone, how many sides to the story do you have?"

I thought of my dad's court comments. "At least two."

"And if you have ten witnesses, how many other viewpoints of what happened do you have?"

"Another ten," Austin answered before I could.

"Exactly. It's human nature to interpret events uniquely. We all have different life experiences and sympathies; none of us sees events the same. Law enforcement has learned to use a series of similar questions to determine if people's view of events change from multiple questioning. From varying opinions, they are able to discern what actually happened. The court of law was exactly the same. Testimonies could vary between witnesses, and cross-examination could bring different recollections. Trials could take weeks to complete in order to go through all of the testimony."

"My dad always told me how painful court cases used to be."

"They were painful, long before and often the person with the most money won. But the innocent party always had a chance. Unlike today, when the accused is presumed guilty. Look at your father's trial and the one for the shop-keeper—both farces. The farthest thing away from justice."

"But why? What did they do to deserve to be sentenced? Morall liked my dad—at least that's what he said to me."

"It's not about liking or disliking someone, it's about exposing the truth."

"What truth? Some of the re-enactments involved places and scenes that had nothing to do with our city. One memory involved dinosaurs, and another pirates. Were you showing some old movies?"

"I don't know what you're talking about, Pene." Mr. Stewart looked confused and leaned forward. "The history I sent you involved different interpretations of our city. Not some fantastic renderings from another world. I sent you the negotiations, the underground tunnels, the sleeping citizens.

"Which made even less sense. How could people sleep through the aftermath of the explosion?"

"I don't know." Mr. Stewart shook his head. "These were fragments that I pieced together from varying viewpoints, documents, footage that disputed our version of events. I don't even know if they are true, but they were purposely scrubbed from the re-enactment database. I did my best to piece these memories together and share with you those that involved your mother. I kept myself distant so that others would not suspect my true intentions."

"Which were?" I asked.

"To share with you the truth about your mother. You look so much like her." He hesitated. "But I had to be extremely careful or I'd be caught."

"Like my dad."

"Your dad was getting close to exposing someone and paid the price for it. I have no idea what your shopkeeper friend did—maybe ticked off the wrong type of people or dealt with illegal commodities. What did he sell?"

"Weird stuff," Austin piped up. "He was delusional. Sold things from faraway lands. Claimed that aliens dropped them off."

"Well, he must have come across something or seen someone he wasn't supposed to. Pene, I figured you were next on their list. What did they try to do to you in the Justice Building?"

I thought about the questions posed by Morall, and the evil-looking sphere.

"They seemed less interested in me and more interested in knowing who was helping me. Besides Austin, there was no one else I knew about. And the explosions stopped everything. They scrambled to move me away, and it seemed to really shock Morall that their defenses could be breached."

Mr. Stewart smiled at my commentary. "With the underground tunnels, it's good we can still do some things undetected."

"But why? Why create the explosions and draw so much attention to you? You couldn't know the explosions would set me free?"

"But we did," Austin interjected. "This cavern is the perfect example. Come here." He pulled me out of my chair towards a shelving unit built into a wall. Several monitors showed buildings around the city. I recognized one room.

"That's where Morall was about to inject me. You could watch me the whole time?"

"Not exactly," answered Mr. Stewart. "Because of the infrastructure of drones and cameras, there is the opportunity to piggyback the signal to let others—"

"Like us!" Austin added excitedly.

"To watch the signal as well. But we don't have the same ability to pinpoint locations. We have to target certain areas of the city and randomly hack into footage. It takes hours to find the right location. We only found you a few minutes before Morall arrived in the room. It didn't give us much time to set up a diversion. But once we did, we followed your progress and created diversions that would hopefully stop or delay your interrogation."

"But why take such a risk on me? The explosion could have hurt someone, and now the Justice Department will be after you. There are more important people than me in this city. Why put your people at risk for no reason?" I was happy to be free, but they could all be caught tomorrow.

"You don't understand, Pene." Mr. Stewart leaned towards me. "Morall has taken a special interest in you. I don't know if it is because he was connected to your dad or if he sees something in you that he wants to redeem. He's shared more information with you than with his own staff. He isn't going to let you go. He wants you badly and he will do anything to find you. That makes you very valuable."

"But if he throws all his resources behind him, he will find me, and all of this." I gestured around the room. "How is that going to help the Resistance if you are all caught and charged?"

"We have a plan, trust me. The department's strength is that they have been able to keep all of this information hidden from residents. The tracking of individuals, the falsifying of evidence; if any of this gets out, the whole system goes out the window. Morall knows that. By staying focused on you, he is going to make a mistake. In fact, I think he already has."

"What do you mean?" I asked.

"We were able to listen to some of his interrogation," Austin said. "He mentioned that they used some type of new crown on you to make you think you had escaped when you didn't."

"I remember that part," I replied sarcastically, wondering what point they were trying to make besides making me feel stupid.

"We have never seen the technology so miniaturized before. What if others have been fooled?"

"What do you mean?" But a dark thought crossed my mind.

"You know how hard it is to get a travel visa out of the city," Austin added. "Takes years to process. Then when someone travels and returns, they always make a big deal of publicizing their exploits."

"And they do interviews, explaining all the places they're been. I watched one guy on a bus monitor tell about his ocean voyage. Showed pictures—described his experiences. From seeing those trips, that is what has driven me to explore," I enthused.

"What if," Mr. Stewart motioned me closer, "the trips were manufactured using the miniature crown you wore? You didn't even know that you hadn't left the city."

"It was very realistic." I thought closely about running through the park, which had been all in my head. "I would probably still be there if they hadn't decided to pull me out." I pondered. "That would mean it was all fake. That nobody's travels are real."

"Since the earthquake, travel has become extremely limited. I used to go abroad when I was your age," Mr. Stewart explained. "But in the first few years since the tragedy, no one was allowed to leave the city because the ground was too unstable because of the earthquake. It's only become available to travel to a select few over the last few years."

"But what are they hiding—what's behind the city limits?" Before he could answer, an alarm bell screamed and everyone in the cavern rushed to activity.

"What's going on?" I asked. Mr. Stewart looked at a screen.

"We have visitors. Looks like we weren't careful enough in bringing you here." Mr. Stewart looked at Austin, who was crestfallen. He patted Austin on the shoulder. "Don't worry, we can turn this to our advantage." He motioned to the others to follow him and pocketed his electronic gear.

Austin and I looked at each other and then ran after him. We climbed a ramp that took us out of the bowels of the cavern, into a basement. We turned and climbed a flight of stairs. The door opened and I could see sunlight through one of the arches. The stadium field beckoned.

Mr. Stewart's men were carrying some type of gun. I wasn't sure if they planned to destroy or disable their attackers. As we exited the archway and entered the field, I turned to the reason for the alarm bells. A large flying drone was hovering over the field, its engine generating heat as it lowered itself to the field. Sitting calmly on the back end of the drone, like a man riding a horse, was Morall. He was all smiles, like he didn't have a care in the world. Or he had just caught us with our hands in the cookie jar.

Around him were at least a dozen other drones. They were large, bigger than a full-size adult and easily twice as strong. As Morall landed on the field, they landed behind him, forming a semi-circle. He leapt off the drone like a man half his age.

"Pene, I was worried about you. Seems you took up with the wrong sort after all. Be glad that I'm here to rescue you." His obvious glee made me think that my 'escape' from the justice building might have been staged. "Please introduce me to your friends."

Mr. Stewart stepped forward. "Leave her alone. For a man who prides himself on justice, preying on teenage girls is disgusting. Instead of standing for all that is right, you represent all that is wrong in our society." Morall looked amused and motioned to one of the drones to scan Mr. Stewart. The red glow measured him from head to toe. Morall looked at a small monitor in his hand and frowned.

"A teacher? I'm a bit disappointed. I was expecting someone with higher credentials to be the mastermind. No matter; you and your group will be sentenced. In a few days you will all be older and a lot less wiser."

"I don't think so." Mr. Stewart slowly paced around Morall's drones. "You underestimate human beings and our ability to adapt. The drones can't think for themselves. They can't create, they can only react. They have no defense for this." Mr. Stewart pulled out a gun and fired. The roar was loud. The lead drone's head exploded, exposing circuitry, and sparks rose into the air. The drone collapsed, its circuits littering the ground like metal entrails. This seemed to infuriate Morall.

"I don't how you acquired a gun. They have been illegal for years. You're only delaying the inevitable. You have gone beyond a normal sentence. Every action is damning yourself and your colleagues to death."

"My colleagues are armed as well." Methodically, Stewart circled Morall. "Any move you make to take us in will result in all of your drones being destroyed," Mr. Stewart motioned, and several people on his team armed themselves. Morall seemed surprised but didn't panic. He began pacing around the field, clicking on a small monitor in his hand.

"You are all being recorded. Thousands of citizens will see your crimes, and your punishment will be swift."

"I'm sure the entire length of our discussion will be viewed by the public so both sides of our exchange will be heard," Mr. Stewart challenged.

"Of course—the footage is always representative of what has occurred." Morall smiled. He wasn't going to be trapped into saying anything incriminating. I figured I needed to draw him out. I stepped towards him and several drones moved closer to me. He held up his hand to stop their advance.

"It's okay—she's unarmed." He raised his arms in an embrace, a grandfatherly gesture. "Pene, you don't know how much help you've been. You've led us on quite a chase but because of your help, you have brought the so called Resistance to its knees. This delay," he pointed at the guns, "will soon be over and these people forgotten."

"Like my dad!" I pointed angrily at him. "Will you erase everything about us just like you did to him? Anyone who challenges the truth is sentenced and deleted." I looked straight at a drone. "Will anything I say be left intact?" The drone's eyes stared at me but remained voiceless. Morall came towards me, and this must have seemed like a threat. Lola came running out of the tunnel and charged Morall. Whatever her intelligence, she was able to determine danger. She leapt at Morall, teeth drawn. I felt a deep pride that something electronic could actually feel the need to protect me. The feeling was fleeting. Morall swatted and she fell to the ground at his feet. He stamped his foot, crushing the little dog. The light in the dog's eyes dimmed and it remained motionless.

"No!" Austin yelled and ran towards Morall. A drone went to intervene and one of Mr. Stewart's men fired into its chest. The drone fell to the ground. The other drones surrounded Morall like a mother protects her babies, preventing Austin from reaching Morall.

"Enough! I have let this go on too long. All of you will be convicted of treason! Resist and you and all of your family members will be killed."

"You and whose army!" Austin screamed while trying to evade one of the drones. Morall said nothing but put his electronic gauge in his pocket and motioned behind him.

At first I saw nothing but then I thought I could see hundreds of dots in the sky. The air became shiny as thousands of reflections flashed from metallic bodies. I heard rumbling and watched as motorcycle drones, as well as dogs and other animals rushed into various stadium entrances. The noise was unbearable and I put my hands over my ears to block out the sound. I turned, and Austin, Mr. Stewart and the others had all stopped—the mass of metal drones was a force to behold. As the flying drones landed and the motorized drones rumbled into the stadium, it felt like the ground was shaking.

As I looked around at the sea of drones, I realized that all hope was lost.

30

Overwhelmed

The things I hated most in my life were all around me.

Thousands of soulless machines surrounded me and my small group of friends—or people who had just become friends. There was no escape. We were outnumbered a thousand to one. I felt like an ant as a large foot came down to stamp out my existence. Morall looked smug, as if he had been pulling my strings all along and this end was inevitable. I turned to Mr. Stewart but his face was calm, as if he too had expected this conclusion. He stepped forward.

"I am giving a final warning. Call this off. Kill us here and you will lose all of your humanity."

Morall looked at him like a parent regards a bad child. "Empty threat, teacher. You're not in a classroom and these drones are not your pupils. In a moment I am going to program your death and there is nothing you can do about it."

"Listen to yourself, Morall," I yelled. "Why do you decide who lives and dies? You said you loved our justice system—where is the justice in silencing everyone who disagrees with you?" Drone hands grabbed me from behind, and I was pushed unwillingly forward. With his army of metal, I knew he couldn't resist flaunting his superiority. Morall's red eye stared at me.

"You don't understand! This is how it has to be. Why couldn't you be happy living in a safe society? Do you know how much my generation has worked to look after you? You could have been secure in the knowledge that as long as you followed the rules, you were perfectly safe. You had it all, Pene, and you threw it away."

"Maybe," I replied. "But it was my decision, not one you forced down my throat. To you I'm safe, but having no free will is still a prison. Just make it end." I wanted his chatter to be done. I looked at the drone holding me, which looked exactly like the one that had escorted me at the Department of Justice. I wished there was some way to tell them apart. *Maybe a nametag.* "Release me." I commanded. Its grip slackened but it did not let me go.

"You can't control them," Morall sneered. "Only I can manipulate their actions." He brandished his controller as if to illustrate his power. I had an idea.

"Not quite. I learned that their programming is to escort, not to hurt. And they have some artificial intelligence to make their decisions." I looked at the drone. "Release me, you're hurting me!" Its grip loosened further, and with a good tug, I could get away. But Morall intervened.

"Hold her," he commanded and tapped on his controller. The drone's grip became tighter. I yelled in mock pain.

"You're hurting me. Follow your original programming." The drone head shook left and right as if confused. Several other drones began to tilt their heads as if following our conversation. "What is your programming?"

"To assist humans. To escort guilty people to sentencing."

"She is guilty!" Morall wailed.

"Have I been tried?" I looked at the drone, trying to see behind its eyes. Was there some intelligence?

"No," it answered plainly.

"Then I can't be guilty."

"Ignore her!" Morale typed on a keypad but the drone made no change. It was almost as if it was thinking over its options.

"Listen to me. Can I command you to seize this man?"

"No. You do not have authority."

"Does he have authority?"

"Yes!" Morall answered.

"He provides commands as long as they don't override our initial programming."

"Not to hurt humans."

"Yes."

"No, she's trying to trick you. You are not hurting her," Morall commanded.

"Yes, you are. See these marks?" I pointed to my wrist, where marks had been made by the drone's tight grip.

"Yes."

"That shows that you are hurting me."

"Yes." And immediately its grip was removed. The drone looked unsteady, as if it was confused and about to fall over.

"Capture her. Capture all of these people," Morall yelled while typing instructions. "That is my order!"

"Do not listen to orders that endanger humans. That is against your programming," I yelled. Many drones turned to each other as if having a silent conversation. Whatever I said to this drone was being passed to the others. "Stand down." Thousands of drones came to rest as if awaiting new orders. My hatred of them was always a smokescreen. They were never the enemy. In some respect, I had gained a new appreciation for them. They were here to protect us, as long as the right person was pulling their strings.

However, whatever delay I had created would be short-lived. Morall would eventually get through to the drones with new orders. I hadn't really accomplished anything but stalling.

"You've delayed your sentencing by a few minutes. I signaled for a full reboot. Whatever commands you think you have given these drones will be gone," Morall stated, as confident as ever.

"No, they won't," Mr. Stewart interrupted, pulling his electronic transmitter out of his pocket. "Thank you, Pene. You bought us the time we needed." He put a hand on my shoulder.

"What do you mean?" I asked.

"Your friend Austin gave me an idea. He wanted to find the location of where the drones are kept and then destroy them."

"There is no central location. The drones are always

working all over the city, you fool," Morall answered.

"We know that. So we took another approach." Mr. Stewart was typing into his transmitter. "We knew you would come in force. We knew you would show off all of your drones to put the 'pathetic' resistance down. We just needed time to intercept your signal. You're not the only one who can give commands. Let's just say," he looked at Austin, "we have discovered more than one way to destroy the drones." He pressed his transmitter and simultaneously a thousand drone red eyes went dark.

The drones had been standing at rest, and now scores of metal arms fell to their sides. It was deafening. Then, with no power in their systems, the drones began to fall down.

Most drones tumbled in waves as Mr. Stewart's command ceased their operations. Their metal bodies went slack and toppled to the ground. Drones fell from the sky and drones collapsed. The semi-circle around Morall fell last, like dominos, one after another until the final one collapsed. Morall looked on in panic, lifting a metal drone as if he could reanimate it like a puppet.

"How?" He looked at Mr. Stewart in disbelief.

"We tracked your communications," Mr. Stewart answered. "When you came here, you signaled for reinforcements. We hacked into your processor and turned them off. All devices to the network, including our gear, is shut down." He tossed his device to the ground.

"But the system will reboot. It might take hours, but the drones will come back on. You've only delayed the inevitable." Morall's confidence made me think he was right. Had

302 · JIM KOCHANOFF

we only bought ourselves a few hours to escape?

"Have we?" Mr. Stewart signaled to his group, which began shooting at the piles of drones. Their shells exploded, with circuitry and wires hanging out of their bodies. In the air, a red eye tumbled to the ground. I guessed Mr. Stewart figured you couldn't reanimate a bunch of broken drones. Morall panicked and tapped his phone.

"Vaslor! Bring your men to the stadium immediately. This is an emergency! The drones are under attack!" I heard Vaslor's voice squeak out of the phone.

"Negative. Seconds ago, all of our recording devices went down. It's a system-wide crash—everything in the network is down. Drones have dropped out of the sky across the city. I have no eyes anywhere. We're blind, Morall. Do you hear me, blind! No cameras, stationary or drone recording, are working. I've ordered my men to spread across the city to maintain law and order. Once people know the drones aren't watching, crime will escalate!"

"But I am surrounded by the people who caused this! You need to come now!"

"I can't." Vaslor's response sounded measured, as if he was weighing the variables. "There is more at stake than your safety. We need to show the people of the city that we are here to support them in this crisis. Once areas are secured, we'll send some officers your way. Vaslor out." The phone went silent. Morall looked around at the chaos as drone bodies were destroyed before him.

"Stop it! We'll just build new ones in a few weeks. Think of the damage you'll cause this city when it shifts into lawlessness. You are endangering the life of every resident of the city with your actions."

Mr. Stewart considered Morall's words then raised his hand. The rest of his team stopped firing and the destruction of the drones stopped momentarily.

"Tell us the truth and we'll destroy no more drones. Your secret's safe—all the recording devices have been disabled. Just tell us why this system is sentencing innocent people!"

"No one is innocent," was Morall's cryptic reply. "We did what had to be done." He turned to me. "Your dad pushed too hard. He would have destroyed all of the hard work our justice system had won. People are safe because of the drones. Your dad would have exposed certain 'adjustments'."

"Adjustments! You killed my dad because of adjustments!" I screamed. I hated him and this city.

"Yes." He stepped towards me. "If it had leaked to the public that court footage had been altered, all trust would be lost. You don't understand, Pene. To maintain the city's security, sacrifices have to be made. I loved your dad like a son, but his death was necessary." *There. He admitted his guilt.*

"Why Lou the merchant?" I dug my fingers into my palms and balled my fists. Knowing the truth about my dad was not making me feel any better. Not in the slightest.

"The vendor? He was selling items that presented questions about what is outside of the city. Those items were illegal and he had to be punished."

"It seems important to you to determine who must be

punished for the safety of the city," Mr. Stewart offered.

"It's a burden but my decisions are for the greater good. A few lives are lost so that millions can be safe."

"What if I told you that I also need to make decisions for the greater good? To eliminate the threats from the city."

"If you are threatening to kill me, go ahead. Other justice ministers will take my place." Morall actually beamed. Maybe he looked forward to becoming a martyr.

"Oh, your death would serve no purpose. I'd rather show people the truth. Give them a taste of your footage of explaining how the law actually works."

"What are you babbling about? Cameras and drones are down—nothing to the network is connected. You said so yourself!"

"Correct, all drones and cameras are down. But there are some things that aren't connected to the network. There are some things that are not controlled by you. That are independent." I looked down at Lola's crushed form. Her eyes had never quite faded away and now seemed to glow. Austin moved forward and picked her up. Lola tried to prop her head on his arm, but her neck was broken. I never knew that a metallic creature could make me want to cry.

"I've got you sweetie. I'll rebuild your body," Austin looked around him. "I suddenly have lots of spare parts."

"Upload the footage," Mr. Stewart commanded Austin. Moments later, a small video screen on Lola's side chirped to life. Morall's face looked huge as Lola's camera had been from the ground looking up.

""Yes," he said coolly, "if it had leaked to the public that court footage had been altered, all trust would be lost." His face froze, the footage ready to play over and over again. Morall's face was also frozen in horror in real life.

"You can't play that! It will bring the city to its knees. You release that and you endanger thousands of people. Don't let your petty differences with me hurt others. Destroy the dog and its footage. Let people be secure." Morall's hands were together, as if he was begging.

"It's not my decision to make." Mr. Stewart turned to me. "Pene?" I was surprised that both adults looked to me. I wasn't sure I could make a decision that would affect everyone in the city. I knew what I wanted, but by watching this man, I had come to realize how sick it was to think I had all the answers. Did I really want to be responsible for what might happen to the city if they knew the truth? What if they destroyed everything and people were killed? Could I live with that on my conscience? I stared at Morall.

"I don't want to be like you. Play it! It's about time everyone saw the truth and made their own choices."

"The truth will destroy this city. The walls will come down. The sky will fall. Crime will take over. You will be responsible!" Morall screamed.

"It that's the price of real justice, then it's about time we all paid it! Maybe people are better able to handle the truth than you think." I pointed outside the stadium. "It's time we let them decide." I nodded to Mr. Stewart. He would eventually play Morall's confession in its entirety once the networks came back online. In the near future, video screens across the city would play the truth. I didn't care if people believed it or not. It would no longer be scrubbed by Morall. I looked at him, hugging the main drone at its knees. Its lifeless arms hung at its shoulders, and no embrace was coming back. Morall had dedicated his life to the drones and now they offered him nothing in return. I felt Mr. Stewart's hand on my shoulder.

"Come. We have at best a few hours before the drones are reactivated. You have a small opportunity to leave the city!"

31
Higher

Mr. Stewart handed me a backpack.

"Put your belongings in this. There are enough provisions to last you about a week. Once you get to another city, tell them about the situation here."

"You're not coming?" I asked, although I knew the answer.

"No. I worked towards this day for over ten years, Pene. Morall is right in some respects. People will handle the truth in different ways. Crime will increase. But when the drones reanimate, I need to make sure the process is transparent rather than being controlled by someone who thinks he knows our best interests." He put both hands on my shoulders. "Do you know where to go?"

"I'm headed west. This little piece may have caused Lou his sentence." I pulled out the concave piece of glass. "I want to see why it has caused so much trouble."

"Then go. But make sure you come back soon. I've tried to give you information on your past. A lot didn't make sense to me but maybe you'll come back with some answers." Mr. Stewart hugged me, turned and then he was gone.

I ran over to Austin, who was working on Lola's legs. The dog's metal tongue stuck out, touching the back of my hand. I could see why he loved this dog so much. He looked at me.

"You're going, aren't you?" I nodded. "I wish I could go with you."

"Then come," I begged.

"I can't. There is too much for me here to do. People need to know what has been happening. I can't just leave my family." He looked into my eyes. "This is your dream. See the world. But make me one promise."

"Anything."

"Take this with you." He handed me a small phone-like gadget. "It will record everything you do and see on your travels."

"Ahh, I'm trying to get away from being under surveillance." I was unsure of Austin's gift. He punched me in the arm.

"You choose what to record. That's the difference. Consider it a scrapbook of your travels. When you come back, you can show me the world. Deal?"

I kissed him, and no further answer was needed. In our embrace, I was having serious doubts about leaving. Figures—I spend my entire life trying to leave the city and when I finally get the chance, I had to meet him. We opened our eyes and I knew he was conflicted in letting me go.

"Make sure you come back to me!" I left his embrace and

immediately began to run. I had no courage to look back to see if he was watching me leave. If I looked into his eyes again, I might change my mind.

Ten minutes later, I was running across the commons of downtown. All transports were offline and sitting idle. I'd have to get around the city the old-fashioned way. There were people standing around everywhere, some poking at the piles of drones, almost waiting for them to become active again. My pace was steady—I wasn't going to exhaust myself. I was confident that I could escape the city before the drones were reactivated. I rounded a corner and ran straight into a barrel chest of a large man. He reeked of alcohol and sneered down at me.

"Where you going?" He looked me over and smiled. Not a nice smile. "Want to spend some time with me?" As he said it, I knew he wasn't asking. His hands groped around my waist. I guess Morall was right in some respects. People were becoming less inhibited without the drones around.

"Leave her alone," an older woman yelled. The man turned and was greeted by the flash of a phone camera. He was startled and released me. "I'm sure the police are going to love a picture of this." She clicked her phone. The man seemed less eager for an audience and walked away, embarrassed either by his actions or by getting caught.

"You okay, dear?" the woman asked and reached for me. I nodded. "People are getting a bit cheeky with those drones down, aren't they?"

"Good thing you were here."

"I guess we can still handle ourselves," she smiled. I grinned back and realized that Morall's dire prediction might not take place after all.

By the time I had made it across town, the late afternoon sun reflected off the West Gates. Drone bodies littered the area like garbage, and some of the boxes they were carrying lay strewn across the ground. Most human workers were absent; they must have either gone home to check on their families or were busy trying to find the cause of the drone collapse. I dashed through an open scanner. A red light flashed as I entered but no alarm screamed.

"Hey, you can't go through there." I turned and saw a heavy-set man wearing a hardhat gesturing at me. He didn't look like he could catch me so I didn't slow down. He took a few steps but gave up in moments. Before I knew it, I had crossed the boundary of the city. My heart thumped, I felt so alive. I had been waiting all of my life for this. Within minutes, the walls of the city faded into the background and no drone was following me. I was free!

I checked the coordinates that the Wildman had given me. Although I couldn't climb there like he had, by passing through the city boundary walls I would be able to reach my destination. I wasn't sure what I was going to find but I'd better do it before it got dark. I pulled out the spyglass that Lou had given me, a relic from the past, and looked towards my future. The peak of the west mountain. Something glimmered in the sky, yet it was too light out to be a star. I used that point to focus my journey.

After two hours, I was dirty and sweaty but near my

goal. As I reached the peak of the mountain, the clouds rolled slowly to the east, fluffy and fat. The view was amazing and a little bit scary. A huge chasm opened up into a valley below. One false step and I would fall hundreds of feet.

I looked up at my focal point. The glimmering in the sky looked different now. Its edges reflected light but its center was dark, like a hole. As the cloud crossed it, it seemed to skip across the hole, like a rock skimming the surface of the water. A large pine tree grew near the peak of the mountain, one of the few trees on top of the slope. I grabbed the lower branches, my pack still on my back. I climbed from branch to branch until I was near the top of the tree and reached skyward towards the raw, sharp hole. Were my eyes playing tricks on me?

I stretched upward and ran the ragged edge along my hand. Its shape looked very familiar. I reached into my backpack and pulled out the glass I had purchased from Lou. It looked like an eye looking back at me. Like Chicken Little, I wondered if the sky was falling. I grasped it and inserted it into the sky. The hole immediately vanished and the illusion was complete. Clouds rolled by without interruption. As I reached up, the sky was cool and glassy to my touch. Even now, with the evidence staring me in my face, my brain couldn't process it.

My hands touched a glass roof. The clouds ran along my fingers, as if the projection was trying to use my hands as a screen. I suppressed the urge to scream. My hands continued to grope the sky. Near the place where the piece had fallen out, my hand touched something hard and round. *Maybe this caused the piece to fall out in the first place?* I tried to turn it sight unseen and it spun counter-clockwise. A portal opened in mid-air down below, a hole into darkness. It was impossible. I turned and looked at the city miles beneath me. Could anyone see me? Could anyone understand what I was doing? Everything looked so small and unimportant below. I swallowed and climbed down the tree.

I sat on the ground and rocked my body back and forth, trying to prevent myself from hyperventilating. This was too much to absorb and I felt my life flashing before me. Could this be why no one left the city? There was nowhere else to go? Was the earthquake so many years ago a cover for something else? Sleeping people and a black sky to hide what really happened? I had wanted to leave the city but none of this made sense. But there was only one way to find out the truth.

I stood up and I stepped towards the edge of the cliff. In order to reach the door I had opened, I had to walk across open air. It might be a projection, but it looked real to my brain. If I stepped forward and was wrong, I would fall to my death. If I was right, I would reach the open door. The chasm kept people from learning the truth. The opening beckoned me but was a good thirty feet away. I was going to take a running jump, but instead leaned out over the cliff and touched the air between me and the door. The air was solid, like a concrete floor. As hard as I pressed, the air impossibly resisted my touch. It was all fake. Everything I thought I knew was a fake as a reenactment. With that knowledge, I crawled, looking at the ground below me, and for the first time since my dream, I almost felt as if I could fly. If I spread my arms, I felt I could glide back to the city. But I wasn't going back there.

I scrambled forward, reaching the half open door where one shouldn't exist. I entered the opening and stepped into a narrow hallway. I looked back at the only home I had ever known and silently said goodbye. Where my city ended, a new place had begun. As I walked forward, the door closed suddenly, trapping me in my new environment. I had wanted to explore some new places all right. *Be careful what you wish for.* The hallway in front of me was long and sterile with little natural light.

I walked forward. A sickly green glow came from the end of the hall. I was drawn to it, and as I got closer, I thought I could hear a voice. I stepped towards the illumination and stepped into a large room with rows of chairs and monitors. A laboratory—and the city was its subject. A semi-transparent screen looked down onto my home below. If I squinted, I could make out a few familiar landmarks. Suddenly a voice filled the room through overhead speakers.

"Standard protocols apply. Breach in sphere 39X— resource team ETA—fifteen minutes. Approach subject with caution." A steel door closed over the entrance I'd come in through. I wouldn't be able to return to the city the same way I had come in. I didn't have much time to decide my next move.

The voice overhead was female and familiar. Her information was confusing. Where was she? I turned to the right to a bank of video screens.

The screens were in rows of ten by ten and showed scenes from places that both thrilled and scared me. Some of the images I recognized. The dinosaurs. The pirates. The war battle. *Do these places actually exist?* Numerous other images played like a series of movies, with scenes and characters that my deepest imagination could never create. *Someone accessed actual video feeds from other places and sent them to me?* My city was only one of many that were being observed. These fantastic places were real!

Then the voice from the speakers spoke from one of the monitors. Her image was clear and showed the top half of her body. I looked into the screen and my mother's face stared back at me. It was her as she was about fifteen years ago. There was a reason her body was never found. Why hadn't she tried to communicate with me and Dad? Why hadn't she aged? She must have escaped to here. Wherever here was.

"Please make your choice." She stared back at me as if daring me to do something. Her voice looped again. "Please make your choice." As my mom's computer image spoke, a huge graphic filled the screen, and it looked like a huge molecule with many spheres existing independently of each. Were these where I saw the other video feeds?

"Five minutes to team arrival!" the overhead speakers blared. I had to go. A team was coming. I didn't know if the team was soldiers, drones or scientists, but they were coming because of me. And I didn't want to find out what they would do to me.

I had to get out of here. Could my mother be out there, in one of these other places? If she was, I'd find her and find out why she left us.

I heard noise from the far end of the hall, from the doorway I entered. I wasn't going to be captured, but there was so much I didn't understand.

To the far right, there were five doors along the wall. Each had a schematic diagram describing the place it opened to. Strange pictograms with images I didn't understand. I pointed my finger along each door, trying to decide which one to take.

Let's. Go. Here.

I opened the door and stepped through.

THE WORLD SERIES

Continues in…

CLAN WORLD

Pene escapes her home only to enter a world she thought she had imagined. A world where humans and prehistoric animals exist simultaneously as technology is falling apart. She must cross this strange land where bands of people will try to stop her from reaching the Cradle—the birthplace of this world's civilization. To find her mother and learn more about who created the drones, she must survive… Clan World!

For more details and information,
visit www.SilverLeafBooks.com

ABOUT THE AUTHOR

Jim Kochanoff has been writing for over a decade—his specialty is action / adventure, putting the reader into adrenalin driven stories. He signed a contract with Toonz Animation, Asia's largest animation company for an animated pilot. He has also worked in television as a production manager coordinating animated children's shows to live action science fiction.

Kochanoff currently serves as the Chairman of the Nova Scotia Society for the Prevention of Cruelty to Animals and is passionate about saving the lives of animals. He prefers book adventures over book signings and will bring his remote control drones to a bookstore near you for his latest novel, *Drone World*.

CPSIA information can be obtained at www.ICGtesting.com
Printed in the USA
BVOW04s0655070816

457912BV00001B/5/P